Cornflower Blue

CHRISTIAN SCHÜNEMANN, born in 1968, is a journalist who has worked in Moscow and Bosnia-Herzegovina. He received the Helmut Stegmann Prize for Journalism in 2001.

JELENA VOLIĆ is an academic, lecturing in Modern German Literature. She divides her time between Belgrade and Berlin.

Cornflower Blue

A Case for Milena Lukin

CHRISTIAN SCHÜNEMANN AND JELENA VOLIĆ

Translated by Baida Dar

First published in English in 2015 by
HAUS PUBLISHING LTD.
70 Cadogan Place, London SW1X 9AH
www.hauspublishing.com

Originally published in German as
Kornblumenblau: Ein Fall für Milena Lukin
Copyright © 2013 by Diogenes Verlag AG Zürich

Translation Copyright © 2015 by Baida Dar

A full CIP record for this book is available from the British Library

Printed in Spain by Liberdúplex

Typeset in Garamond by MacGuru Ltd

ISBN: 978-1-908323-96-5
eISBN: 978-1-908323-97-2

Acknowledgements

The authors would like to thank the Robert Bosch Foundation who made possible the research for this novel through a *Grenzgänger*-grant.

The translator thanks her fellow translator and true wordsmith Peter Lewis for his unfailing editorial flair.

This novel is based on a real case: on 5 October 2004 two soldiers died in mysterious circumstances in the grounds of the Belgrade barracks where they were stationed. According to the army's internal investigation, one of the men allegedly first killed his comrade before turning his weapon on himself. An independent enquiry later concluded that the two soldiers had been shot from very close range by an unknown third party.

The characters and events in this novel, however, are entirely fictitious and, accordingly, any similarities between them and actual characters or events are entirely coincidental.

1

Sacks of potatoes sat propped up against a pile of rocks from which nettles were growing – shapeless varities, lazily slumping there and waiting for Samir to lug them down the flight of eighteen narrow steps to the kitchen. Their size and bulk were way out of proportion to his flyweight frame, but the fact that he looked like a damned squirrel when he shouldered them bothered no one here. Here, the only thing anyone was interested in was seeing the potatoes peeled and boiled by the end of his watch, so they'd be ready, at precisely 12 noon, to be slapped onto their plates as one of two veg sides.

It was still early. Samir lit a cigarette and scurried across the barracks yard. No Serb who harboured even the faintest glimmer of national pride would have pictured this place as quite so derelict, with patches of missing cobblestones and deep potholes in between, where water pooled when it rained. When the next rain would fall, though, heaven only knew. As it was, the air was filled with the deep bass buzz of blowflies, blackbirds and thrushes were singing merrily, and the sun was gathering its strength before blazing down again across the whole region, including this spot in the middle of Topčider, Belgrade's city forest, and turning it into a sweltering oven, from which there had been no escape over the past few days.

A sandy path linked the main building with the officers' mess. Behind it lay a meadow, which plunged steeply downhill behind the trees. Strictly speaking, this area on the far side of the path was out-of-bounds to him. But the dark, moss-covered nook below the stone steps leading down or even up here, in the shadow of the wall, were places where he and his comrades could crouch down and enjoy a quiet smoke. So far nobody had noticed his excursions over this way or told him off.

He ground his fag butt into the sand with the tip of his shoe. An early morning mist blanketed the meadow and with every step the dew moistened the canvas of his shoes. As he passed he ran his hands over the tree trunks, over the channels of rough bark that ants were using as pathways. It smelt of pine resin. He pushed some branches aside, stumbled over roots, slid down the slope, got sand in his shoes, grabbed hold of tufts of grass to steady himself – until finally he was there. Nature had laid out a little terrace for him here, with a hummock of grass forming a comfy seat.

Samir loved this spot and the view of the Sava River, shimmering and meandering through the landscape beyond the fence and the barbed wire. This panorama made up for all the slog: the head chef's barked orders, the bad moods and fighting of his older comrades, the constant steam and the stench of Brussels sprouts and onions simmering down into the same old slop in the dented pots and pans. Sitting here now, though, Samir did not mind that his back hurt from all the carrying, that his jacket was stiff with grime and grease and that his family was far away.

He lent back, crossed his arms behind his head and stretched out his legs. He didn't have much to complain about, really. His brother was an unemployed painter and decorator who was scratching a living delivering winter coal to people in Novi Sad, while his mother was a toilet attendant at some motorway service station or other in Hungary. And since his sister had announced that she was emigrating to Austria in search of a better life, nobody had heard a thing from her. He was worried. Dragaš, their home village in southwest Kosovo on the border with Albania, was now deserted except for the grandparents and a few goats, and it was in the lap of the gods whether the family would ever be reunited there, even in the cemetery.

Samir plucked a blade of grass and wound it round his finger. There was another way of looking at his situation: he had done something nobody else in his family had ever done. Aged 20, he had a job, a pension and a uniform, even if it was only that of a chef. And he wasn't serving up grub for just anybody, either. He was part of an elite Serbian unit, providing sustenance for the Guard of Honour. Samir's family proudly recounted how he'd already achieved more than anyone like him might dream of achieving in a whole lifetime. He ought to be thankful. And by the same virtue, he dared not tell anyone what his real dream was.

It was a dream that haunted him every day. An impossible, presumptuous dream: he longed above all to wear knee-high boots, black trousers with red stripes down the seams, gold braid on his chest and the Serbian coat of arms on his sleeve. He dreamt of the jacket, which was as blue as the cornflowers that grew in the fields of his homeland, as bright as the cloudless sky over the Danube. Samir dreamt of one day wearing the uniform of an elite Serbian guardsman.

He stood up and dusted off his trousers. The potato sacks were waiting for him. Even so, he allowed himself one last detour: a stroll along the narrow path that wound around the hillside, before cutting diagonally through the bushes back to the barracks kitchen.

He was a complete idiot and should stop daydreaming such nonsense. For a start, to serve in the Honour Guard you needed to be a Serbian national, which he wasn't, nor did he have the necessary education or any helpful connections. To cap it all, he was at least fifteen centimetres too short. He'd never get any closer to his dream than the kitchen at the battalion's barracks; there he'd be the happiest man on the planet if only the head chef would allow him to serve food to the troops on a regular basis rather than just once in a blue moon, because at least then he'd get the chance to admire his idols at close range. It would be a gift to be granted such a privilege.

Samir only saw the obstacle after he'd tripped over it. It was something hard and firm, which he desperately clutched at to try and regain his balance. Material as blue as cornflowers, marred by a brown stain that had eaten into the fabric and caused it to tear across the chest. Samir was so close to the guardsman that he could see his dead eyes through the mass of flies and bugs that were teeming over the corpse's face.

Samir's scream reverberated around the grounds, up to the barracks and down to the river. Gasping, he staggered to his feet. He ran and stumbled again.

The second body lay in the grass, its legs twisted, and with a round, black hole in its forehead.

2

Milena Lukin might have heard the mobile phone ringing in her handbag if Vera hadn't buried it under the light Merino-wool jacket. Her phone, handbag, mother and the woollen jacket were all sitting on the back seat of the Lada Niva, which Milena was attempting to weave as fast as she could through the dense traffic of Belgrade's rush hour. In truth, it was quite impossible to pick up speed. Buses, cars and lorries stood bumper-to-bumper, all trying to leave town at the same time. If this traffic jam did not by some miracle ease after Brankov Bridge, a well-known bottleneck, she'd never make it to the airport in time. The flight from Hamburg was due to land in half an hour.

'Maybe I should have made some goulash for him instead.' Vera's voice sounded anxious. 'With green peppers and mash.'

Milena checked the rear-view mirror, indicated and changed lane.

'If only you'd brought me that strong Pecorino cheese like we agreed,' Vera moaned, 'and not that stuff from Hungary.'

'I'm sorry! How many more times do I have to say it?' Milena sighed. If only she'd made the detour via the big supermarket. But the crisis meeting at the institute had dragged on and made her late, so she'd just picked up a packet of grated cheese from the corner shop, with no thought that its quality would of course in no way measure up to the fantastic noodles Vera had laboured over the whole afternoon. It was amazing what energy this old lady could summon up when it came to preparing one of the favourite dishes of the household's only male. She'd spent hours on end kneading the flour, eggs, warm water and a pinch of salt, cutting the thinly rolled dough into equally thin strips, and carefully laying them out on a starched white cloth to dry. What a fandango!

Finally they were past Brankov Bridge, but the traffic still wasn't moving any faster. Sluggishly the long queue of cars pressed forward, making little headway. There was no sign-post indicating an exit but Milena knew the way alright. It was their only chance.

Her secret rat-run led along a row of electricity pylons. Milena grasped the steering wheel tightly with both hands and pressed down hard on the accelerator. Although the Lada was relatively new and its boxy shape made it look like a real 4×4, unfortunately this basic model did not come with back-seat suspension fitted as standard. The old lady bounced wildly up and down, together with the earrings that she only wore for special occasions, as she valiantly tried to maintain some kind of balance, swaying in sync with the wild zigzag manoeuvres that Milena was executing to avoid the worst potholes. Vera didn't complain. Quite the opposite: trying to make up the lost time was just what she wanted.

The engine was still running when Vera flung open the door and dashed into the arrivals hall, clutching her woollen jacket. It took only a few seconds for her salt-and-pepper coloured hair to disappear from sight, swallowed up by the crowd. Milena reached for her bag on the back seat. Her phone showed three missed calls.

A taxi driver drew up alongside her, wound down his window and started hurling abuse at her – something along the lines of 'tomatoes over your eyes' and 'straw inside your head' – before giving her the finger.

'Keep your hair on!' Milena got out, turned her back on the Serbian macho moron and smiled. Adam had just appeared through the sliding doors, wrapped in a warm cardigan and gesticulating wildly, with Vera behind him dragging his suitcase. Wow, the boy had grown – his head now came up to his grandmother's shoulder!

Milena waved and Adam ran towards her. She held out her arms, caught hold of her beautiful boy, hugged him, kissed him and ruffled his long hair, which tumbled in pretty locks across his forehead and down his neck. She and Vera had been forced to spend three weeks without their son and grandson, and had sat like owls in the flat, biding their time and forever waiting for the next call. They'd voraciously pounced upon every morsel of information he'd tossed them from far away, excitedly sifting through every crumb, studying it from every angle and regurgitating it until they'd extracted the last bit of nutrition. But those times of deprivation were now over. The family was whole once more, reunited. Then Milena's mobile rang again.

Damn it all, she should just hang the bloody thing round her neck.

'How's Fiona?' Adam shouted, 'did she miss me?' His high-pitched voice all but drowned out the roar of a passing bus, which had enveloped them in a cloud of diesel fumes.

Milena rummaged through her bag. 'Fiona's fine, she missed you terribly. We all missed you terribly.'

'Is my basketball still there?'

'Hello?' Milena pressed her phone to one ear and stuck her finger in the other.

'Where are you?' It was Siniša Stojković, the lawyer. 'I have to talk to you.'

Milena took a few steps aside and sheltered behind a column, thinking it might be a bit quieter there. Two women came by, laughing out loud and pushing a luggage trolley, and only just missed clipping Milena's heels. 'What's up?' she asked.

'Not on the phone. It's a bit...'

'Hello?'

'...a bit of a delicate matter.' On the other end of the line, Siniša was now yelling to try and make himself understood. 'When can we meet?'

'Siniša, all your matters are delicate, and I don't have a lot of time. Adam's just come back from his summer holiday and, guess what, I have to deal with another delicate matter called the renewal of my contract.'

'Sweetheart, you never have a lot of time! But this one's really urgent, believe me.'

'At least give me a clue.'

'Topčider. The two guardsmen. Remember?'

'What's that got to do with me?'

'Meet me tomorrow, 2 pm Café Le Petit Prince.'

Milena stuffed a set of jump leads behind a box filled with files and squeezed the little suitcase between a bag of cat litter and a crate of apples.

They hadn't even reached the motorway before his grandmother started grilling Adam. Milena knew her mother's litany of questions by heart from when she'd been a child herself: What did you have to eat? How's your digestion? Did you clean your ears? Were you cold? Did your father have a warm bedcover for you? – in Vera's eyes, all the things a person could possibly wish for – even on holiday – for a life of happiness and ease.

While Adam did his best to answer his grandmother's interrogation, on the far side of the Sava River the Kalemegdan Fortress came into view, the hill at the northern end of the old town, terraced by high walls. Turks and other peoples had erected the fortress over many centuries, a succession of rulers had defended it and extended it by adding new redoubts, wells and churches. On the uppermost terrace the Messenger of Victory monument soared into the sky, the statue on top holding a dove of peace on its outstretched arm and marking the spot where the Danube and the Sava converged. It was a favourite haunt not only of tourists but also of Belgraders; old men sat there playing open-air chess, women gossiped and passed around thermoses and children played hide-and-seek under ancient trees. Vera always maintained that Milena took her first steps on the Kalemegdan, but then she also told the same story about Adam. Milena knew for sure that the boy had actually taken his first steps on the Wilmersdorfer Strasse in Berlin.

A lorry overtook them, blocking the view of the fort out of Milena's side window. Hemmed in between two buses, they crossed Brankov Bridge into the old town. In Serbian, Belgrade means 'the white city'. Milena knew every street and every house here, at least that's how it seemed to her. In old books, illustrated with photographs from bygone eras, it all looked very different from this grey heap of stones, punctuated with billboards. What Serbs, Turks and Habsburgs had crafted and built over many centuries had suffered extensive damage in a German bombing raid on 6 April 1941, before being completely flattened by the Allies in the first months of 1944. All that now remained from past centuries was the odd magnificent building, stucco-fronted and decorated with pillars, lovingly preserved for posterity and surrounded by symmetrical flower beds, elegant park benches and genteel babbling fountains. The majority of these beautiful old piles were reserved for the elected representatives of the Serbian people and servants of the state bureaucracy – or wealthy hotel guests from abroad.

Milena had to opt for one of the arteries that pumped traffic through the city, so switched on her indicator and got into lane. Their route took them past building sites where wrecking balls loomed over half-demolished walls, with no one seemingly able to decide whether to finally seal their fate. At the turn of the century – the 19th to the 20th that is – these buildings had reflected the wealth of their owners, men who controlled the flourishing trade between East and West. Nowadays they either stood totally empty or were home to small institutions with sad, downtrodden employees, or to music teachers, who wrapped themselves up in thick woolly cardigans to stave off the chill and damp while their pupils struggled to play instruments with fingers numbed by the cold. The external walls of these façades provided plenty of space for free expression, their plinths pissed on by dogs and drunkards and their upper sections spray-painted by street artists.

Over the past few decades, the gaps between the magnificent mansions and the ramshackle buildings had been filled in with whatever necessity dictated and contemporary taste came up with: blocks constructed from prefabricated wall and window units, whose drab colours and schematic decorative patterns feigned the same kind of modernity and progressiveness as the latest stepped or daringly angled wonders of new architecture, built of mirrored glass and faced with granite slabs. Whenever such an iconic building was constructed, one of these little apartment blocks with blind windows would usually spring up right next to or diagonally opposite it. Like forgotten weeds they lurked in the shadows, settling for sloping walls and low roofs and recalling a time when there was still room for a yard with hens and rabbit hutches. And yet these diminutive houses with their tiny rooms, set as they were in such exclusive locations, were the secret luxury of this city.

Milena kept a wary eye on the traffic, the lunatic drivers who erratically switched lanes without indicating, cut sharply in front of her and then jammed on their brakes. She was rummaging around in the glove compartment for Adam's favourite CD and some chewing gum when she remembered the phone call earlier: what did Siniša have to do with the guardsmen in Topčider? That had happened weeks ago, hadn't it?

'Mum,' Adam shouted, 'guess what? Dad's got a new girlfriend. And her boobs are like *this*!' His hands mimicked full breasts.

'I'm delighted to hear that,' said Milena, switching on her headlights as they entered a tunnel. 'Just thrilled.'

When they got closer to their apartment block, she slowed to a crawl. She got lucky, someone was just pulling out. Milena indicated.

'You won't get in there,' commented Vera from the back scat.

Adam craned his neck.

Milena let a green tram rattle by, then reversed, locking the steering wheel, spinning it back, and juggling with the accelerator, clutch and brakes as she swung in. With one wheel she had to mount the pavement, which had been blocked – totally idiotically – by the bin men, while on the other side a tree with a sloping trunk was in the way.

'Precision work,' said Adam approvingly.

Milena pulled on the handbrake. 'Close your window and be careful when you open the door.'

Around this time, just after the end of the working day, car drivers tended to split the street into four or five lanes without paying the slightest heed to the road markings. Milena, Vera and Adam scurried across like hares, though Milena took the opportunity to remind Adam to be sure always to go up the road a bit and use the pedestrian crossing in the normal course of events. 'Yeah, Mum, I'm not an idiot,' he said, taking the keys from her hand and leaning his full weight against the metal frame and security glass of the apartment block's front door.

She collected the post from one of the many mail boxes inside the glass porch as Adam told them about his excursions with his father, climbing the tower of St Michael's Church in Hamburg and visiting Hagenbeck Zoo. His excitement at seeing the harbour cranes stretching all the way to the horizon and the porcupine babies, who had not yet grown their spikes, echoed around the high stairwell.

All three of them, plus their suitcases and the bag of apples they were carrying, squeezed into the lift, which as usual sagged down a few centimetres under the weight, almost as if the cabin was supported on a bed of cotton wool. Adam pressed the button whose number, 5, had been rubbed off by decades of use and announced: 'When I grow up, I'm going to be a zookeeper.'

'Wash your hands,' Milena said as soon as she had unlocked the last of the three locks on the door to the apartment. 'And take your suitcase to your room.'

Fiona was waiting to greet Adam at eye-level. Picture-perfect, the cat was perched on top of the chest of drawers between the straw hat, postcards and a dried-flower arrangement that Milena had put there as decoration. The boy scooped up his beloved Fiona in his arms, pressed his nose into her long, fluffy fur and whispered sweet nothings into the animal's ear. Today, however, Milena was not on the best of terms with the cat. She'd spent half the night meowing, complaining about the closed door to the living room, which Milena had kept shut because Vera's pasta was draped over the sofa there drying. In this flat the couch was the only place where the noodles could be laid out flat and straight on a starched tablecloth. Every other nook and cranny was occupied by shelves, hanging closets, and wardrobes with sliding doors, and since Fiona had moved in over a year ago even the last remaining bit of free space in the hallway had been taken up with a cat scratching post while the half a square metre under the sink was where the litter tray lived. To make matters worse, this family did its utmost to turn this pretty and affectionate animal into the most tyrannical creature imaginable: Vera prepared it an array of culinary delights, from chicken breast fillets to calves' liver, and Milena was dispatched to the far end of town to fetch scented Italian pine sand for its litter. Adam carried Fiona around in his arms or over his shoulder and let her sleep in his bed. How was such a spoilt animal supposed to understand why the door to the living room should suddenly be closed overnight because of noodles?

The apples from Uncle Miodrag's garden, which Milena was planning to turn into a strudel, went into the vegetable crate on the balcony. When the sack of potatoes had gone down enough to be stowed away under the garden chair there would be enough room again for the rotary clothes drier. She dreamed of having a larder. Or a dining room with space enough for a big table. Or, come to that, a biddable mother and a son who didn't always simply close his ears to things he didn't want to hear.

'What are you doing?' Vera shouted from the bathroom. 'Stand up, boy! A Serb stands up, otherwise he's not a real Serb. Is that what you want? Don't you want to be a real Serb?'

In his high-pitched voice, Adam replied: 'Dad told me it's not right, though!'

Vera came into the kitchen shaking her head. 'Every time he comes back from Germany, his head's full of these stupid fads. What will his friends at school think of him if he starts peeing sitting down?' She put the pot on the stove.

The sauce Milena had secretly been hoping for was poppy seed and raisin, which Vera usually cooked in milk scented with a vanilla pod. But that sort of pasta dish needed to have ground walnuts added to the dough. Instead, Vera had gone for a classic tomato sauce, a safe choice where Adam was concerned, blanching and steaming the really juicy beefsteak tomatoes that came from the south of the country, seasoning them with a pinch of sugar and adding some basil right at the end, chopped so finely that it would hopefully be barely noticeable. Adam hated everything green. Her subterfuge worked: he polished off two large portions. By this stage, he'd already had his bath, blown his nose, washed his ears and applied 'Pavlović Ointment', which had been prepared exclusively since time immemorial by Pavlović's Pharmacy on Zmaj-Jova-Street, to his arms and legs for his mild eczema.

While Adam was brushing his teeth in his pyjamas in the bathroom, Vera clattered the dishes in the sink. 'Did you see it?'

'See what?' asked Milena.

'The book. It must have been his father's idea.'

'What book?'

'If you ask me, that sort of reading material can't be good for the boy.'

'*Encyclopaedia of Bad Pupils*,' Milena read on the cover and began leafing through it. The bad pupils turned out to be great men like Napoleon, Leonardo da Vinci and Winston Churchill – this was probably quite a comfort to Adam, with his poor command of spelling and grammar.

She slipped it back under the pillow where, as usual, Adam had also stashed a slim silver torch.

One slipper crashed into the radiator, the other landed on the small suitcase. Adam jumped into bed. Milena fluffed up the duvet around him. 'Are you happy to be back home?'

He nodded.

'You and your Dad – you got on OK, didn't you?'

'More than OK.'

'And Dad's girlfriend' – she straightened out the blanket – 'is she nice?'

'Her name's Jutta. We took her sailing. She asked if she could come along and we said yes.'

'You went sailing with your Dad?'

'We started from the Outer Alster Lake, went into the Inner Alster and then turned back. But next time we want to go through the canals and maybe out into the Elbe. Shall I show you on the map?'

'It's alright,' said Milena, but in fact it was very far from alright. It was madness. Her boy in that little cockleshell of a boat, in the middle of the vast Outer Alster in amongst cruise ships and water taxis. Sure, Adam knew how to swim, but he was completely out of practice. How could Philip do this without first checking with her? Wasn't she the only one who could judge whether Adam was ready for such an expedition? No, this sailing trip was definitely too risky. Philip Bruns! It was time for another telephone conversation.

'When the Outer Alster freezes over we're going to go ice-skating. And Jutta wants to take me to a climbing wall.'

'We'll talk about it.'

'Please, Mum, can I go to Hamburg again over the autumn break?'

'We have to talk to Dad about that when things have calmed down a bit.'

'He told me to ask you.'

She forced a smile, though she felt like crying. Sailing, skating, climbing – all that belonged to a world that she could not offer him, and was clearly so exciting that his eyes were shining bright with the myriad of things whizzing round his head. Sleep was the last thing on his mind right now. Who was she kidding? She wasn't really concerned for his safety. She was jealous, through and through.

Milena stroked her son's soft hair. 'You like Jutta, don't you?'

'A lot!'

'Is she pretty?'

Adam pondered a bit and weighed his words. 'She looks totally different from you. Her hair's...'

'Blonde?'

'Yeah.'

'And her eyes? Blue?'

'Yeah.'

In other words, this Jutta was a typical German, super-sporty, fighting fit and pretty much the exact opposite to her. She should offer Philip her warmest congratulations when they next spoke. Milena kissed her son. 'Now, go to sleep.'

'You know, Mum...'

'What?'

'I'm happy that Dad isn't on his own anymore. You're so much better off than he is.'

'How's that?'

'You've got me.'

'You're right. Now, close your eyes.'

'Mum?'

'Yes?'

'Promise me something.'

'What?'

'That you'll stop smoking?'

'I'll try. Yes, I promise. Sweet dreams.'

She left the door ajar so Fiona could jump onto his bed whenever she wanted.

The tea was an infusion of ginger and mint, to which she added three drops of lemon juice and covered the mug with a saucer, placing it with a napkin on top of the living-room table, within easy reach of Vera.

'Thank you, dear.' Her mother was staring at the television screen, transfixed by an orchestra of sobbing violins and a love story that was just about to reach its climax.

Milena bent down to straighten the rug on the polished parquet floor. There it was again, that backache. Well, she was pushing fifty. Maybe she should finally take up some kind of sport, too. 'Good Morning, Belgrade' was the name of the initiative that gave everyone free access to the city's public baths for two hours every day. But that would mean getting up even earlier. Anyhow, when was the last time she had gone swimming properly? That messing around in the water on their holiday in Istria didn't really count.

With a pot of coffee in her hand she went to her room and switched on the computer. While it was booting up, she opened her wardrobe. Her bathing suit lay at the very bottom and dated from her time with Philip, in other words it was ancient. She pulled it out and held it up against her body. The way the fabric stretched from hip to hip distorted the dot pattern into a grotesque design. She had always had broad hips, but this thing definitely wouldn't fit her anymore. She flung it back into the wardrobe.

As she did so, she came a bit too close to the mirror on the inside of the wardrobe door, and caught sight of the wrinkles around her wide mouth and the shadows under her reddened eyes. But the day had been strenuous and the light here was not exactly flattering. Her thick dark hair had a beautiful lustre when she was fully made up. In the mornings she usually didn't have time to do anything except put on a bit of lipstick, a warm umber colour, which went well with her eyes. And as far as her clothes were concerned she also preferred warm, muted colours: a crème twinset and the brown cashmere jumper, fitting attire for an intellectual woman of her age. On the other hand, she loved bright red lipstick, her azure-blue blouse and her latest acquisition, a grass-green, knee-length coat which her best friend Tanja, with a disapproving shake of her head, had adjudged 'a bit out-there'. But for Milena colours were an expression of her *joi de vivre*. She closed the wardrobe. Right now, though, she'd have preferred to wrap herself in a black cloak.

She lit a cigarillo, blew the smoke into the room and stared at the desktop – a green landscape strewn with files. Although the separation happened ten years ago – a period exactly matching the age of her son – hearing that Philip was far from unhappy still filled her with burning rage. As did the fact that other women continued to figure in the life of her ex. How she had loved that man! The first time she met him, she had to keep her arms folded to stop herself from grabbing hold of him. Philip with his full lips and his alluring hooded eyes – the potbelly had only appeared later. At first she hadn't noticed how he was withdrawing from her. Yet it had happened all the same, back when the war in Yugoslavia began. When wave after wave of refugees started flooding into Germany, and her friends and relatives came looking for a safe haven under their roof in Berlin. All those late-night tears, and earnest discussions in a language that Philip did not understand and which excluded him. Milena had under-estimated the problem, which in any event was dwarfed by the one facing these people who had lost everything – their homes and their homeland. It stood to reason that they should sleep in his study, use his computer until late at night and drink coffee from his favourite cup in the morning. It was a fraught, exciting and sad time. When she became pregnant, Milena thought that happiness would return to her life.

That same evening he'd confessed to having an affair with

Susanne or Sabine or whatever the bitch's name was. His admission came completely out of the blue. Had she been blind? He just had time enough to spot that she'd laid the table in celebration with their best china and the large wine goblets, with folded napkins and candles, before, in her fury, she took hold of the table edge, lifted it up and smashed the whole lot against the wall. She left the flat without clearing up the mess, or telling him about the child she was expecting. And without having the faintest idea where she was going. The worst thing was that he made no attempt to stop her.

Milena stubbed out the cigarillo, opened the internet browser and typed in the search terms 'Topčider', 'Serbian elite unit', and 'Guards'. She paused for a moment before adding another word: 'Dead'.

The entries with the most hits were various articles from the regime friendly newspaper *Politika* and a report by the leftist magazine *Vreme*. She had followed the case of the two dead guardsmen at the Topčider – which Siniša was now somehow involved with – in the newspapers, though she could not recall all the details. Milena also scanned the headlines in the tabloid *Kurier*. The two guardsmen Nenad J. and Predrag M. had been found dead in the early hours of the twelfth of July in Topčider city forest, inside their barracks compound. Like all the troops in this elite unit, they were highly trained, physically fit and psychologically stable, were well-liked by everybody in their regiment and came from good homes. The night before they died they'd been put on night-watch – a routine duty every guardsman had to perform. The findings of the investigating judge Jovan Dežulović – a member of the Military Tribunal – stated that one of the two guards had shot the other at close range and then committed suicide. The involvement of a third party was ruled out and the investigation concluded with the verdict that the two young men had most likely died while performing a ritual of some obscure religious sect.

Milena leaned back. Physically and psychologically healthy. Victims of a ritual suicide.

Fiona leapt onto the desk, skipped lightly across the card index with her soft paws, brushed the scented candle with her bushy tail, turned around smartly in the length of her own body and rolled up next to the stuffed Rolodex.

Milena shut down the computer, window by window. 'Go to sleep,' she told herself. 'What's keeping you? Adam's back safely and his door's open.'

Fiona stared at her with her grey, inscrutable cat's eyes. Not for the first time, Milena wondered whether this dumb animal was simply that or whether it knew and saw something hidden from her, the creature who was endowed with the power of reason.

3

The brown of the envelope was the same shade as the short-crust pastry that formed the solid base for layers of custard, jam and cream. The Constantinople-Slice was finished off with a layer of dark chocolate, a finger's width deep. It took a certain determination to slice straight down through the brittle chocolate coating with the prongs of the pastry-fork. But Milena possessed such determination. And that was despite her all-too recent embarrassing run-in with a designer chair. The incident had occurred in the smart new meeting place on Terazije Street, where Tanja had taken her for a drink last month. When Milena tried to get up, her hips got stuck between the chrome armrests. For seconds the chair had hovered in the air as if it was stuck to her bottom. All the hip people around her, with their gelled and over-styled hair, saw it and smirked.

But here, in the Café Le Petit Prince, people were more concerned with cakes, tarts and reading the newspaper and Milena's wooden chair had no armrests, just a backrest, on which the solicitor Siniša Stojkovič now laid his hand, smiled, as probably only men from Montenegro could smile, and said in a way that made Milena really want to believe him: 'Milena, I swear you get more beautiful every time we meet!'

She unfolded the silver arms of her spectacles, brushed back a strand of hair from her forehead and put the glasses on her nose. 'Institute for Ballistics and Firearms Technology, Ludwigshafen' was the return address on the envelope.

She took off her glasses again and looked at Siniša: 'What, may I ask, have you got to do with this institute?'

He waved at the waiter, pointed at the cappuccino cups and raised two fingers in the air. 'I've taken on the case of the two dead guardsmen. The parents of Nenad Jokić and Predrag Mrša are my clients and, I think I can now safely say, my friends. We're not going to rest until we've established how the two boys were killed. The circumstances are more than mysterious.'

'Mysterious? I read that they might have joined a sect or something. That they performed some kind of ritual.'

'Utter rubbish. The guys weren't into rituals or religious stuff.'

'What if they were?'

Siniša's dark eyebrows formed a sharp contrast to his silver-white hair. 'You don't believe that nonsense, do you?' he asked.

'Thank you.' Milena smiled as the waiter placed the cup in front of her and set it straight on the saucer.

'Believe me,' said Siniša, 'these are the lies of a regime in which the military can still do as it pleases. This was no ritual, no suicide. What's really behind the deaths of Nenad Jokić and Predrag Mrša is a totally different story.'

The sugar trickled out of its sachet and sank into the frothed milk. Milena stirred her coffee. She liked Siniša and admired his courage and the tenacity he had displayed even back when he tried to make the impossible happen and get the dictator's criminal son locked up. Accessory to murder had been the charge that Siniša, at that time still Chief Prosecutor, had brought. Soon after, he found himself dismissed and having to fend for himself as an independent solicitor. The dictator had long since been ousted, and his son had left the country, but Siniša was still a driven man, filled with hatred for the decrepit structures and those criminals in uniform who refused to acknowledge the war crimes committed by Serbian troops during the Yugoslavian conflict of the nineties. Whenever Milena – in her scientific papers, her newspaper comment pieces or as a guest speaker on some podium or another – called for the mass executions of Muslims in Bosnia and Albanians in Kosovo to be investigated, she knew for sure that Siniša was on her side. What she didn't like about him was his tunnel vision.

'Anyhow,' he continued, reaching out and placing his hand flat on the table as if he wanted to prevent Milena from getting away, 'after I took on the case, it took me no time to get an independent commission to reinvestigate the whole saga.'

'My compliments. How did you manage that?'

'The usual cat-and-mouse-game.' Siniša gave a pained smile. 'Unfortunately I wasn't allowed to chair the commission. That job went to a henchman of that incompetent crook Dežulović, the examining magistrate.'

'Wait a minute. You manage to set up an independent commission, but you aren't yourself a member of that commission?'

'That's right.'

'Then this is anything but an "independent" commission.'

'Precisely.'

'So what now?'

'I've done all I could. I made sure that the autopsy reports, the interview protocols, the pictures of the bodies *in situ* and the crime scene, in short everything which Dežulović uncovered in his investigations, was sent to Ludwigshafen and disclosed to the Germans. A triumph for me; a total humiliation for Dežulović.' Siniša laughed cheerfully.

Milena was baffled. 'But if there was really something fishy about the death of the two guardsmen, then surely Dežulović would have made sure he falsified the investigation's findings to start with, wouldn't he?'

'My dear Milena,' Siniša wrung his hands, 'what would you have done in my shoes? Nothing at all? Just sat back and watched while these gangsters did whatever they wanted? If we mean to expose what this sleazebag Dežulović has tried to sweep under the carpet, then I see no alternative but to poke their dunghill.'

'So what dirt have our colleagues in Ludwigshafen dug up?'

Siniša gave a sigh. 'On the face of it they confirm the findings of the military tribunal. At least that's what the official Serbian translation of the German report says.' Siniša leant forward, so close that Milena could smell his spicy aftershave. 'But here, in this envelope,' he said in a lowered voice, 'is the German original. I managed to get hold of it through some back channels. Can you translate it for me? Word for word. And if it differs one iota from the official version then I'm going to kick up a massive stink about it, rest assured.'

Pensively, Milena pushed together fragments of chocolate and cake crumbs on her plate. A massive stink – she knew what that meant. Siniša would parade himself, most likely in an open coat and flowing silk scarf, in front of the TV cameras as the tireless champion of just causes. However, he wouldn't hesitate to bend the truth a little here and there, just as his enemies did. If need be, he'd even exploit the pain, grief and despair of the victims to his own ends, if that helped him expose his opponents. She'd known him too long to have any illusions.

'Maybe there's a totally different explanation for the deaths of those two young men,' she suggested.

'Like what?'

Milena got up to leave.

Siniša laughed. 'You mean that they were in love with one another? That they were gay?'

'That's just one of several possibilities.'

'Predrag was a renowned womaniser.'

'What about the other one, Nenad? Maybe there were drugs involved.'

'Nenad wanted to train as a pilot.'

Milena stuffed the envelop into her bag. 'I'll call you.'

'When?'

'When I've finished the translation.'

He helped her on with her coat. 'Tonight?'

'I'll do my best.'

*

Her parking spot under the birch trees behind the institute was possibly the most beautiful in the whole of Belgrade – and it was taken.

Irritated, she swung around the square with the monument, past the little petrol station with its single pump – but found nothing, everywhere was full. If only the people from 'Tanjug', the state news agency housed in the vast office complex, had been about to knock off for the day. The city was simply not designed for this many large cars. Thank goodness not everywhere had tackled the problem in the same way as King Alexander Boulevard, formerly Revolution Boulevard. There, the venerable plane trees that had once lined the street in their hundreds were simply declared diseased, felled with chainsaws, and serried rows of parking bays installed in their place. All the protests and signatures collected by irate Belgraders had run into the sand, stifled by city bureaucracy. Vera had called the street the 'Boulevard of Horror' ever since.

Milena had no choice but to park at a sharp angle near the Red Cockerel. When the weather was good people sat here in their finery with their laptops, outside the open bar. Now the wind was blowing the first dry leaves across the square and a light rain was falling on the deserted tables and chairs. Only the old woman sitting on her flattened cardboard box remained. Day after day she sat at the corner and used a potato to demonstrate to people hurrying by the efficacy of the peeling knife she was selling, though she could barely hold it in her gnarled hand. Milena turned off the engine. Her place of work was directly opposite. If she was forced to park illegally, then at least she'd make sure it was convenient.

Over the decades the rain had washed all the colour off the front of the building on the corner, turning it a greyish-brown hue that would not have actually looked so bad if only the plaster hadn't started flaking off all over in smaller or larger chunks. Then there were the weathered wooden roller-blinds, which were hanging all skew-whiff in their frames, especially on the ground floor. The Institute for Criminology was so dilapidated and run-down that people had to steel themselves to enter it for the first time. But that made the pleasant contrast they encountered inside all the more surprising.

A dome of frosted glass, with coloured sections which formed a naïve pattern and produced charming light effects throughout the day, spanned the head of the stairwell. The walls were whitewashed, the ceilings were decorated in stucco, the windows were high and the parquet floor creaked with every step. There were times when Milena, ensconced in her little room almost at the end of the long corridor, felt like she was in a castle. And although the location of her desk made it a bit draughty, she had an even better view than the head of the institute up in his tower room; from her window seat, she overlooked the grey monument of Duke Vuk, hero of the liberation struggle, who was clutching his moss-covered rifle and storming ahead for all eternity, though never getting anywhere.

Milena hung up her umbrella on the hook, put a potato peeler in the bottom drawer, next to all the other potato peelers she had bought, and pulled on a cardigan. But the cold draught was coming from below. She got on her knees and crawled under the desk.

Where was her head today? Before she could turn on the electric space heater, she first needed to boil a kettle for an all-important cup of coffee. If she turned on both electrical appliances at the same time they would blow the fuse.

Of late, she'd been dialling the international code for Germany and the number in Bonn virtually every day. The German Academic Association paid half her salary, but whether that arrangement would continue in future heaven only knew. For the past few weeks and months Milena had been engaged in documenting her work for the bureaucrats in Bonn in a series of analyses, diagrams and reports. She had been employed to develop a department for International Criminal Prosecution and Jurisdiction – a task that had met with considerable obstruction on the part of the Serbs. That was yet another of the many paradoxes of this country, since officially the Serbian Ministry of Education was financing her work. The political will was there to demonstrate to the European Union that Serbia was ready to confront its past war crimes. But there was no appetite for matching this theoretical willingness with any substantive measures. The people from Bonn were different but not much better in their own way.

'I'm sorry,' said the lady on the other end of the line. 'I can't find your file. My colleague Blechschmidt is ill, I'm only standing in for him.' Something in her voice made it apparent she was sitting in an office with thick carpets, nice furniture and curtains in the windows. 'When did you say your deadline was?'

'Deadline?' Milena was determined not to raise her voice. She wanted to appear as calm and collected as the woman she was speaking to, though this endless foot-dragging by Bonn, this thoughtlessness bordering on arrogance was driving her crazy. Damn it, her livelihood and that of her son and mother were at stake here! 'My contract expires at the end of the year, if that's what you mean.'

'I understand. You need to speak to the planning security department. What was your name again?'

'Milena Lukin.'

'And you are in...'

'Belgrade. The capital of Serbia.'

'One of my colleagues will contact you in the next few days.'

Milena hung up. Her eyes were inflamed and sore. With her thumb and index finger she squeezed the bridge of her nose and concentrated on her breathing. With her other hand she pulled her bag towards her, reached blindly inside it and rummaged around until she found what she was after. Without touching it, Milena squeezed a jelly banana straight out of its cellophane wrapper into her mouth. Instantly the sweet, dark-chocolate coating began to melt. Then she used her tongue to dissolve the caster sugar layer beneath and reach the firm core of cool jelly. Milena closed her eyes.

She was making hardly any progress with her own research anymore. 'The Criminal Prosecution of War Crimes in the Territory of the Former Yugoslavia between 1990 and 1999' was the title of her thesis, which was meant not only to shed light on the darkest chapter of the country's recent past but also hopefully one day to earn her a tenured professorial post somewhere in the world. It didn't have to be Berlin. Boston,

CHRISTIAN SCHÜNEMANN AND JELENA VOLIĆ

maybe. She had no objection to relocating her family across the Big Pond, moving into a brownstone with a bay window, dining room and front lawn, and receiving a far higher monthly salary than she could ever dream of getting here. And above all she finally wanted to gain some recognition for her work, which nobody here appreciated.

There was a knock at the door. Without waiting for a reply, the head of her institute entered – a rude habit she could never seemingly get him to break. Boris Grubač's tie was already slightly undone, and the peppermint smell on his breath signalled that he had already pre-empted the end of his working day with a glass or two.

'How's it going?' he asked in a tone that was meant to show that he took an active and solicitous interest in Milena's work. Neither was actually the case. 'Have your colleagues in Bonn finally given you the green light?'

'It's looking very good.' Milena lied, deftly sliding the brown envelope from Ludwigshafen under a folder: 'They have assured me that they'll keep supporting my work here.'

'And you have that in writing?'

'A mere formality. It will be here in the next few days.'

Grubač handed her a small envelope made from expensive handmade paper. The eagle of the Federal Republic of Germany was discreetly embossed on the back flap and on the letterhead of the card inside. An invitation to a reception. The new German Ambassador requests the honour of your presence, Friday 3 September.

Milena handed the envelope back to her boss. 'I don't have the time.'

'You could make time. Do a bit of lobbying. Networking – ever heard of it?'

'I simply haven't got the patience to stand around all night making small talk. Why don't you go? Take your wife.

Have a nice evening.' Milena smiled at her boss, this little man with hair combed over his bald patch, and conjured up an image of his wife Itana at his side, a Bosnian who was not even from Sarajevo: Itana with her small plump hands, her small plump feet and her fatal attraction to garish reds and violets and oranges. She expressed her taste in colours not only in her billowing clothes but also in her choice of hair dye. Mr and Mrs Grubač in the midst of the black-white-grey milieu of the German embassy – Milena had fun picturing the scene but, at the same time, was ashamed by her own malice.

'My dear Ms Lukin.' Now it was Grubač's turn to smile. In fact he smiled so broadly that his nostrils expanded and exposed the growth inside even more than usual. 'Why on earth should I stand around at the German Embassy all night – as you so appositely put it? After all, I don't need the Germans. My job is secure. Have a nice evening.' He had already reached the door when he turned around again. 'And do yourself a favour and don't go burning the midnight oil. You look really done in.'

Milena gulped down the black coffee, pulled the telephone towards her once more and dialled her home number. Adam picked up.

'Sweetie,' she said, 'don't wait for me with dinner. I still have work to do here. Is everything alright with you? Hello?'

He was mumbling something incomprehensible, his mind obviously elsewhere, probably on one of those mobile phone games.

'Can you put Grandma on?'

There was a rustling sound, and then silence. 'Hello,' Milena called into the receiver, extending every vowel and then whistled.

Finally Vera came on the line. 'Good of you to call,' she

said. 'You promised to pick up some cat litter, remember. Did you?'

Milena closed her eyes and told herself that she loved her family, yes she really and truly did, despite everything.

After she finally hung up, she eased off her tight-fitting shoes, switched on the lamp on her desk and leant forward to look at the computer screen. She clicked around in the word processing program until she'd securely opened, saved and filed the new document. She emptied the brown envelope on to her desk – forty-five stapled pages – put her glasses on and folded back the covering sheet. She started typing as she was reading.

Re: Cause of Death of Nenad Jokić and Predrag Mrša... Based on the findings of the Forensic Science Institute of the Military Court of the Republic of Serbia...

It was long past 6 pm by the time Milena finally got down to the brass tacks of the sober analysis that the German scientists had come up with concerning two deaths on Serbian soil.

4

He lay on his bed fully clothed and listened with his eyes closed. He could hear the sound of his own breathing and, in the distance, the roar of traffic. Somewhere, a dog was barking.

Next door, in the office, the lock of the desk drawer was turned – once, twice. Then the desk key was dropped into the briefcase, and almost simultaneously the clasps – right, left – were snapped into place. Chair legs on lino. A squeaky hinge: the cupboard door was opened, then closed again. At the count of ten at most, the back door would be locked. Pawle counted. By the time he'd got to eight, Momčilo was gone.

Pawle opened his eyes. He saw the water stains on the ceiling and the plaster which was peeling off all around them. He turned his head. Beneath the basin, just by the bend in the downpipe, was his roommate, the spider. For days she had been sitting there in her web, always in the same position. It seemed like a pretty stupid place to build a web.

He got up, put the bucket into the basin and turned on the tap. In his work he followed orders, but he preferred to be left to his own devices in how he carried them out. He did not care for onlookers, nor was he accustomed to having any.

With the scrubbing brush stuck under his right arm he lugged the bucket along in his left hand. One time when he'd walked into the room, keen to get started, he suddenly realised there was still somebody there. One of those baby-faced Belgrade types, fearless and stupid. Because they hadn't seen anything of the world and Mummy still made sure no harm would come to them, they thought the world out there was some boy scout camp. That was the sort of cretinous expression the bloke had on his face when he had approached him, said something and then suddenly stretched out his paw to him.

He hated it. The chatter, the stupid questions and always being stared at. And where there was one, suddenly a whole crowd would appear. Like rats. But if a rat didn't disappear on the count of three, it deserved to have its neck broken.

Hold on a minute, he had told himself. Don't panic. After all, it was just some babyface.

So he did what he had been instructed to do under these circumstances: keep your hand in your pocket, count to three, mutter something, count to three again, then mutter something else. That was all it took. The message came across loud and clear. The bloke cleared off. It never failed to work.

He put down the bucket, grabbed the chair closest to him, turned it around and slammed it onto the table, seat down. All with his left hand and with a deft flick of his wrist, a single movement, like a conveyor belt. Chair after chair. He took the scrubbing brush and pushed the limp bristles under the water. Small bubbles came gurgling to the surface.

He stared into the water. He saw images. Fishes splashing about in shallow water. Blue shimmering skin between the stones and around his naked feet. His hand, his right hand, plunged in to grab them.

Jerking the handle and rag of the mop out of the water, he cursed as he pressed the dripping cloth into the strainer that was fixed to the side of the bucket. Turning the handle, he twisted the rag and wrung it out with all his might until the flow of water abated and finally not a single drop came out of it. The images had dissipated. He tried to breathe regularly.

He looked at the roster. Four tiles made one square. He

kicked away the wastepaper basket and worked his way across the room, square by square. The further he went the more obstacles appeared: the rusting cardholder. Boxes full of catalogues, a few of which must still be lying in the display window at the exit. One time, he'd leafed through one of these catalogues. Hardly any pictures, but full of stuff about comradeship and common goals. Complete twaddle.

The guys must have got these tables with their scraped metal runners from some school or another. They still had the hooks for satchels on the side. Those damned hooks. It was here that he'd experienced the visions for the first time. Without warning, pigtailed girls wearing flowery dresses and skipping along appeared in front of his mind's eye. Boys in short trousers kicking a can along and running after it. Pictures without sound. They pursued him. They took his breath away.

Rag under water, rag into the strainer, mop up. Tile after tile, square after square, up to the desk, up to the washed-down blackboard. Don't think. He took the chairs off the tables again, working efficiently, positioning everything neatly again, edge against edge. He checked the symmetry of the 'U' shape of desks he had created, took out a cloth and wiped the surfaces of the tables, the declarations of love, the obscene phrases and graffiti doodled and carved by all those who'd spent time here lounging around on their arses. Milksops.

He poured the dirty water into the loo and pissed on it.

He walked back into the big room, up to the entrance door. He rattled the handle. Securely locked. The crack in the pane of glass had been glued over, probably by his predecessor. A brawl, a break-in? Actually he couldn't care less; it had happened before he'd been posted here.

The curtain in front of the kitchenette had a pattern,

waves in the material which were now in motion. Utter nonsense. Or was it?

He jumped up and tore the curtain aside with such force that it came off its rail and hung loose at one end. He cursed. He had two options: either to hope that nobody would notice the damage. Or report it straight away. He couldn't decide which was better. He only knew that he dare not draw attention to himself.

He flicked the switch, extinguishing the neon strip lights. Only the sign in the window was still on. He leant against the doorframe. The light was warm and beautiful like the big yellow moon of a summer's night.

He walked to the back door, put on the chain and the padlock and went to his room. He unbuttoned his trousers, hung them over the chair and lay down on the bed. The springs squeaked with every movement. He didn't mind. He had learned to be unobtrusive and not to move even when he was asleep.

He listened. Rain dripped from the bars on the window and made a hollow knocking sound on the aluminium of the windowsill. There was no rhythm. He heard his breathing and in the distance traffic noise. Somewhere the dog barked, gave a yelp, then started barking again. He had never set eyes on the animal. If he ever got his hands on it, he knew exactly what he'd do to it.

He wrapped himself in the thin blanket. One day it would all blow over. One day he'd get out of here. Until then he just had to keep going. And not make any mistakes.

5

Milena tugged at the brass catch until, finally, the window sash flew open. Fresh air streamed in and rustled the papers on the desk. She took a deep breath. Her throat was parched.

The asphalt reflected the glare of the streetlamps. It must have rained heavily just now. The chef from the restaurant The Spring was standing outside, with only the glimmer of his lit cigarette to show that he was alive and breathing. Milena drank the remaining coffee from her cup, which was by now cold and tasted bitter.

She had translated non-stop, retracing how the German scientists had painstakingly pieced together the facts from the patchy material that their Serbian colleagues had handed over to them, highlighting inconsistencies and inaccuracies and revealing piece by piece the true picture that lay behind outward appearance. In truth, she hadn't expected too much to come out of this process. But in paragraph nineteen, there was the telling statement: *Considering that the angle of the bullet into the entry wound was less than twenty-five degrees...* – The telephone rang.

She knew straight away who'd be on the other end of the line, itching to hear what she'd discovered. 'Siniša?' She coughed. She hadn't spoken for almost four hours.

'Do you know what time it is?' It was Tanja's voice. 'Listen,' she said. 'Shut down your computer right now, get your arse to the car and get over here.'

'What, now?'

'Yes, right now. I've got a surprise for you.'

Tanja's house was set way up above the rest of the city, high on the escarpment over the harbour, and could only be reached by a steep flight of steps. These could be a bit treacherous after wet leaves had fallen, and even more so during winter when covered with ice and snow. But Tanja really loved her place, this old barracks she'd discovered and purchased last year and was now busy turning into a gem of a house.

Tanja hugged her, pressing her close like it had been an eternity since they'd last seen one another, rather than the fortnight that had actually passed. She had tamed her wild curls by trapping them in a practical elasticated hair band that forced them into a frizzy, sticking-up brush. The copper tone of Tanja's hair was similar to the colour of the gladioli in the vase on the floor and complimented the green nail polish on her toenails. Her grey silk jumper was a bit tight over her full breasts and the faint scent of fresh lime deodorant she exuded during their embrace made Milena think of the dark patches of sweat under her own arms, which fortunately were nothing she had to feel ashamed of in this company.

'I met Siniša.' Milena slipped out of her flat shoes, which were so worn out of shape they looked like boats next to Tanja's strappy silver sandals. To make them look less conspicuous, Milena pushed her shoes next to the pair of walking boots that Tanja had bought for a tour of the Montenegrin high plateau. The soft house-slippers for guests at the end of the long line of shoes were clearly a new acquisition – a dream of pale pink snakeskin. Milena could not resist.

'Siniša, the shyster?' Tanja exclaimed from the kitchen. 'Is Philip giving you grief? Listen, if you need a lawyer, I'll get you one, but one who's really hot shit. It's about time somebody started putting the bite on your ex.'

No matter how much she tried tucking in her toes, there was no way she was getting into the slippers. Milena's clodhoppers and Tanja's dainty little feet – two different worlds.

A cork popped in the kitchen and Tanja called out: 'And by the way, you shouldn't be hanging around at that institute of yours all hours of the day and night, slaving away for other people!' With splayed fingers, she arranged sushi on a big plate, licked her index and middle fingers and turned around to smile at Milena.

'Your underfloor heating is heavenly,' said Milena, taking the glass Tanja handed her.

'To us!' The thin glasses clinked together delicately. Tanja's searching eyes scanned Milena as they drank.

'Be honest: have I gained weight?' Milena stepped back.

'Not in the least.' From the shelf over the sink, Tanja fetched down little bowls stacked in leaning towers between colourful food packages and herbs from all over the world. Milena liked this mess, the hanging cupboard sitting on the floor, the folding chairs leaning against the wall, the accumulation of empty bottles and the naked light bulb dangling from the ceiling.

'You're a beautiful woman with voluptuous curves,' Tanja said. 'There are hardly any women like you left. You belong to a most precious species that needs protecting, 'cos it's threatened with extinction. Believe me, I know what I'm talking about. But let's eat now; I'm famished. Can you grab the glasses, please?'

Milena was content with that response. Tanja was an expert in such matters. After all, she was raking in money as a plastic surgeon who pandered to the delusions of beauty and fashionable *ennui* of people who came to her from far and wide, who disappeared behind the thick hedgerows and high walls of her private clinic to emerge weeks later smoothed, taut and rejuvenated – and lighter to the tune of a few thousand Euros. It had taken Milena a long time to get her head round Tanja's decision to take over the clinic in the chic suburb of Dedinje and specialise in plastic surgery. Prior to that, her friend had always worked where she was really needed: in provincial hospitals where medication and qualified personnel were in equally short supply and, after the outbreak of war in Yugoslavia, in crisis areas where she spent her time removing bullets and shrapnel from wounds and amputating limbs. Even so, she was unable to save a lot of her patients. Tanja figured that she'd seen enough pain and suffering in that period to last her a lifetime.

Latterly, though, the two girlfriends had been able to while away many happy hours steaming in the Finnish sauna on the roof and flicking through gossip magazines as Milena had Tanja show her the cosmetic nips and tucks she'd performed on various glamorous, *nouveau-riche* celebrities.

They flopped down onto the couch in almost perfect sync. Lit candles were strewn over the low glass table, their twinkling light reflected a thousandfold by the windowpanes. Magazines and books were piled high on a cowhide next to the lounger. The sound of a jazz trumpet filled the room. Milena tucked her feet up and Tanja stuffed some colourful cushions behind her back. 'Are you alright?' she asked.

Milena smiled. 'Yeah, just dandy, thanks.'

'But...?'

Milena shook her head, took a sip of wine, put her glass down and began: 'You know, Vera asks me where the cat litter is, which I've been carting around in my car boot for days. But it's not just a simple question: it's like the family's whole life depended on it. She's got no idea what's really going on. What if they don't extend my contract? Once again, I find myself fighting for our very existence. I struggle and struggle, but sometimes I get the feeling there's no end in sight.'

'Sweetie, don't get mad with me, but that's not exactly news. Don't tell me that's the reason why you're all out of sorts today.' She popped a rice roll into her mouth. 'It's because of Philip, isn't it? The tuition fees. That pig hasn't transferred any money again, has he?'

'I dunno. Probably not.'

'How much do you need?'

'No, Tanja.'

'Let me. This is important. It's the least I can do for my godchild.'

'Hold on a minute, you're doing everything as it is. Without you, we'd have to either scratch his guitar lessons or his basketball club membership. Probably the guitar would lose out. No, really Tanja, I'll take care of his tuition fees.' Milena wiped her hands on the napkin, picked up her glass and took another sip. 'The German school,' she said, 'maybe it was a crazy idea. Of course Adam should learn to speak German, as fluently as possible. If he knows German he'll have a better chance later in life, won't he? But let's not kid ourselves: this German school's not our world. Do you imagine one of Adam's school friends would ever come to our flat in town for his birthday party? Out of the question. None of them are going to leave their villa or gated compound. They've heard about our area and are convinced we live right next to a slum. Believe me, Tanja, that's what they think! So what do we do instead? We bake cakes and make lemonade and drive up to Dedinje, where these people live. Because they won't come to us, we go to them and organise a picnic in the park for these mothers and their spoilt kids. Vera spends her time dutifully running after the German snot-noses with ironed handkerchiefs, then comes back to me and mocks these tarted-up bitches for neglecting their brats so badly. And I skip from one to the other, trying to please everybody and hoping to pass muster with the German ladies. Once again, I can guarantee I'll be the only mother who misses the lantern run, and who can't say for sure whether she can make the Christmas handicraft hour, which will actually turn into a Christmas handicraft afternoon, and then a Christmas handicraft evening. These German yummy mummies with the lists they make, the cakes they bake and the nice trips they organise – they're driving me round the bend.'

'Forget them.' Tanja put her plate down. 'Even if they showed the slightest interest in you, they couldn't understand the first thing about your life. And believe me, dear, you don't want to trade places with them.' She reached for the cigarillos. 'But you could still learn something from these women and their talent for organising. If you ask me, you're badly in need of a bit more calm in your life. Promise you won't hit me if I try and put things in a nutshell, but honestly I think you need a man, not another Philip, but one who has your back for a change. It doesn't have to be forever.'

'Yeah, that really would be quite a change,' Milena muttered, helping herself from the flat, square box with the cherry-flavoured cigarillos. 'It's your turn to tell now,' she said. 'How were things in Cyprus with Stefanos?'

Tanja's new lover was fifteen years younger than her and drop-dead gorgeous – like all the men in Tanja's life. And as always, Milena pulled her punches as to what she really thought about Tanja's conquests: that none of them ever came close to Dejan. The blond, slim Dejan, who could sing so beautifully and play the guitar, who smoked a pipe and came from one of the most renowned families of doctors in Belgrade – Tanja's first great love. Unfortunately, he not only adored Tanja, but many other women as well, ultimately a Russian tennis player. Tanja first got wind of the affair after reading about it in the tabloid press. By the time she packed her bags and left him, unaware that she'd be turning her back on Belgrade for quite some time, Milena was already living in Berlin, prompting Vera to ask: 'What's the matter with you two? You're like pumpkins – you don't seem to have any roots!'

Milena smoked as she looked at the digital images of Cyprus and Stefanos on Tanja's mobile. So much sun, tanned skin and blue sea. The breeze, which you could feel just by looking at the screen, was already a blessing. Tanja did so many things so well. She worked hard and at the same time grabbed life with both hands. And when Milena told her about the plight of displaced ethnic Serbs from Kosovo in the Gunzati reception camps Tanja didn't hesitate for a moment, whipping out her chequebook to sponsor some refugee child in Serbia, ensuring they were provided with a winter coat and warm shoes. 'Milena, now I'm a rich-pig capitalist , you're my guilty conscience,' she used to say.

The wine fizzed in the glasses, the cushions were soft and the view over the harbour, the Sava and the lights of the city was breathtaking. Milena felt wrapped in a warm cocoon, high up, secure and pleasantly tipsy, and giggled like a silly girl listening to Tanja's stories and looking at the snaps of Stefanos, posing on a cliff-top, diving into the water and looking for all the world as if he could turn pirouettes as well.

Suddenly a gift landed in her lap, the surprise she'd been promised, Tanja's little present from Nicosia. Still laughing, with the cigarillo between her lips, squinting and wreathed in clouds of smoke, Milena undid the ribbon and opened the box.

Inside was a confection of silk and fine lace, so sheer and gossamer-light it felt like nothing in Milena's hands. She'd never owned a négligée like this before. All of a sudden, her throat tightened and she was gasping for breath. It was as if she'd been snatched up by a wave that had carried her away and washed her up in a landscape where everything beautiful had been replaced by ugliness. On the one hand was this superfluous luxury, and on the other, two young men who'd still had their whole lives ahead of them. Suddenly it all came flooding back: two bullets – one to the heart, the other through the skull. Milena covered her face with her hands, pressing her fingers against her eyes.

'Sweetheart!' Shocked, Tanja leant forward and put her hand on Milena's knee. 'Whatever's the matter?'

'I'd hoped...' Milena's voice trembled. 'I'd really hoped,' she repeated in a somewhat steadier voice, 'that Siniša was just imagining things. That he'd just got a bee in his bonnet as usual. But the angle of the entry wound...' She tried to sit up straight and breathe deeply. 'The angle from where the shot was fired...'

'Fired?'

'The German report states clearly that a third party must have fired the shot.'

'I don't understand.'

Milena put the lid back on the box. 'It was murder.' She gave Tanja a peck on the cheek. 'The underwear's beautiful. Thank you.'

6

The straggly grey tussocks growing in the craters between the high-rises and the old garages were blades of grass that had never seen the sun. With their flat roots they were trying to bind together the crumbling soil – a combination of broken asphalt, mud and rubble – which was strewn with garbage cans and wrecked cars. Cannibalised and stripped of their wheels, these heaps of rust were the perfect home for a colony of feral cats who were breeding uncontrollably between ripped-up seat cushions and old batteries. It was into this damned, godforsaken terrain that the petrol-blue Lada slowly advanced, drawing to a halt between a wooden shack and a large water butt.

Milena pulled on the handbrake and switched off the engine, before gathering her glasses, purse, chewing gum and mobile from the passenger seat and the glove box. She slammed the car door shut and locked it. Taking a big step across a puddle, she slipped on the mud but regained her footing on a flat stone. From there, she jumped to the next one and continued her progress to the street in similar fashion, leaping from stone to stone. Behind her, the cats occupied the Lada, stretching out contentedly on its warm bonnet.

All along Milja-Kovačevič-Street, the main road to Bucharest, the pavement was lined with wooden shacks, which had been turned into makeshift shops by the addition of windowpanes and corrugated-iron roofs. The merchandise was displayed in buckets outside: opulent bunches of roses and gypsophila, slim gerbera, modest asters and plump dahlias. Milena stuck her nose into one of the big blossoms, closed her eyes and breathed in the scent and for just a few seconds had the feeling that she was not standing beneath this dirty awning on a rainy day in August, but was under an umbrella in a beautiful garden, with the wind gently caressing her cheek.

'Can I help you?'

Milena opened her eyes. A short man in a thick jumper and an even thicker padded vest was looking inquisitively at her through filigree-rimmed glasses.

She was undecided what to buy. Today was Parastos – the commemoration of the dead. Forty days had passed since the two guardsmen Nenad Jokić and Predrag Mrša had been buried here in the New Cemetery in the borough of Pallilula. A truly biblical period: the Flood had lasted forty days, for forty days Moses and his people had crossed the desert to reach the Promised Land, and there were forty days of Lent. For forty days the souls of the dead had remained on earth to bid this life farewell. Now they were free to ascend into heaven. The families would gather around the graves of their sons, bring provisions and something to drink for the journey, and would light candles to illuminate their way. Such were the rites of the Serbian Orthodox faith.

Milena opted for white roses. One for Nenad Jokić and one for Predrag Mrša. The salesman wrapped them in thin paper with little bunches of flowers printed on it.

The New Cemetery was in fact the oldest in Belgrade and covered a vast area. Milena wandered slowly along the wall of brown-red bricks and dirty-yellow, square sandstone blocks. With its stocky pillars and squat, round arches, the graveyard resembled some gloomy fortress shielding the realm of the dead from the world of the living. The heavy iron gate had a high roof over it, surmounted with a cross.

There had been a time when she and Vera would walk along this little paved street every Saturday. Saturday was the day when Christ died; Saturday belonged to the dead. The heart attack had struck down her father and wrenched him from this life when Milena was only sixteen. Almost the whole family gathered in the section of the cemetery beyond the hill, around the black, polished granite slab, and together broke the Pogača bread that Vera had baked the day before – without any yeast but with the requisite pinch of salt – and drank the tea or coffee which Milena passed round, along with scented handkerchiefs. She had been a good daughter even though she hated Saturdays. She would much rather have gone to the swimming pool with her friends or to the Illustrators' Café, where grand plans for the future were hatched. Instead, she had stuck it out beside the blubbing aunts, while the uncles had lit a cigarette for the deceased and placed it on his headstone, where the wind had fanned the glowing amber tip until it was totally consumed. Even nowadays, on his birthday, Vera still took a bunch of red roses to the grave of her beloved.

Siniša stood under an elm and, checking his silver watch like this was a court hearing, announced: 'Dead on time.' The only thing missing was his briefcase. 'We've got time. The remembrance ceremony will take about thirty minutes. After that there will be lunch at the Jokićs', Nenad's parents, with Predrag's parents too, of course, the Mršas, who, by the way, live in the same house, on Béla-Bartók-Street. Do you know where that is? And if your schedule permits...'

'OK then.' Milena took his arm, forcing him to take smaller steps. 'With pleasure.'

The layout of the cemetery, which spread right round the hillside, assigned a plot of a few square meters to each corpse, at the head of which stood a headstone, a cross or an obelisk, depending on what fashion prescribed, faith permitted and the relatives of the deceased deemed appropriate and affordable. The clumsy-looking grand sepulchres that influential Belgrade families had erected for themselves and their dead relatives in centuries gone by stood at prominent corner sites where the paths crossed. When Milena was younger, these tombs used to spook her with their busts, reliefs and inscriptions, but over time they had shrunk to familiar old acquaintances, with moss growing from all their ancient nooks and crannies.

'What's on your mind?' asked Siniša.

'You know,' Milena began, 'there's only one way of finding out what really happened that night in the barracks. We have to fly in the experts from Ludwigshafen and have them perform an autopsy.'

'For an exhumation we'd need the families' permission.'

'That's right.'

'Not an easy step.'

'A nightmare.'

'But you're right,' said Siniša. 'Maybe it's our only chance. If I put it to the parents, explain it as calmly as possible, they might understand. They trust me.'

'Even if they agree, that still leaves the military coroner.'

'Dežulović.'

'You reckon he'll give it his blessing, then?'

Siniša laughed. 'Of course not! He'll move heaven and earth to prevent an autopsy.'

Milena was almost relieved. 'Then there's no reason to bother the parents with a request for an exhumation and autopsy.'

'Right again.'

'I have another suggestion,' Milena said. 'We confront Dežulović with the original German report. My translation of it, that is.'

'And then?'

'We point out every mistake the military made, every omission, every piece of inaccurate and tendentious wording in their translation. We'll put my translation and theirs side by side, together with an affidavit and anything else you think is necessary, and I can assure you: the result will be crushing for Dežulović. He can't ignore facts. He'll have to cooperate. He'll have no choice.'

'You really think so?'

'And then we'll take it from there.'

'Listen to me.' Siniša grabbed Milena's arm and held it tightly. 'I can assure you he won't cooperate. Do I need to remind you? The people we're dealing with are soldiers. They follow orders. Our information is dynamite and the Serbian military will do anything to prevent it from coming out, anything that doesn't suit their purposes.'

A priest's solemn chanting filled the cemetery as it slowly rose and fell, wrapping the mourners in its deep, melodious tones. Holding lit candles, they crowded around the graves of the two dead men.

'If we're planning to corner them, then there's no way we're doing that alone,' Siniša whispered. 'Understood?'

Milena did not know which was the stronger in that instant – her disgust at Siniša's words, which were basically telling her: Look, there's nothing we can do, this is too big for us to tackle; or her resentment at the priest with his tall black *kalimavkion* and long beard, swinging his brass thurible and wafting the scent of incense all around; it descended sweetly and heavily on her thoughts and told her: Let it go. What will be, will be. We are all in God's hands. And lo and behold, the dead are redeemed!

Accompanied by the priest's sonorous singsong the people knelt down and placed plates and dishes of fruit and cakes on the ground. The priest's richly decorated vestments parted and an arm unfolded like a wing. Crows rose from the straggly pine trees and soared cawing into the white-grey sky. Wine, the Blood of Christ, dripped onto the earth. The mourners crossed themselves. Milena, who stood to one side clutching her flowers, got the strong impression that here death was celebrated and exalted above life.

Among the uniformly black garb of the mourners, one point of colour stood out brilliantly. The guardsman in his cornflower blue uniform stood so upright that the material seemed to support him like a corset. He was holding his cap, respectfully doffed, in front of a chest decorated with medals. Strands of thinning grey hair, combed tightly back, could scarcely conceal the many liver spots dotted across his skull.

'Who's that?' Milena asked quietly.

'Colonel Danilo Djordan,' Siniša whispered.

'You know him?'

'Not really.'

While bread was passed from hand to hand and shared, Milena observed the gold braid, the knee-high boots, the red stripes down the seam of the soldier's trousers and the Serbian coat of arms on his sleeve. She stepped aside a bit to get a better view of his face. He had deep shadows under his eyes, and his mouth was a thin line under a carefully trimmed ice-grey moustache. Nothing in his expression, not a single twitch of a muscle, revealed whether he was simply attending in his capacity as the Honour Guards' commander or had come out of human compassion.

Siniša took Milena's arm and said quietly: 'I have a proposition for you. How about we grab the bull by the horns, but cover our backs while we're at it? We'll contact the media. Everyone needs to be told what rogue elements there are in our elite unit. And at the same time media interest will be our life-insurance policy, understand? Milena, are you listening? We'll go public...'

'...we'll go public, yes, right.'

Natural justice had been violated and a myth shattered: two young men with their entire lives in front of them were dead, laid to rest by their mothers and fathers. Once a year had passed, two tombstones would be erected, two little photos attached and names, dates and inscriptions engraved. Everything meekly followed a canon of unwritten rules.

By now, the priest was leading the way back to the church, walking at a measured pace. The mourners slowly fell in line and followed the procession. Two men hung back at the graveside. Shaken by some unseen force, one of them kept his arms tightly folded across his chest as if to prevent it from bursting, so tightly that his fingers were digging into his black shirt. The other had fallen to his knees, with his forehead resting on the ground, and was clawing at the earth. His weeping sounded almost inhuman.

Milena recalled the professional mourners at her father's funeral, women in white robes who had knelt at his grave, beating their breasts, wailing and tearing their hair. At the time, she had been furious at how these women, whom she did not know, were trying to hijack grief. She didn't care that the wailing women's performance was an ancient tradition for which they were not formally paid, but were still amply rewarded with gifts. In ancient Egypt the mourners had been organised in a kind of guild and with their songs prefigured the chorus in Greek tragedies. These women turned grief into poetry and pain into melody.

What these two men were doing, though, was unprecedented. They had usurped the role reserved for women and professional mourners. They had sacrificed their position in

Serbian society and catapulted themselves out of a hierarchy in which men were on top. Milena was shocked by the power of their grief and the determination of the two fathers to display it. They did not want to go on without their sons. Men who cried in public wanted to die.

'Mrs Lukin?' The woman in black brushed back a strand of blonde hair and tucked it beneath her scarf. Her eyes were rimmed with a thin, inflamed red line, so precise it looked as though it had been drawn with an eyeliner pencil. 'I am Sonja Jokić,' she said, 'Nenad's mother.'

Milena clasped her hand. 'I am so sorry.'

'Mr Stojkovič told us about you. Please come home with us. You are cordially invited.' Saying this, she glanced over Milena's shoulder, and if there had been the hint of a smile on her face, it died in that instant.

Milena followed her gaze and caught a glimpse of the colonel, the cornflower-blue dot as it hastened away and presently disappeared between the tombstones.

7

Milena stood in the Jokić family bathroom, washing her hands, and thought of the dead. After every visit to the cemetery they clung to the living. Try as she might, she could not suppress the thought. The dead were demons – you had to protect yourself against them. Like all demons they shied away from water. The place where a coffin had stood had to be sprinkled with water, and once it had been carried out of the home, a bucketful of water had to be emptied out behind it. She did, however, draw a line at taking a detour to shake off the dead; she'd simply lost her way from the cemetery to Béla-Bartók-Street.

Just as in the bathroom, the mirror in the hallway had been shrouded with a black cloth. The pendulum of the grandfather clock stood still, its hands in all likelihood showing the time when news of the deaths had been received. On a table covered by a lace tablecloth stood two framed portraits next to an oil lamp; they had been arranged in such a way that they seemed to be looking at each other. Milena took one in her right hand and the other in her left and looked at them.

The young man on the left had finely drawn eyebrows, which lent his handsome face an almost girl-like tenderness. Through dark eyes he gazed out at the world as if faced with a serious problem. But maybe one should not underestimate him. There was something in his attitude, his straight back and the clarity of his gaze, which showed that he was tough and determined to accept any challenge. He would fight and probably not for the first time fulfil all the expectations placed upon him.

His friend was the exact opposite. Little laughter lines around his eyes and mouth betrayed that his head was full of ideas, but ones that were less likely to change the world or make it a better place. One flash of inspiration followed another, but you'd likely wait in vain for the real eureka moment. His flights of fancy were almost as hard to control as his unmanageable curly hair. Life was supposed to be fun, and it was – that was all that mattered to him.

Milena put the two portraits back on the table and turned them to face one another. Her assumptions about the two young men were as different as the photographs. She had never seen or met them. She did not even know which one was the womaniser and which the pilot.

'Praise be to God.' Whispering people entered through the open door of the apartment and paraded past the portraits decorated with black crepe. Milena followed them.

The curtains were drawn, the five-armed chandelier and the lamps to the right and left of the sofa were lit. The table, laid with white linen and the good china, extended through the connecting doors into the next room.

Time after time, Siniša rose to his feet, embraced relatives and friends of the family, calling them by name: 'Anđa' – 'Jovan' – 'Maja' – 'Srećko'. Spotting Milena, he beckoned her over, indicating that she should take a free seat diagonally opposite him.

Milena introduced herself to the lady sitting next to her, an old woman who had knotted her headscarf tightly under her skinny chin and kept the top button of her matted cardigan firmly clasped with her hand, as if she was afraid someone might take it from her. Milena knew these kind of women, aunts like them existed in every family, though they normally did not sit at grand tables like this but on the kitchen bench. That was where they sat all day, quietly, and ate whatever was put in front of them: warmed-up leftovers and the end slices of cakes, because they would never dare ask for more. These women lived off the misery of others, which they sat patiently waiting for. Consequently, it came as no surprise when the old woman suddenly leant over to Milena and whispered: 'I was never blessed with a child and my husband was a drunkard. But that misfortune is nothing compared to the sorrow around this table.' She took the corner of her scarf and dapped away a tear from the corner of her eye. Her voice was very high now: 'They won't see their sons getting married, they'll never cradle a grandchild in their arms and nobody will carry on their line. The shots hit the heart and we should be thankful for that. Others were buried alive up to their necks and their heads were cut off and they played football with them. Can you imagine?!' The old woman fell silent and observed hungrily what other women – most likely her neighbours – were busy bringing to the table: bean stew with rice and meat in a pan, cabbage-wrapped roulades, eggs garnished with red paprika, fried aubergine slices, roasted courgettes and steamed tomatoes. Men who had taken off their jackets, rolled up their sleeves and cut the suckling pig into thick slices and poured *Rakija* into small glasses. Women ladled fish soup into bowls and handed round white bread.

Sonja Jokić walked along the wall behind the tables and disappeared into the adjacent room, before emerging again. She put a sweater around her husband's shoulders. Finally she sat down. Her hands lay on the table like broken wings.

Milena reached across and gently touched her arm.

Sonja Jokić smiled. 'Siniša tells us – you have a son?'

'Adam.' Milena nodded. 'He is ten now.'

'May God protect your boy from all the evil in the world.' The old woman dabbed spittle off the corner of her mouth with the corner of her scarf.

Mr Jokić raised his glass. 'May the boy have a long life.' His voice was so hoarse that the conversation around him stopped. All raised their charged glasses.

'May the souls of Nenad and Predrag rest in peace,' Milena said.

'May the earth be light for them.'

The clear *Rakija* burned the throat and warmed the insides. 'We dragged our kids out of the Bosnian hell,' Mr Jokić continued. 'That was in 1993. Like cats we carried them in our mouths and fed them with our love. Big and round is what they should have become. Instead they became beautiful and strong. Now Dragan is the only one left. Dragan, come over here. Where are you?'

With his fork hovering motionless above his plate the boy looked up from behind his thick eyebrows. Above his obstinate upper lip there was a faint shadow, the first hint of stubble. Indignantly he turned his head.

'I knew my Predrag was dead,' said the man who had cried next to Mr Jokić at the graveside, 'I knew it the minute those guys in their uniforms appeared at the door, I knew he was dead.'

'Later, when they brought us the boys in those lead coffins...' The woman, whose large spectacles covered almost her entire face, fell silent. As she was trying to regain her composure and search for the right words, a hush fell on the room. Then, after a few seconds she announced in a firm voice: "Your sons have voluntarily chosen a dishonourable death." That's what they told us.'

'We weren't allowed to open the coffins. They were sealed. We could only see Predrag's beautiful face through a little window.'

Mr Jokić interjected into the outraged murmur that swelled up around him: 'We couldn't touch our Nenad, couldn't kiss him.'

'I had to kiss a dirty little piece of glass.'

'I wasn't allowed to wash Nenad. Wasn't allowed to dress him in the good suit that was hanging in the closet for his wedding day.'

'Nobody could tell us what our children were wearing. Whether they were lying stark naked six feet under and were cold down there or whether they were dressed in rags.'

'We were stupidly proud when our sons became guardsmen in the elite regiment. "It's your holy duty", I told Nenad and thought of the splendid uniform and the white gloves he was going to wear. "It's your job, and a great honour to boot." God will punish me for these words.'

'We're not letting Dragan join the army, that's for sure. Listen to me, boy! Forget about it – I won't allow it. We won't give Dragan away, he's the only blessing left to us. When they come to get him I know what I've got to do. I'm prepared. My pistol is ready in the drawer. I'm keeping it for that very day.'

The old folks made the sign of the cross and folded their hands. A hush descended.

Mr Jokić began his mournful tale. He told the story of Nenad and Predrag, the two friends who were like brothers, born two weeks apart and named after the Serbian heroes Nenad and Predrag who had fought against the Turks for freedom and in the end paid the ultimate price. One after another the men joined in. It was a litany that grew in strength and touched the hearts of all those present. Siniša had closed his eyes and held his folded hands pressed against his mouth. The old woman next to Milena swayed and whimpered, and the other women sobbed.

Milena had tears in her eyes as well. God dammit! What a fool she'd been. The great Battle of the Field of Blackbirds had been fought and lost over six hundred years ago, and only Serbs were able to link their current suffering to this historic defeat and commemorate it over and over again.

Dragan, the son of the Jokić family, looked at all these people as if they were ghosts. He saw the tears, the flushed and red faces. He looked over the good china and heaps of food. Nobody reacted when he abruptly pushed his chair back and left the room.

Milena laid aside her napkin, murmured an excuse and got up.

The front door was open and Dragan was already outside. Hastily Milena grabbed her coat, in the process knocking into the little table and causing the frames with the pictures of the dead boys on it to wobble violently. The gentle hands of Sonja Jokić stopped them from falling over.

'Please excuse me,' Milena said, 'I didn't mean to impose on your wake.'

Sonja Jokić took her hand and squeezed it. 'Come back and visit us soon. And bring your son. It would be a great pleasure for us to get to know him. Our house is so quiet and empty.' She squeezed so hard that Milena thought this stranger's fingers might stop the blood from coursing through her veins.

'Goodbye,' Milena said, 'all the best.'

In the stairwell she could still hear Dragan jumping down the last steps, and still see his hand sliding down the banister, but by the time she'd reached the bottom of the stairs, the sound of his steps had ebbed away.

The entrance door to the flats was made of solid iron. It had loose windowpanes, and Milena would surely have heard if it had closed behind Dragan. The images of horses stuck on the walls here probably dated from a time when there was still a difference between the colour of the ceiling and the wall. The door leading to the courtyard at the back stood open. The weatherboard at its base was made of wood and, warped by the damp, had jammed against the floor.

She stepped outside onto a mat of verdigris that looked like an old worn rug. A clothesline was stretched from wall to wall, with clothes pegs on it and a single rag. In front of the wall, which bordered the yard on the opposite side, stood two chairs, a table with an ashtray on it and a discarded fridge. Furnished like this, the place resembled a room, untouched by a single ray of sunshine, and whose shabbiness was mercilessly exposed by daylight.

Dragan could have climbed on top of the fridge and escaped over the wall. But why would he have done that? Milena had a feeling that this boy had something to say. The problem was that no one was listening.

She was on her way back into the house when she noticed a doorway that looked like the entrance to the cellar. She rattled the handle.

The racket made by the door as she opened it was huge. Someone must have put the dented birdcage behind it on purpose.

She pushed the obstacle aside with her foot. 'Dragan?'

A steep staircase led down, but Milena could not find the light switch. Step by step, she groped her way along the wall, which had been covered by fungus in a pattern of small pimples. Downstairs a little daylight seeped in through narrow windows and the slits between the wooden screen of boards, casting faint lines across the long corridor. Milena glanced into the storage rooms: junk, shelves, bottling jars. And a very faint smell of something alien to these cool, humid surroundings but still very familiar: cigarette smoke.

'Are you there, Dragan?'

Not a sound.

'It's me, Milena Lukin. I'd like to talk to you.'

She squeezed past an old pram, but then found her way blocked by a pile of dirty pallets. She turned around, took a left turn, turned right – or had she been here before? She struggled to get her bearings. Something was different here. She took a few steps forward. This storeroom had been so artfully covered with newspaper and cardboard that no light shone into the corridor.

'Dragan?'

Through a narrow gap, she saw a crate of oranges which had been turned upside-down and now served as a table for a thermos. Cutlery protruded from an open can. Torn-open packages, burned-out tea lights, well-thumbed magazines and dried-up leftovers lay next to a mattress. The legs lying on top of it were clad in black trousers with a crease down the middle. An ashtray rose and fell, balancing on top of a stomach. Two fingers held a lit cigarette.

Cautiously she pushed her hand against the planks. The draught made the thin column of smoke tremble.

At that moment the ashtray flew across the room. Dragan screamed, leaping to his feet so quickly that Milena had no time to withdraw.

'Sorry...' Milena stammered with half-raised hands, as his fist hovered in front of her nose. 'I called out but...'

Confused, he took a step back, let his fists drop and tugged at the wires dangling in front of his chest, removing two minute plugs from his ears. 'Are you crazy, startling me like that? Shit.' He bent down, picked up the cigarette from the floor and fell back onto the mattresses.

'Can I come in?'

He exhaled. 'No, get lost!'

One of the crates seemed stable enough. Milena picked up the clothes lying on it, turned around and placed the bundle at the foot of the mattress. Dragan followed her movements in silence.

'I'm worried,' Milena said, putting down her bag.

'I told you to get lost!' Was that his voice breaking, or was he just still agitated?

She sat down. 'Siniša and I – we want to find out what happened to Nenad and Predrag in Topčider.'

'Are you a cop or a social worker?'

'I work in the Institute for Criminology and Forensic Science and have better things to do than run around after scallies like you. But what happened to your brother at the barracks is preying on my mind.'

'Your problem. Nothing to do with me. So piss off.'

She searched in her bag for her cigarettes. 'Did Nenad ever talk to you about his army service?'

'Are you deaf or something? Piss off, and while you're at it you can take your lawyer friend with you, too. He makes me want to throw up every time I see him. He's always sucking up and showing off and he gets on my tits with his constant yakking. I'm not one of your bloody victims, got it?'

'Nenad must have told you something about his life in the camp at Topčider at one time or another.'

'Maybe. But I probably left the room at that point.'

'Why's that?'

'The Honour Guard's really not my kind of thing.'

'Okay, but maybe you picked something up all the same. Something about what they get up to there, or if he liked it, say, or had any problems?'

'Zilch. Is that it?'

'No. Have you got a light?'

'I dunno what you're after.' Reluctantly, he handed her his lighter.

'Does the name Danilo Djordan mean anything to you?'

Milena blew a stream of smoke vertically upwards and looked at him. In the midst of all that rubbish, the boy was sitting on his mattress like a raft. Suddenly he started laughing.

'What's so funny?' asked Milena.

'I'm just remembering how they blubbed when Nenad swore his oath of allegiance. They cried the same way they're crying now. That's funny, isn't it?'

'They loved your brother more than anything, the same way they love you.'

He lit the little flame of his lighter, let it burn for a second then extinguished it. On – off.

'And you?' she asked. 'What about you?'

He shot Milena a furious glance. 'What do you want from me? Want me to start blubbing too? I'll tell you something right now: they can take all this hero-worship stuff and shove it up their arses for all I care. Okay, he was my brother, but he was a shit brother. I've got nothing else to say.'

'Have you got any other brothers or sisters?'

He groaned and shook his head.

'Nenad was older than you. The older brother's the crown prince. You're the baby of the family. You can do as you please. That's how it is in all families. Everybody has their place. And that's how things should be.'

Milena stood up. She had a stiff neck, but what she still didn't have was even the beginning of an idea what murky business Nenad Jokić had been mixed up with at the barracks in Topčider. What had she expected?

Dragan was still staring fixedly at the lighter in his hand. 'If you ask me – it all has something to do with Bosnia.'

'Bosnia?'

'Nenad was born in Bosnia. That was his big advantage. You should see what happens when Bratunac is mentioned. Tears in their eyes straight away – the lot of them! I was born here in Belgrade. That was much later. Nothing special about that.'

'Have you ever been there, to Bratunac?'

'What for? There's none of us left there. All gone, and whoever didn't get out and was stupid enough to stay was killed by the Muslims. Ever heard of that? Muslims are Serb-murderers.'

'Now listen to me.' Milena sat down again and held her palms pressed against each other vertically. 'The Serbs were a minority in Bratunac and had to flee from the Muslims, you're quite right. But why was that? They had to get away from the Muslims because just a few kilometres away Bosnian Serb troops were slaughtering Muslims.'

'And what does Nenad go and do? He joins the Honour Guard, puts on a pretty uniform and has the girls admire him on parade outside the presidential palace. How bogus is that? What's the point of that? I wouldn't dream of doing that, anyhow.'

'So tell me what you would dream of doing.'

Dragan held up his hand like a stop sign. 'Know what?' He got up and stuffed the packet of cigarettes into his pocket. 'That's none of your business.'

*

The rush-hour traffic had already clogged up the roundabout, so Milena decided to go via Zoran-Djindjić-Bulevard and avoid Mihajlo-Pupin-Boulevard. At the traffic lights she slipped her favourite CD from Germany into the player and pressed the button until the display showed track number seven.

She loved the male voice, the clear pronunciation, the tone of the mouth organ, and knew the lyrics by heart: *And after dinner he said, I'll just run out to get some cigarettes...* She sang along quietly, steering with her right hand and propping her left elbow on the window surround. *I've never been to New York, I have never been completely free...* She was sad and was longing for something. For a better world? When she discussed current affairs with her ambitious students, she'd bang on about freedom, about a basic democratic order, about human rights; she'd make grandiloquent demands for these values to be embraced by Serbian institutions and upheld in society. But what was she supposed to say to a young man like Dragan? He had experienced first-hand how his brother and his best friend, the boy from next door, had been surreptitiously murdered, how the killing had been denied by the authorities and how the investigation had been botched. The lad was in shock, devastated, and would have had all his illusions shattered. All her talk about safeguarding minorities, parliamentary democracy and everyone being equal before the law would just be hot air to him. But what could she say to him, then?

...and never walked through San Francisco in ripped jeans. On the other hand, Dragan was still young and his opinions not yet set in stone. He was still open to all kinds of influence. So she really oughtn't give up quite yet.

'Get a move on, girl!' Milena yelled at the woman driver ahead of her, who was slow on the uptake when the lights changed. 'Or are you planning on staying here all night?' She swung the steering wheel around and pressed hard on the accelerator. Too late, the lights had already changed to red again.

And Nenad and Predrag? Which side had they been on? Had they obeyed the law or as elite guards thought themselves above it?

The parking spot she finally managed to secure was not, as she'd originally thought, in a shallow puddle. When Milena opened her door, she realised it was in fact a lake, with the Lada an island in the middle, and all easy access to the dry cat litter in the boot cut off. Milena picked up her coat.

As Milena deposited the heavy sack in the hallway, Fiona was the only one who at least deigned to acknowledge her feat with a glance. The booming volume of the television was only occasionally drowned out by Adam's laughter, and every laugh – sometimes a high-pitched giggle, and sometimes a low chuckle of *Schadenfreude* – would have been enough to convince you that this was the best TV show ever, which it would have been unthinkable to interrupt. From the kitchen the aroma of celery and carrots that had been simmering for hours with a sizeable piece of beef and bone marrow wafted towards her. And then Vera's voice: 'Where have you been all this time? We tried calling you!'

Milena hung up her coat and stuffed newspaper into her sodden shoes. On the chest of drawers a pale green envelope was propped up against the pretty straw hat – the electricity bill. And the beautiful bunch of dried flowers was now acting as a chock stopping Adam's basketball from rolling off. She'd deal with these thoughtless additions to her stylish interior décor presently.

Washing her hands and looking at the dark rings under her eyes in the mirror, she thought how Adam was privileged in a way that other young Serbs could only dream of: speaking German and having a German passport he'd have the choice of living in Serbia or Germany. To put it another way: if a Dragan, a Nenad or a Predrag rubbed someone up the wrong way here and could see no way out, he'd be completely at the mercy of this country, its laws and its lawlessness. Adam, though, would always have a bolt-hole.

'Look,' he shouted, pointing at the screen. 'This bloke really is as thick as pig shit!'

'Mind your language,' Milena told him. She leant over, gave him a peck on the cheek, then bent down to straighten the rug. 'Did your father teach you that expression?'

From the kitchen, Vera, with her glasses balanced on the end of her nose, adjusted the temperature of the stove and called out: 'Sit yourselves down.' She ladled soup into a deep tureen and scattered finely chopped parsley over it – a remedy for high blood pressure. She then brought the bowl through, set it down in front of Milena and said: 'Now eat.'

Left-over noodles were swimming in the rich, clear broth. Because they looked like fringes, at some stage they'd started calling the soup 'fringe-soup'. Ever since childhood, Milena had always loved fringe-soup.

Vera put the ladle in the sink and the lid on the pot. 'Fiona needs to have her claws clipped. If you don't do it soon, I'll go ahead and make an appointment at the vet's. That cost forty Euros last time, remember?'

'I'll take care of it. Has Adam been practising his guitar today?'

Vera wiped the outside edge of the stove with a cloth. She was smiling.

'Has he done his homework?'

'He's been involved in a fairly lively exchange of text messages.'

'Who with?'

Vera placed the bulbous pepper mill on the table. 'I believe her name is Katinka.'

Milena let her spoon sink into the soup. 'Adam!'

Vera looked at her daughter, tilted her head to one side and shrugged her shoulders.

Adam came in holding the cat. 'Zoran's got new basketball shoes.' He sat down, still cradling the cat in his arms. 'They're brilliant. They cost seventy-nine Euros.'

'Go and wash your hands, please.'

'I'm thirty-six Euros short. Can you give me an advance? Please, Mum! Twenty-five would be a big help. Or twenty at least.'

'Do as you're told. We have to get up early tomorrow. We're going swimming.'

Milena's eyes followed him as he left the room.

One day, it would be his turn to make sure things improved in this country. She would prepare him for this task as best she could. But at the same time she was going to make sure that the bolt-hole remained open.

From the steaming water, Vera lifted out corn cobs crammed with succulent yellow sweet corn. 'Tomorrow we'll have corn hash for breakfast,' she said, 'with *Kajmak.*' She glanced up at the kitchen clock and then down at the stove. 'Or would you prefer basil?' Her beady grey eyes looked inquiringly at Milena. 'For tomorrow's lunch, as a side-dish with the veal goulash?'

Milena sighed. 'I don't know. I really don't. *Kajmak* or basil – you decide.'

Vera shooed the cat off the chair, sat down and picked up her napkin. Turning to Milena, she asked: 'Who ever told you that you always have to be trying to save the whole world? Was it your father? Did he put those thoughts in your head?'

All the strength suddenly drained out of Milena, like Vera had opened a tiny, hidden valve. She had no stomach left, no voice.

Vera looked at her daughter and pondered for a moment, weighing her words carefully. Eventually, her face cracked into a smile. 'On the other hand,' she said, 'if anyone can do it, you can.'

8

Milena closed the office door behind her, took off her velvet jacket – the best item in her wardrobe – and hung it up, neatly tucking the silk scarf into the sleeve. In her high heels and pencil skirt, she thought better of crawling under the desk today to turn on the electric radiator.

In the normal course of events, Friday evenings (and, if she was lucky, some afternoons too) were reserved for work on her postdoctoral thesis on Balkan war crimes in the 1990s. All her colleagues had left the office by that stage and there were no little chats, coffee breaks or phone calls to distract her. She'd done all her tasks for the week and peace had finally descended, which is exactly what she needed for her research. But today, Friday 3 September, was exceptional, and her computer would stay switched off.

She wrapped the cardigan around her shoulders, filled the kettle with water and put two heaped spoonfuls of coffee granules into her mug, then added another one for good measure. Outside, two girls were loitering at the foot of the monument to Duke Vuk, directly below his moss-covered gun, and drawing lines in the sand with a stick. Milena looked at her watch: 5.30 pm. Fat chance of reaching anybody in Bonn now.

Holding the phone to her ear, and listening to the dial tone, she began searching around on her desk for the little embossed envelope.

'Blechschmidt.'

The large catalogue with advance information of all

forthcoming legal publications slid off the pile and hit the floor. Milena leapt up in surprise. 'Mr Blechschmidt!'

'Who's calling, please?'

'Lukin. Milena Lukin from Belgrade. How wonderful to speak to you.'

'Ms Lukin – of course. What can I do for you?'

'Well...' With the kettle in one hand and the receiver jammed between her ear and shoulder she attempted with her free hand to keep hold of the cardigan, which was about to slip off the sheer silk of her blouse. 'It's about my contract...'

'Your contract extension. Yes, of course. Do we have your report?'

'It's been on your desk for the past eight weeks.'

'Including the strategy paper, the evaluation, prognosis and the written statements?'

'I have also prepared statistics, and a set of diagrams showing the development of student numbers. I thought it would be interesting for you to see that in the past year, aside from the seminars and the colloquium ...'

'I understand...' He hung on the word. 'Just a moment, please. Stay on the line.'

As she listened to an electronic version of Mozart's *Little Night Music*, the cogs began turning in her head, bringing to the surface all the questions that she had asked herself a million times: Why did she always have to deal with bureaucrats? Why should these people decide her future? Why was she, with all that she knew and had accomplished, beholden to these people?

'Ms Lukin?'

'Yes?'

'How would it be if I called you back as soon as possible? At the very latest by the end of next week.'

Totally numb, Milena stood by the window, the receiver still in her hand, and smelt peppermint behind her.

'Still nothing?' Boris Grubač enquired. 'I feel for you, Ms Lukin.'

'Thank you for your sympathy, Mr Grubač.' She carefully bent down, picked the catalogue up off the floor and put it back on the desk.

'The Germans are really messing you around! They're holding you at arm's length and letting you starve.'

If she wasn't going to be late, she really had to get going. Now, where the hell was the...

'Tell me, have you had your hair done?'

Between a pile of essays and her mail tray was an apple and beneath the apple the little envelope she'd been looking for. As she slipped it into her bag, her fingers felt the discreet embossing on the handmade paper, the Federal Eagle. 'That's right, Mr Grubač,' Milena replied. 'I've had my hair done.'

'And who, may I ask, have you got yourself dolled up so nicely for?'

She knotted the silk scarf loosely around her neck and let him help her into her velvet jacket, without gracing his impertinent question with a reply.

'Of course,' he said at length. 'Lobbying, networking at the German embassy. Very good, Ms Lukin. People like us should leave no stone unturned. We should grasp every opportunity going. But if I could give you one little piece of advice: don't be so aloof tonight. Why not be really charming for a change? Try coming out of your shell, flatter some people. Now, don't go pulling such a face. Little tricks like that work wonders with us men.'

Milena picked up her bag. 'Tonight's not about wonders. It's not even about whether I'm going to flatter anybody or whether I'll still get my puny little salary next year. Tonight's all about something much more important. And if you want to do something for me, then wish me luck.'

Forty-five minutes later Milena joined the receiving line that had formed on the pavement of Count-Miloš-Street, the road leading to Sofia. The line lead to a modern building, whose façade was made up of thirty-five honeycomb-shaped panels, seven horizontally times five vertically. A web-like construction comprising bulky columns and connecting braces mirrored the monotone box arrangement and made the ugliness of the building even more apparent to those who might initially have overlooked it.

In front of the building stood two blondes in black suits standing behind high desks and two men in the uniform of a security firm. The women were typing people's passport numbers into a laptop, while the security guards searched bags. One of the blondes ticked a guest list, while the other returned the passport and the invitation, smiled and said: 'The Embassy of the Federal Republic welcomes you.'

'Thank you.' Milena replied, zipping up her bag.

From the makeshift cloakroom a staircase lead down to the foyer, the former basement car park. All round the room, with small gaps between them, standing tables had been arranged, with flower bouquets on and laid with long, champagne-coloured tablecloths tied tight at the bottom. Behind a folding wall, which was pulled back halfway, stood rows of chairs. In the centre of the stage stood a lectern decorated with the flags of Germany, the EU and Serbia.

Milena looked for a seat on the end of the final row, giving a nod of recognition as she did so to her right, where the ladies and gentlemen from, if she was not mistaken, the German business delegation were sitting. After greeting the head of the cultural institute, she sat down and read in the little folded card that had been left on top of the thinly padded seat that the introduction of the new ambassador was to be followed by a farewell speech by his predecessor, a welcome speech by the second minister of the foreign office and a concert for violin and flute. At the end of it all came the reception proper.

She took out her little make-up mirror and checked her lips, which shimmered with a discreet shade of gloss lipstick, and her eyes, which the eyeliner made even bigger and more expressive. What about her hair? That was still in good shape, with a half wave over her forehead. She slipped the mirror back into her bag, smoothed down her skirt and crossed her legs. Good, there was no run in her tights, everything was perfect.

Milena was determined to get through this evening and press as much flesh as possible. She wanted to use the opportunity and gain the support of influential representatives of an influential country. Siniša words came into her mind: 'Everyone needs to be told what rogue elements there are in our elite unit.'

9

He had spotted the damn dog – nothing more than a bag of skin and bones. Shaggy coat, torn ears, the skin around the tip of his pointy muzzle a shiny pig-pink. Only his black, lacklustre, bloodshot eyes looked menacing; and of course there were the three legs that this creature hopped and hobbled around on. All three legs were trembling, barely able to sustain the animal's fly weight. What a wretched, laughable animal it was. Locked out by its owner and then forgotten. Someone should just shoot it or beat it to death. It would best all round.

He lugged the bag with the groceries into the kitchenette. The six-pack of beer, the milk and the mustard jar went into the fridge. The box of cereal and the tin of sausages up onto the shelf. And now for the real bargain he had picked up at the superstore checkout. Pawle gazed at the colourful image on the cover of the DVD: a jeep, two guys in camouflage fatigues and on the back two chicks, similarly clad in battledress. Utter nonsense, of course. But tonight, when Momčilo had finally gone out, he'd set up the projector, put it on Movie XXL format, and veg out in front of it, watching this trash.

He crumpled the bag into a something resembling a snowball, pulled open the drawer and hid the DVD at the very back near the roll of garbage bags.

A quick glance out into the hallway. The door was still closed. Momčilo had been in there for hours. Most likely playing pocket billiards and inspecting each receipt individually. Monday was payday. Fucking bookkeeper.

He picked up the box with the 40-watt bulb, pulled the step-ladder out from the gap between the sink and the wall and dragged it into the hallway. By the time Momčilo finally emerged, it would be pitch-black outside, and he needed to gain a few brownie points after what had happened with the curtain.

He set up the ladder underneath the light fitting with the blown bulb, adjusted its position and checked that it was steady.

He climbed the steps, extended his left arm and grasped the bulb. The thread squeaked as he unscrewed it.

When he finally got the light bulb out, he shook it to make sure it had blown. The filament rattled faintly inside the opaque glass; behind the closed door of his office, Momčilo loudly exclaimed: '...but that's crazy!'

Pawle froze.

Again came the sound of Momčilo's voice: 'And what if we still need him?'

As soundlessly as he could, Pawle stepped back down...

'So why the hurry?'

...and tiptoed up to the door.

'Okay, he'll have to go, then...yes! But before...– exactly. Keep your eyes peeled. And if he does it again...– that's right. One mistake, and...– right. But let's not do anything hasty. Me? Why me? You've got far more clout than I have.'

This had to do with him, Pawle. He was sure of it. They were deciding his fate in there. The bulb in his hand turned into a wet, slippery something that suddenly developed a life of its own and slipped from his grasp, fell to the floor and shattered.

Pawle swore silently, crouched down and began collecting the glass shards in his cupped hand. Too late.

The boots were suddenly so close to him that he could make out in the pale light from the open office door the cracks in the leather and the flecked pattern of the laces. He looked up and saw the receiver in Momčilo's hand and the grey eyes glowering down at him. Pawle ducked.

'Are you snooping around?' The words stabbed him like a knife. The bookkeeper's boot heels ground the shards into little splinters. 'This will have consequences. Just you wait.'

The door slammed shut. 'It's nothing,' he heard Momčilo say. 'Now, where were we?'

It took an eternity for Pawle to stand up again, reascend the ladder and, with a trembling hand, screw the new bulb in.

Mechanically, he folded up the ladder, carried it back and shoved it into the gap between the fridge and the wall.

In his room he lay down on the bed. The springs squeaked. He rolled up in a ball. The spider under the sink did not move. The damned dog was whimpering softly.

He had to become invisible. Not budge an inch. And make no mistakes.

10

In the heat her feet puffed up like lumps of bread dough, pressing against the inside of her pumps and steadily expanding out of that confined space. Her skirt, tight over her hips, began inching its way up, while her tights started to travel in the opposite direction. With a complex series of tweaks and tugs, Milena attempted surreptitiously to counteract both problems, simultaneously shifting her weight from one foot to the other, smiling inanely, and desperately trying all the while to avoid looking like a stork. The man from the cultural institute whose name always escaped her was talking nonstop. The saliva he produced with every sibilant he uttered formed little specks on her silk blouse, already disfigured by the fluff from her office cardigan. And she hadn't even seen the new ambassador yet!

She had nipped outside briefly between the speech by the junior minister and the concert for violin and flute. Every call from home jangled her nerves. With good cause. Vera, it transpired, had put Adam's super-cool and much-loved Alba-Berlin baseball cap into the machine at ninety degrees, and he was beside himself. Vera was mortified and Milena – after having calmed things down a bit on the phone – needed a smoke. The cigarette led to a chat with the cloakroom attendant, also a smoker and also a mother, whose son had got it into his head that he wanted to study law. Showing motherly solidarity, Milena had given the woman her office telephone number – just in case she needed any advice.

When she came down to the foyer, people were already helping themselves to the Flying Buffet.

Milena had grabbed a glass of water (though she'd have preferred a cup of coffee) and almost immediately struck up a conversation with the head of the office of the Bank for Reconstruction and Development. The same faces were always milling around on these occasions. One of the men from the delegation of the German Industrial Federation soon joined them. The new Serbian legislation on foreign trade proved a fertile topic of conversation, but Milena made her excuses – 'we must go into this in more detail some time soon' – and left. She chatted to the representatives of all the political foundations, one after the other, and without much preamble raised the subject of the dead guardsmen in Topčider. But naturally these little mice in their elegant suits did what they always did in such situations: expressed their consternation and then swiftly changed the subject.

Her next target was already in her sights: a field-grey, ironed uniform jacket with medals on the chest. A *Bundeswehr* dignitary, a recruiting officer or a German military *attaché* maybe. By now, he was standing slightly apart from the main throng and letting himself be admired by his gold-chain-bedecked female companion.

Using a finger to ease her swollen heel back into her shoe, Milena set off towards him. As she made her beeline across the room, she suddenly found her way blocked by the Director of the German School. Undeterred, Milena sidestepped him, called back 'Let's talk in a minute!' and kept on going.

She extended her hand towards the man with the medals on his chest, smiled and said: 'Good evening. Milena Lukin, Institute for Criminology and Forensic Science. Can I bend your ear on a certain matter?'

The woman at his side was playing with her necklace and staring at her with her mouth half-open. Milena shook her hand, too.

'What matter might that be?' His clean-shaven face glowed.

'It is about the two guardsmen from the elite Serbian regiment.'

'Topčider?'

'You've heard about the case, then?'

'Only very indirectly.'

'They were found dead in the bushes.'

'Right.'

Milena adjusted the strap of her bag on her shoulder. 'The case is about six weeks old, the official investigation is long closed and their bodies have been buried. Allegedly it was a suicide, or murder and a subsequent suicide. But there are several loose ends. The lawyer of the family, Siniša Stojković – do you know him by any chance?'

His face was now shining like it had been rubbed down with bacon rind. He shook his head.

'He called in the Institute for Ballistics and Firearms Technology in Ludwigshafen. Their report clearly states –'

'Excuse me, Ms...'

'Lukin.'

'I'm terribly sorry. I'm sure you know that the matter you are referring to is an internal affair of the Republic of Serbia, and we, the Federal Republic, aren't in any position –'

'We're talking murder here, the violation of human rights and –'

'Now steady on, Ms...'

'Lukin.'

'Look, if you'd like to put all this in writing and send it to me, I promise to pass it on.' He gave her his card. 'Nice meeting you.'

The woman at his side took his arm and laughed as they walked off.

'My pleasure.'

Her bag was so heavy it felt like she had tons of people's business cards in it. The skirt pinched and she'd have loved to toss her shoes into the corner. She was tired. And was heading in the wrong direction. The cloakroom was the other way.

At least she'd be able to report back to Siniša about having made contact with – she glanced at the card – 'Klaus-Dietrich Seemann, Lieutenant General'.

The cloakroom attendant smiled at her. Milena smiled back.

What had she been thinking? That her concern was so pressing that the Germans would drop everything to help her?

She was struggling to get her arms into the sleeves of her coat.

'Excuse me. May I?'

Milena turned around and looked into deep blue eyes set in a finely cut face.

The man took her coat. 'Milena Lukin – it really is you! Leaving already? We haven't had a chance to speak yet.'

'Do I know you?'

'Balkan Conference, East European Institute, Berlin.'

'Excuse me?'

'At that time you were academic assistant to Professor Hoensbruck, in the international law department, and I was in the legal division of the German Foreign Office.'

'Get away! That was years ago now.'

'I remember it well. You were sitting to the right of the professor, all in black and with your hair pulled straight back. During the conference you barely spoke and when you did it was straight to the point. I also remember that I failed to get a single smile out of you the whole time.'

Milena slowly knotted her scarf. Of course she remembered that conference. Slovenia and Croatia had just left the Yugoslav Federation and declared their independence. Germany had rushed to recognise these states without considering the consequences. It had only served to catalyse developments that then gained a momentum of their own. Milena had not been the only one back then who saw dark clouds looming over the multi-ethnic state of Bosnia and the future of the whole Balkan region. But what all that had to do with the man with the blue eyes... He stood there looking like he'd swallowed a wasp. – 'I'm sorry,' Milena said.

'Take two. Berlin, Balkan Commission.'

'You mean the think-tank of the German Foreign Office? Just after the protests in Belgrade...'

'You, Ms Lukin, were part of the so-called Balkan Taskforce. You presented us with a crystal-clear analysis of the situation Serbia's democratic opposition found itself in, along with some pretty specific recommendations on how the German policy makers should handle it, which I can still recall today. You really caused the scales to fall from our eyes back then, I mean the eyes of the Western Balkan department.'

'You're exaggerating.'

'Not at all. That's just how it was.'

'I still don't remember you.'

'Maybe it's because I had a beard at the time.'

'Were you the guy...'

'... who kept on inviting you to join me for a coffee.'

'And I...'

'You kept on turning me down.'

'I probably didn't have time, or something like that.'

'I was so happy to see your name on the guest list today and...'

'You must excuse me if I interrupt you, Mr...'

'Alexander Kronburg.'

'So what brings you here now?'

The astonishment in his face and his eyes, which scanned hers for several seconds as he tried to work out if she was kidding or not, caused Milena's face to blush violently as it suddenly dawned on her. 'Wait a minute,' she said, 'you're not the new...?'

He laughed out loud, revealing a set of impeccable teeth.

'Call me,' he said. 'We've got a lot of catching-up to do. I want to know so much more about you!'

The people who now pounced on him – it was only now Milena noticed them – had kept a discreet distance until they had finished their conversation.

✳

Milena hung up her jacket, took off her shoes and gave a soft sigh. Purring loudly, Fiona mooched round her legs.

Adam was asleep, with his mouth half-open, and one leg outside the blanket. The Alba-Berlin baseball cap lay next to him on the pillow. She smoothed out the duvet, put the cap on the bedside table and kissed him gently. She left the door slightly ajar.

In the living room she adjusted the reclining chair, closed the listings magazine and put it on top of the television, and took a plate with left-over grapes on it out to the kitchen.

The little light over the stove was still on and in the pot she found what she was hoping for: some dregs of cold coffee.

Fiona followed her, scurrying into her room. Milena closed the door, put the mug on the desk and opened the window. She sat down and pulled the keyboard towards her. The computer was in standby mode, as she'd let Adam play one of his online computer games on it that evening.

She typed *Alexander Kronburg* into the search engine and fished out her spectacles.

Did you mean: Alexander Ferdinand Ludwig Graf Kronburg?

Milena clicked, scrolled down and read: *Aristocratic family originally from the Tyrol, moved to Southern Germany during the Thirty Years' War. Grandfather: August Friedrich – Ambassador to India. Father: Maximilian Alexander – Diplomat in Norway.*

Milena pushed Fiona aside, reached for the flat box, took out a cigarillo and lit it.

Alexander Ferdinand Ludwig. Born in Oslo. Grew up in Munich, Cairo, Washington. Studied law at Cornell. Joined a law firm. Returned to Germany, entered the foreign service. First secretary at the German embassy in Beijing and Manila. Returned to Bonn and Berlin. Ambassador in Ankara and Budapest. Currently Head of the German Mission in Belgrade, Republic of Serbia.

She leant back. Underneath the desk lamp, the cat was purring contentedly with half-closed eyes. Milena smoked, clasped her mug and pondered.

Back then in Berlin she had been invited many times to the German Foreign Office for consultations. Around the same time, those who directed European foreign policy took the decision to integrate South Eastern Europe into the EU and a heated debate had ensued about how and when this might happen. In Political Division Two of the Western Balkan Department, all manner of scenarios and contingencies were drawn up and subsequently dropped. Among the German delegates there had indeed been someone who kept challenging her with his – admittedly, in part, not uninteresting – theses, who wouldn't let things lie and kept asking her opinion.

She clicked on his photograph. His smooth hair was combed back and neatly parted; it had probably been a bit fuller back then. His nose was slender and maybe a bit sharp, but those eyes! Of course her head had been full of other things at the time. The separation from Philip was one big running sore, Adam had just been born and Vera – who had arrived in Berlin with the buggy in her luggage to provide support – was a bit lost and just another headache for her. This had been the time when she'd had to decide whether to return to Belgrade with her small family. She'd said goodbye and got on the move before she fully knew where the journey was going to take her. Concern for her future and the future of her country weighed heavily on all her thoughts. And trying to separate the one from the other had sapped all her strength.

Milena enlarged his photograph, and cupped her chin in one hand. He probably wore bespoke suits, silk socks, Italian shirts and English shoes. She traced the fine laughter lines around his mouth with the cursor. He was slightly gaunt. His beautiful teeth were unfortunately not on display in the official diplomatic photograph.

Again she scrolled through the biographical details. What a life.

Marital status – she had totally overlooked that section before.

She clicked and closed window after window. She was a silly cow. What did she expect? And besides she had plenty of other things going on in her life to worry about.

She opened a new message in her e-mail inbox and started typing: 'Dear Philip.'

She then deleted this and wrote instead: 'Philip! If you want make your son happy...'

Again, she deleted her words and began afresh: 'Philip, could you please send your son a new baseball cap straight away, one with the Alba Berlin logo on, preferably size M. Thanks.'

She sat back and thought for a bit before furiously hammering in a sign-off line: 'I'm doing just fine'. Exclamation mark.

Her 'Sent' folder showed the message to Philip Bruns had been successfully transmitted.

She took off her earrings, got up to open the window, and stared out at the grey concrete wall opposite.

Was it the case that she was forever charging ahead without ever actually getting anywhere? And in the process not only missing the sights along the way but also the exit signs to her destination? She spent her time collecting temporary contracts and business cards, while skating over the real treasures.

She switched the lamp on her bedside table on. Every so often, it might be a good idea to stop, take stock and get her bearings.

She sat down at the desk again, took out a piece of paper and picked up a pen.

Nenad Jokić and Predrag Mrša. Born in the Bosnian town of Bratunac. Loved and sheltered by their parents, envied and admired by their brothers. Commissioned as guardsmen in the Serbian elite unit. Ordered to take the night watch of the eleventh to the twelfth of July. Found shot in the early hours of the twelfth. The entry angle of the bullets indicates that a third party must have fired the shots. The Serbian military tribunal has closed the investigation.

Milena pulled the keyboard towards her one more time, opened her e-mail and typed: 'Good morning, Siniša. The visit to the German Embassy was a complete waste of time. I'll try the direct route now. Milena.'

11

In the centre of the roundabout, two green giraffes stood and glowed in the morning sunshine. The ivy, which had entwined itself around the steel frames, dangled down at the end of the long necks, looking for all the world like snot hanging from the giraffes' noses.

The second exit was Duke Putnik Street. Milena joined a short queue behind a slow bus. Through her open window scraps of music – trumpet, tuba and tambourine – drifted in on warm waves of late-summer air. Gypsies were playing outside the Church of St Peter and Paul for a wedding party. The bride was floating in the bridegroom's arms a hand's-width above the ground, the guests were clapping along in time with the music and a child in short trousers was roaming barefoot around trouser-legs and swinging skirt-seams, begging hat-in-hand for a few dinar for its clan.

Near the old maple tree Duke Putnik Street merged with Rakovica Way. Over the centuries the branches of the maple had assumed the size of large-diameter pipes, and shown a propensity for growing sideways rather than up. In amongst the ingenious system of iron crutches erected over the years to prop up the golden canopy children were playing hide-and-seek, while their mothers were busy chatting and opening plastic containers as they prepared a picnic.

Just a few streets away, in the suburb of Dedinje, was where the beautiful, rich and powerful lived. The president, various ministers, and pop and tennis stars barricaded themselves in villas built like fortresses, had the borders of their compounds watched by surveillance cameras and the entrance gates controlled by security personnel. This is where the widow of a murdered politician lived, only a stone's throw away from the widow of a murdered Mafia boss.

Milena turned her car into a long bend and the sunlight illuminated in all its unpleasant detail the mess left on the windscreen by Belgrade's pigeons. There was no sign or marker of any kind pointing to the driveway with the barrier.

Milena slowed down, indicated and let the cars behind her pass. After executing a three-point turn, she drove back a few hundred metres before pulling over onto the grass verge and turning off the engine. She glanced up at the rear-view mirror, then picked up her bag.

The fence was over two metres high and impenetrable to any prying eyes. It was topped with several rows of barbed wire. Sandbags were piled high outside a corrugated-iron hut.

She had not even reached the barrier before the sentry emerged, making the same hand gesture that Milena used at home to shoo away the cat. 'Get lost,' he shouted. 'Go and walk somewhere else.' Dressed in camouflage fatigues and black boots and with an automatic rifle slung over his shoulder, he came towards her.

'Good day,' Milena said. 'I want to see the colonel.'

'You can't come in here. The compound isn't open to the public.' Using his machine-gun, he ushered her impatiently towards the verge. Behind her, a tank transporter with giant wheels pulled in and, with its engine roaring, stopped at the barrier.

Another soldier, also in battledress, walked over to them. 'What does she want?' he asked the guard.

'I want to speak to Colonel Danilo Djordan. My name is Dr Milena Lukin.'

The barrier was lowered behind the transporter. Through the open door of the hut a third soldier was clearly visible, who was just in the process of taking his feet off the table and straightening his black beret.

'We don't keep regular office hours here.'

'I'm aware of that.'

'Are you from the papers?'

'No, I'm from the Institute for Criminology and Forensic Science.'

'Your papers.'

'I am a member of the European Research Project. We investigate war crimes that were committed in the former Yugoslavia. I am working with the International Tribunal in The Hague.'

The men looked at one another. All three of them were now standing in a semicircle round her, in their uniforms and clutching their weapons, while she rummaged among the jelly bananas in her bag and tried to make up her mind whether she should show her Serbian passport or her German identity card. She'd brought along both; belt and braces. Eventually she handed over the Serbian passport and said: 'If I were you I'd think very carefully before obstructing me in my work; you'd be much better advised to call the colonel.'

'Step back.'

The men leafed through her documents. She couldn't decipher their muttered conversation. Then they walked back to the corrugated-iron hut. One of them disappeared inside, while another stood outside, barring the door. The third patrolled in front of the barrier.

Milena took a few steps towards them. The soldier outside glowered at her. She got the impression that his comrade inside was standing to attention while speaking to a superior on the phone. A row of monitors transmitted pictures from a multitude of surveillance cameras. As she craned her neck to see, the soldier pointedly blocked her view. 'The Lada, the blue one – that yours?'

'Should I park it somewhere else?'

'Your bag.' He reached out his hand. 'Hand it over!'

She followed his order.

'Stay where you are.' He disappeared with her bag and all her paraphernalia into the hut. The patrolling soldier kept a close eye on her. Milena thought it best not to move an inch.

Suddenly the soldier who had been on the phone emerged and called over to her: 'Come here!'

Milena hesitated. Had she been arrested?

'Well, what are you waiting for?'

Milena marched behind her escort and passed the barrier. The patrolling soldier did not cast another glance at her.

She was in. Inside the tightly sealed compound of the Serbian elite guards unit. Nobody, not even she herself, had thought that possible. But her triumph was tinged with a faint sense of fear. Without her bag and identity papers, she felt remarkably vulnerable and exposed. She started thinking that maybe she ought to have told Siniša a bit more about her planned visit here. But he hadn't answered her e-mail, and she hadn't called him again.

Her hope that the flat-roofed building right ahead was where the colonel was going to receive her was quickly dashed. With another abrupt hand gesture, the soldier motioned her to get into a jeep.

Milena grabbed the metal bars to the right and the left, placed one foot on the footrest and tried simultaneously to push herself off the ground and hoist herself up into the jeep. She made it on the second attempt. The seat was high and everything was so very open.

The rough, unmetalled track led up through a pine forest. To steady herself on the bumpy ride, Milena clasped the door handle with one hand while bracing herself against the seat with the other.

Somewhere behind the hill was the Sava River.

After a few minutes of silently bouncing around together in the jeep, Milena asked the soldier, in what she hoped sounded like a jokey tone, 'You are taking me to Colonel Djordan, aren't you?'

No reply. Evidently the soldier was under orders not to talk to her.

Finally, after another bend, a building came into view, its façade adorned with pillars, pilasters and the Serbian flag. They passed it and turned into a courtyard completely paved with cobblestones. A number of civilian cars were parked amongst military vehicles.

The driver switched off the engine and got out of the jeep. Milena grabbed hold of the bar, jumped down and followed him as he marched, swiftly and with a military bearing, towards a side entrance, as a group of about twelve soldiers came running around the corner. With their heavy boots, they sprinted across the courtyard, along the path, onto the meadow and then crossed through a line of trees at the double until their helmets disappeared from sight, one by one, down the slope beyond.

The driver waited in the doorway, looking at her impatiently. Well-worn steps led them to the first floor and down a long corridor. The doors to their left and right were shut, and neon strip-lights flickered nervously. The only sound to be heard was the echo of the soldier's boots.

The hallway ended at a door whose windows had been replaced by pieces of hardboard. The soldier pushed one of the wings open and looked back to make sure that it did not hit her in the face as it swung back – a small courtesy that put Milena's mind slightly more at ease. She also noticed that he was not carrying a weapon.

They stepped into a wide oval space, from which an ornate staircase led to the upper floors. Three galleries were surmounted by a cupola roof, and sunlight streamed in through high old windows. Somewhere quick footsteps could be heard, followed by a door slamming. Milena almost bumped into her companion.

'Step back!' He straightened his back, waited a second, knocked at a door and entered. Milena heard the heels of his boots click before the door closed.

Under normal circumstances, she would have taken out her mobile to check whether she was still in touch with the outside world. But she was in Topčider and it was as though the earth had swallowed her up.

The door swung open. The soldier did not look at her as she entered, but stepped briskly outside, closing the door behind him. He was gone in a second.

The first person her eyes lighted upon was the Serbian president. His portrait hung in a narrow wooden frame next to the national flag, emblazoned with the double-headed eagle of Serbia with a white cross on its chest, against a background of red, blue and white horizontal stripes.

'Sit down.' Danilo Djordan stood bolt upright behind his desk. She remembered him as being taller. His uniform jacket was not cornflower blue today but mouse-brown with a black belt.

'Thank you,' said Milena. 'I know it's not the done thing to just turn up at the barrier and ask to speak to you.'

'Indeed. You were at the funeral. The lady with the flowers.'

'That's right.' Taken aback, she smiled.

'What can I do for you, Ms Lukin?' He waited until she had sat down before taking a seat himself.

She scanned his face to try and determine if he was well-disposed towards her or not. In vain. Maybe it was down to the moustache that almost completely covered his thin lips.

'Do you have children?' she asked, without having really thought about it.

'I beg your pardon?' His eyebrows and moustache moved.

'You know, my son's ten years old. If he ever told me he wanted to join the Serbian guards, I'd move heaven and earth to dissuade him.'

'I'm sorry you think that way. We train our soldiers to be responsible and decent people. But it might be a bit soon for your son to be thinking about such things anyhow.'

'Look, I'll be perfectly frank with you.' Milena leaned forward. 'The death of Nenad Jokić and Predrag Mrša affects and bothers us all. This ritual that they're supposed to have acted out together, the murder-and–suicide-theory – let's be honest now, neither of us really buys that, do we?'

He stared hard at her. In that instant Milena realised how incredibly dangerous it was to suggest a double murder, and so question the findings of his investigating authority. She was on a military base, in unfamiliar territory, and really ought to adopt a more diplomatic tone.

She struggled for words, the palms of her hands grew moist, but there was no way she was about to wipe them on her jeans.

The colonel continued to fix her with his gaze. 'Did Stojković ask you to come here?'

'I'm doing nobody's bidding here. The entry angle of the bullet and the distance from which the shot was fired prove that a third person was involved.'

'Interesting. And who gave you this information?'

'That's of no concern right now. But you can't just allow basic facts to be ignored and swept under the carpet, if it means that a crime is hushed up.'

'I'll hold you accountable for such allegations.'

'You have to make sure that the investigation is reopened!'
Milena hoped he didn't notice the tremble in her voice. 'Only
a very restricted group of people has access here. The compound's strictly guarded, so it's by no means easy to get in.'

'Will you just hold your tongue for a moment!'

Milena crossed her legs and waited.

The colonel rolled a fountain-pen between his thumb and
index finger, back and forth, seemingly mulling over how to
get rid of this woman, who had ambushed him in his own
barracks, as quickly and discreetly as he could. Or was he just
trying to unsettle her?

'Before we start,' said Djordan presently, so loudly that he
could have been heard by someone at the other end of the
room let alone sitting right in front of him, 'be assured that
we have also been deeply affected by the death of Corporals
Jokić and Mrša. Number one. Number two: it was suicide,
of that there can be no doubt. If you have access to other
information, then the facts have been misrepresented or
wantonly misconstrued. Certain circles – and I regard your
friend Stojković as chief among them – go out of their way
to try and present me and the guards unit to the public in
a particular light. These people simply ignore any facts that
don't corroborate their view.'

'Do excuse me.' Milena did not want to be unnecessarily
provocative. 'But what facts might those be?'

'The families of these young men experienced the war and
have seen dreadful things. You don't have to be a psycholo-
gist to know that such trauma can continue to affect the next
generation and even the one after that.'

'I see,' said Milena. 'So according to your theory there are
at least two young men in the elite unit who were traumatised by the war.'

The colonel laid down his pen.

'And who committed suicide as a result.'

He stood up and pulled his uniform jacket tight.

'But of course that's not the image of the unit you'd wish to convey to the public.'

'I'll tell you this for your own good: you should leave this instant and let this matter drop.'

'Is this a threat or a warning?' Milena asked.

'It's a request, Ms Lukin. Just a request.'

Outside, she looked over towards the meadow and the trees. She'd have dearly loved to ask the driver to wait while she had a cigarette. But he had already climbed into the jeep and started the engine.

On the drive back, using her tried-and-tested method to cushion the bumps, she had to admit to herself that she'd rather screwed up the interview with Danilo Djordan. She'd had the chance to meet the colonel of the elite unit on equal terms. With a little more tact and diplomacy she might, for instance, have claimed she was sceptical about the conclusions of the German report, since they'd relied on the somewhat patchy forensic evidence that the Serbian authorities had grudgingly provided. That way, she might have achieved her aim: namely, to get him to commit himself to reopening the inquiry and reinvestigating the deaths. As it was, she'd completely fouled things up.

As they were approaching the pine forest, she caught sight of a figure walking along the track, a man in civvies wearing an oversized jacket and carrying a plastic bag that dangled from his wrist. He hailed them, but they sped past him so close that the poor man was forced to leap aside.

'Don't you have eyes in that head of yours?' Milena was enraged. 'He just wanted to hitch a ride!'

The driver pretended not to have heard and kept on looking doggedly straight ahead.

'Stop!' Milena exclaimed. 'This instant!'

The driver braked hard.

The young man – Milena reckoned he couldn't have been more than about twenty – flung his bag onto the rumble seat and clambered in. 'Thanks!' he said. He had close-set black eyes. If he hadn't also had a potato-shaped nose, Milena might have taken him for an Albanian.

When they reached the barrier, the guard was already waiting for them. With a deadpan expression on his face he handed over her handbag with the words: 'Please check to see if there's anything missing.'

She knew what that meant: they had searched her bag and discovered not only the jelly bananas and the potato-peeler but also her German passport. Milena assumed that all her personal details, including her car registration, had been carefully noted.

On the way to her car – she was finally able to light that cigarette – she noticed the young man again. He was standing at the bus stop. 'Can I give you a lift?' she called out. 'I'm going into town.'

Without hesitating, he came over.

She unlocked the passenger door for him and threw her bag on the back seat. He got in, reached under the seat and pushed it back.

'Buckle up, please.'

He complied.

'Look at me, giving out orders left, right and centre!' Milena said. 'Your army life seems to have rubbed off on me.'

The traffic on the main road into town was streaming past in such an unbroken procession that Milena finally lost patience, stepped on the gas and pushed her way into the queue. Once there, she opened the window. It was warm in the car and smelt of fried onions.

'May I?' The boy pointed at the pack of cigarettes lying on the dashboard.

'Help yourself.'

'Lada Niva. Solid car. But quite a gas-guzzler, isn't it?'

'You can say that again! But I got it converted. Autogas is a whole lot cheaper than petrol.'

'And what's up with your windscreen washer?'

She looked over at him. 'Are you the barracks mechanic or something?'

'Actually, I work in the kitchen. Samir.' He extended his hand. She reciprocated, giving him her name, and then asked him: 'Are you Gorani?'

'Well spotted.'

'Which region?'

'Dragaš.'

'In Western Kosovo, right?'

'South-western. Near the border with Albania. Do you know it?'

'Only by reputation.' The Gorani people were a minority ethnic group in northern Albania, but some of them also lived over the border, in Kosovo. The Gorani she had met during her time at the refugee agency had always been at pains to distinguish themselves from Albanians.

When they reached the motorway she changed into fourth gear and said: 'I was meeting the colonel today to ask him about the two dead guardsmen.'

He smoked in silence.

'You hear about that?'

No reaction.

'Don't tell me you didn't know about it. The whole city was talking about the deaths in Topčider.'

'Are you from the police?'

Milena laughed. 'Do I look like a policewoman?'

'So you're a PI?'

She looked at the wing mirror, indicated and changed into the overtaking lane. 'A good friend of mine is a lawyer. He's found out something fishy about the deaths of the two guardsmen.'

Samir said nothing.

'We simply want to find out the truth.' Milena said, getting into the right-hand lane. – Had she really just said 'simply'? If only! – 'I believe,' she went on, 'we owe it to the two dead men to at least clear up the circumstances in which they died. And we owe it to their families too.' She glanced over at him. He kept looking straight ahead, like he was trying to memorise every mark on the windscreen. 'What are you afraid of?'

'It was me who found them. – Hey, watch out!'

A cyclist – Milena swore. 'You found the bodies? I thought you worked in the kitchen?'

Silence again.

All of a sudden, he launched into his story: 'It was early, before I started my shift. I went for a walk down to the Sava River.'

'You mean where the land slopes down?'

'That's right. So, I'm just strolling along there, on my usual route, and there they were. With bullet wounds. One in the chest, the other in the forehead. I'd never seen anyone who'd been shot before.'

'What did you do?'

'I ran back like a madman and told my boss. He raised the alarm. And then the military police came.'

'Did they interrogate you?'

'Interrogate me? I got a bollocking, more like!'

'Why?'

'Because those parts of the compound are out of bounds for me.'

Milena shook her head. 'And the police?'

Samir gave her a sideways glance. 'All I did was come across the bodies. That's it.'

'No interrogation, no questions?'

'Why would they do that?'

'Because you're an important witness. It's essential, and quite normal procedure, for the police to question you.'

He clicked open his seat belt. 'There, over by the traffic lights, can you let me out?'

Milena indicated, pulled over and stopped outside the entrance of a fast-food restaurant. 'You can get out now and go on your way. Or you could try and help me. We could eat a burger together and talk. How about it?'

He opened the door.

'At least take the cigarettes.'

'Thanks.'

He had already got one leg outside the car when Milena asked: 'When you found Nenad and Predrag did you notice anything unusual?'

'I'm sorry, I can't help.'

'What about the day before?' Milena called after him.

He slammed the door.

Behind her, someone tooted their horn angrily. 'What's your problem?' Milena screamed into the rear-view mirror. 'I can't vanish into thin air! And I can't fly either!' In front of her was a concrete bollard and behind her a small queue had built up. She tried to judge how much room the guy in the car behind, whose road rage had got the better of him, had left for her to reverse when there was a knock on her window. She wound it down.

Samir leant in. 'The evening before, we served lamb.'

'Lamb?'

'Orders from above.'

'You mean Colonel Djordan?'

'From the very top! Special request. I don't know any more.'

'And the lamb?'

'Was served bang on time.'

'Who to?'

'Definitely not the regular troops.'

'Who to, then?'

'Top secret. And frankly, I don't want to know. And if anybody asks: you didn't hear it from me, right?' He looked around. The cacophony of honking was increasing. He slapped her door with the flat of his hand. 'I think you need to get away from here.'

And then he was gone.

'Alright, alright.' Milena raised her hand in conciliation. She put the car into reverse and carefully inched backwards.

A secret feast inside the compound of the Topčider. The next morning – two dead bodies. Slowly she manoeuvred the car out of the space.

Once again, precision work.

12

The bench was situated above the Roman Fountain and the King's Gate, on roughly the same level as the Victory Monument, and was the most beautiful spot on the Kalemegdan. Nowhere else on this fortress hill afforded a better view of the Danube looping in its majestic arch from Hungary, merging with the Sava River and then continuing its journey onward to Romania and ultimately the Black Sea. As Milena sat here looking down on the river, she fancied she could comprehend things which at other times remained a mystery to her, and see connections that otherwise eluded her. As she sat there in her reverie, decades and centuries seemed to flow by with the river, whole epochs in which wars were waged and frontiers redrawn, and in which civilisations rose and fell.

Siniša didn't even give himself a chance to sit down before launching into his diatribe: 'What on earth did you think you were doing?' Only the two little ice-cream tubs he was carrying stopped him from wringing his hands in anguish. 'Barracks aren't shopping malls – you can't just barge in there! Topčider's a high security compound and the men there are armed to the teeth. Plus, those guys aren't exactly squeamish at the best of times, and since the deaths occurred there they've become very twitchy indeed.' The tubs were resting on his knees now. 'Promise me one thing,' he said to Milena.

'What?' she asked.

'Before you go gallivanting off like that again, tell me first, and not in some e-mail with waffle about direct or indirect approaches or stuff like that. Tell me exactly what you're up to, what you're planning and I'll do my best to get you an appointment with the colonel or whoever else you want to speak to. That's the only way I can be sure nothing bad happens to you.'

'Nothing did happen to me, Siniša.'

'Promise?'

'Yes.'

He handed her the tub of Amarena cherry ice-cream. The silver watch on his wrist showed just before five.

He passed her a little plastic spoon. In return, she forbore to tell him that never in a million years would she have got an appointment with Colonel Djordan if Siniša – the lawyer of the Jokić and Mrša families and one-time instigator of the Commission of Inquiry – had asked for it. Siniša was well-known and despised in equal measure in Topčider circles.

Siniša sighed, swung his arm over the back of the bench, smiled and said: 'But who could refuse a woman like you anything? No one. I can just imagine how you marched in there, leaving the boys gawping open-mouthed at you.' He shook his head in admiration. 'Terrific.'

Milena rummaged around in her bag, dug out her calendar and the spectacle case and put her glasses on. 'The operation wasn't completely futile. With your permission, I'll give you the low-down.'

Siniša stretched out his legs and linked his hands behind his head.

'Well,' Milena began, leafing through her calendar. 'The situation is this: in the early hours of the morning of the twelfth of July, the kitchen boy Samir finds two dead guardsmen in the long grass in the compound; both have been shot.'

'So what's new?'

'Listen up. The day before, the eleventh of July, the barracks kitchen receives an unusual order: lamb. We don't know who's behind it. All we know is that the order came from the very top, though not from Colonel Djordan.'

'Interesting.'

'We also know that lamb is traditionally served on feast days. At those kind of banquets plenty of things happen, with all the alcohol, singing and dancing. We can assume that the celebrations went on well into the night, maybe until the early hours of the morning.'

Siniša grunted approvingly.

Milena went on: 'That evening, Guardsmen Nenad Jokić and Predrag Mrša were detailed to take the night watch. According to the evidence given by the kitchen boy, the banquet was top secret and only for a very select group. Our two guards might not even have been aware it was going on inside the compound when they came on duty that night.'

'What kind of feast was this supposed to have been, by the way?' Siniša asked. 'Some kind of long-service award ceremony, or what?'

'An anniversary.' Her mobile buzzed.

Siniša sat up straight and looked attentively at Milena.

'During the Bosnian War, it was the eleventh of July when Bosnian-Serb forces marched into Srebrenica. They overran the city and presented it, as they put it, to the Serbian people. Eight thousand Muslim boys and men were killed. I'm afraid it's not beyond the bounds of possibility that, on the anniversary of that date, the worst war crime perpetrated in Europe since the Second World War was celebrated in Topčider with a lamb feast, copious quantities of alcohol and raucous nationalistic songs. So, I ask you: what if Nenad and Predrag stumbled upon this event? And saw something they weren't supposed to see?'

'What sort of thing?'

'Men who've had international arrest warrants issued against them.'

'You mean war criminals? The General?'

Milena put away her calendar and looked at her phone. A new message.

Siniša leant forward. 'Would the kitchen boy, this...'

'Samir.'

'Would he be willing to give evidence in court?'

'I doubt it.'

'Do you have his last name? Address, telephone number?'

'I'm afraid not.' She slipped the phone back into her bag and zipped it shut.

'Where are you off to now?'

'I've got another appointment. I'll call you.'

On the way to the exit on Paris Street, Milena passed the little square tables in the park where old men were playing chess, surrounded by onlookers. On a mild evening like this they'd sit there moving the pieces until it got so dark they could no longer tell their knight from their rook.

Not far away stood the monument honouring the French with an inscription in Cyrillic: *Let us love the French as France loved us in 1918.* The First World War, the alliances and enmities between the Kingdom of Serbia and France, Austria-Hungary and the German Empire – all such a long time ago now. There were also other monuments commemorating Serbia's more recent past. For example on Takovo Street, the headquarters of Serbian State TV.

Like an open dolls' house, two walls on the wings of this building were missing. And all the rooms on levels one to four were burned-out shells. Sixteen journalists between the ages of twenty-seven and fifty-four had been killed at their desks, when the TV station became one of NATO's principal strategic targets. Four years after the end of the Bosnian War, the international community had resolved not to look on passively once more when a new conflict erupted four hundred kilometres south of Belgrade, this time between Serbian and Albanian nationalists. Once again, five decades after the end of the Second World War, warplanes were in the skies over Belgrade and thousands of citizens took to the streets to stand on Brankov Bridge, the entrance to Belgrade, to act as human shields and protect it from destruction.

Back then, missiles hit Duke Miloš Street and completely destroyed the military archive. When Milena looked at the ruins today, with trees growing out of the rubble, and walked along the hoardings where concert posters and flyers had been posted, she found herself overcome by a strange melancholy. Between these ruins and the old monuments a huge chasm yawned, a black hole, into which the whole world had disappeared. It was the world of the former Yugoslavia, with its red socialist pioneer scarves, white socks and the rooms of her childhood, peopled with strict aunts and jocular uncles and warmed by the love of attentive parents, a world that smelt of *Gugelhupf* and hot chocolate. The illicit experience of smoking her first cigarette, on a summer holiday on a Croatian island, and her first kiss, in a chalet in the Bosnian mountains, had been all but wiped from her memory by a dull sense of disappointment, and all the photos from that time expunged from the album. Half a century of an entire nation's past had been erased from the blackboard of world history and every individual had forfeited their right to sentimental memories because the generals and politicians had been allowed to rewrite history. Life back then had been played out in another country, whose soil had not yet been drenched and sullied with the blood of the Yugoslavian War.

Milena wandered through Tašmajdan Park, past the colourful carousel, the bouncy castle and the little monument commemorating the children who had been killed in the NATO attacks. She crossed Carnegy Street, pushed open the iron gate and climbed the stairs to the Serbian national archives. To her right and left stone lions sat enthroned, flanked with standards bearing the flag of Serbia.

The porter glanced up from his quiz magazine as she passed. Milena gave him a brief wave. The thick coir runner on the staircase muffled the sound of her steps. On the first floor she turned left, stopped in front of the second panelled door and knocked.

'Come in!' The voice sounded high-pitched, almost girlish in its tone and very familiar.

No matter what time of day it was, the brass-footed lamp with the green glass shade was always lit and the curtains of both windows always drawn. The tall bookcases, the wood panelling and the engraved prints hanging on the walls were all shrouded in gloom.

The only island of light in the room was the desk, every square inch of which was covered with pieces of paper, piled up, bound and rolled, all crammed together. The direct path from the door to the desk was blocked by a black leather sofa and two massive armchairs, but there was no way round the side of these either. Small metal trolleys loaded with books stood there in a long line waiting to be dispatched. When, and in what sequence, that would occur was decided by the person in the pleated skirt. Innumerable chains, necklaces and a pair of half-rimmed spectacles on a cord hung down over her crisp white tailored blouse. Her hair, a mélange of every shade of grey from black to silver, was loosely back-combed and held in place artfully with hairclips. Her cheeks were slightly flushed with excitement at the arrival of her niece. Aunt Borka squeezed past the row of trolleys to greet her. Her gold bracelets jingled when they embraced and kissed. As always, her first question was: 'Shall we have a little cup of something?'

'That'd be nice, Aunt Borka.'

Borka took the tray and scurried away with little steps. Milena picked up a book at random: Isidora Sekulić, *Travelogue, second volume.* The room had always been Milena's cave, where she could sit in the big armchair, dangling her legs, stuffing her face with biscuits and burying herself in any book she fancied. She loved it when Aunt Borka recited from memory whole passages from world literature and the work of her favourite authors like Rilke, T.S. Eliot and Pasternak. Some relatives whispered disapprovingly behind her back that Borka had wasted her life away here, in the archive, buried under all these books. That wasn't quite true, however, as her aunt had had at least one other love: the literary critic Vlastimir, renowned in Serbia and across the whole of the Balkans. Sadly, though, he'd been so advanced in years that he died before Borka could make up her mind whether she loved him enough to marry him. But now, when she went to drink coffee at his grave and read the latest reviews to him, the relatives of the dead in the neighbouring graves would nod to her, giving her the warm glow of feeling she was a real widow like them. Yet Milena got the distinct impression that Aunt Borka was harbouring another secret, a great treasure, hidden away from everyone and buried so deep that it might never come to light.

Vera viewed her sister-in-law through less rose-tinted glasses: 'No children, never married, and a trip to Montenegro is a grand tour for her.' Even so, her basic affection for Borka manifested itself in the form of *Gibanica,* paper-thin sheets of filo pastry layered with a mix of soft cheese, oil and eggs, and plenty of chard. She'd lovingly put two large slices on top of one another in a Tupperware box for Aunt Borka plus another one on its side next to them.

'Oh, she really didn't need to do that,' said Borka, smiling, then turned to the subject of Milena's recent contribution to a *festschrift* in honour of the great political scientist Nikola Tomić. She praised one of Milena's lines of argument, criticised another and then suddenly slipped off her flat shoe: 'Look,' she said. Beneath the heel of her white tights, a half-moon appeared. 'Remember this wedge you once brought me from Berlin?'

'Oh yes, the Dr Scholl insert.'

'Exactly. I've tried everything, but nothing else works. Only Dr Scholls. What kind of patent is that?'

'I'll look into it for you.'

'You are a darling.'

'Have you ever thought about having the ganglion removed? There's a marvellous specialist at the Charité Hospital in Berlin.'

Borka pressed her foot back into her shoe and picked up her keys. 'Come on now, no time to waste. You've got work to do.'

Milena made a mental note: e-mail Philip this evening without fail, and add a pack of Dr Scholl wedges to the order for Adam's baseball cap, size M.

Where the rug ended, a staircase lead up to the attic. Here, in the narrow hallway, the doors and the temperature were much lower than in the rest of the building.

Borka tried several keys, unlocked the door and disappeared into the darkness. Seconds later, another lamp with a brass stand and a green shade was lit here as well. Next to the table where it stood was one of the small trolleys, piled high with books, files and slipcases. There were no curtains here. After the missile attack the windows had been boarded up.

'No one's going to disturb you here.' Borka placed a cushion on the chair. 'Everything in the field you're so keen to research is classified, of course. But we won't let that bother us, will we?'

'Thanks. I'd be lost without you.'

Borka bent down and switched on the electric heater. 'What exactly are you looking for, anyway?'

'If only I knew. I've got to get an overview.'

With her hand already on the door latch, Borka turned around once more. 'And why in heaven's name, my dear girl, are you interested in the barracks in Topčider?'

'That's a long story. I'll tell you it one day.'

'Good luck.' Borka closed the door behind her. The jingle of her bracelets faded with her receding steps, and Milena turned her attention to the material in front of her, all the treasures on the trolley beside her, which she could now trawl through to her heart's content without having to file an official request, which doubtless would in any case have been denied.

She put on her glasses, slipped on some thin cotton gloves and picked up a little leaflet on the far left side of the trolley. The characteristic sweetish aroma of old paper wafted up from its pages.

Milena's watch was showing almost seven o'clock as she embarked upon her examination of the classified material and entered into a realm normally off-limits to unauthorised persons.

13

The spider was dead. He'd checked. It had met a miserable end in its holey web under the hand basin, a completely stupid location it should have vacated in good time. By contrast, the damned dog was much harder to get rid of; the cur kept on barking, yelping and barking again.

Pawle lay there for a long time until he heard the lock of the desk next door being turned – once, twice. The key dropped into the briefcase, then the clasps were closed – left, right. Chair legs on lino. Cupboard door open, cupboard door shut. Pawle counted. On the count of twelve, the back door was closed. Again, not a word.

He got up, fetched the bucket, placed it in the basin and turned on the tap. He watched as the water flowed in. A weekend had passed and then another couple of days since they had discussed his case on the phone. They were probably pissing themselves laughing watching him on tenterhooks like this. They'd probably betted on how long it would take him to make a mistake so they could report him to their superiors. Then that'd be that. The endgame. Of course, the other possibility was that they'd already forgotten about him down here. He didn't know which was worse.

He stuffed the mop under his arm and lugged the bucket into the front room. With his left hand he snatched up the chair and put it on the table. He could just clear off, do a bunk. Today. This very instant. And go where, though? Over the border. And then what? Bullshit. There was no place for him anywhere.

He upended chair after chair on the table. He did his job well, he was reliable. Followed orders. Didn't ask questions. Not so long ago he'd been the key man in the unit. The other guys had looked up to him. And now? He was just snivelling about here. He was a zero. A nothing. He kicked the bucket in fury. The water slopped over the dirty grey tiles.

The chair he'd just had in his hand suddenly flew through the air and crashed against the wall. The next one fetched up in the corner with a crunch of splintering wood. He grabbed a third by the leg and smashed it down violently on the table. Once. Twice. He panted with exertion. He was standing in the corridor outside Momčilo's office. He lifted his foot, screamed and kicked the door open with all his might.

Momčilo's nerve centre. There was a sickly sweet scent in the air. The cupboard was empty. On the desk, a fountain pen, biro, pencil, sharpener and paperclips. A card index with no cards in it. To the left a hole-punch, next to it a letter opener, and on the right the telephone. Pawle swept the whole book-keeper's paraphernalia aside with his hand, slumped down in the swivelling chair, put his arms on the rests and pressed his hands against his skull. His heart was racing.

He rattled the drawer, then picked up the letter opener from the floor, jammed it into the gap, and wiggled it about until he had prised open the lock.

Two pornographic magazines, a third and then another – he flung them all into the corner. Beneath, he saw some papers in a clear document wallet. The clean plastic suggested it must contain something important. He pulled out the sheets, stapled pages, columns with names and ranks, addresses and telephone numbers, all very orderly and clear. Was this a register of members, a list of forthcoming promotions, a hit-list, or what?

He rifled through the document. He couldn't see his name. A broad, coloured band became visible through the thin sheets of paper; on the final page one line of typing had been highlighted.

Rank, last name, first name. Pawle spelled out the name: Colonel Djordan, Danilo.

He got up, leaving both the drawer and the door open. Re-entering the main room, he saw the debris, the broken glass, the water and the dirt, the whole mess he'd created.

The image that flashed before his mind's eye was without a soundtrack but was crystal clear. He saw the dolls lying in the rubble, all over the place, tossed aside, stamped on in anger. He reeled, tried to clear a way through with his feet, stumbled and fell. Shards of glass got stuck in his hands as he crawled along on all fours. He was whimpering. And there was blood on his hands again. He found the wall, groped about for the light switch, and hit it again and again until it was finally dark.

He was cowering on the floor. In the distance he heard the sound of traffic, a constant low hum. Pawle forced himself to breathe calmly, take his hands from his face and look at the sign in the window.

It glowed warm and yellow, just like the moon on that summer's night. Once again, he knew he'd do nothing. Just wait, as he had done then, until they came to find him.

14

Milena took off her glasses, stretched her arms above her head and then to the sides, arched her back and rolled her head around a few times. She looked at her watch. For more than three hours, she had scoured the word index, and skim-read her way through countless essays and treatises. If she'd mastered one art, it was this: digesting masses of written material in a short time and rapidly getting herself up to speed in a subject she'd previously known nothing about. She hadn't realised that the Turks had been responsible for building the first barracks at Topčider before their withdrawal from Serbia in 1867, or that King Obrenović had founded the Honour Guard along Prussian lines, thereby starting a tradition that lasted well into the royal dictatorship period and was then revived by Marshal Tito, of all people. She was sitting here behind high walls and a boarded-up window, working her way through a mountain of Serbian history and amassing knowledge that was probably completely irrelevant to solving of the murder of Nenad Jokić and Predrag Mrša.

She closed the books and put them back on the small trolley. Although she felt exhausted and glutted with information, she forced herself to look at one final document, the old map that she'd kept till last. She put her glasses back on.

There was the Church of St Peter and St Paul and the crossroads, now a roundabout. The Sava River was shown in blue, and she could clearly make out the outline of the Topčider compound. The entrance to the barracks was in exactly the same place as it was today. A large building located inside the compound had no legend or caption, but she recognised it as the place where she had met Colonel Danilo Djordan. In addition, though, there were several larger and smaller numbered squares – presumably also buildings of some kind – which Milena could not fully decipher, and dotted lines criss-crossing the terrain, which she could not make any sense of whatsoever.

Milena leant back. She could not even precisely identify the location where the bodies had been found. For that she would need Samir, whom she had let go without asking for his address or telephone number. Sure, that had been a mistake, which she could not deny when Siniša had challenged her about it. Maybe it was time to delegate certain tasks. She'd ask Aunt Borka for a copy of the map and Siniša would get the job of waiting for Samir at the bus stop. Despite all the setbacks she seemed to be on the right track with her research. She was convinced of that, though as yet she had no idea where this line of enquiry was leading her.

Wearily she picked up the envelope that had contained the map and as she did so felt some resistance. There was something inside, a thin bit of padding. She pushed the paper apart and discovered a small pocket, which had been skilfully worked into the lining, an envelope inside the envelope. Using two fingers, she reached inside and took hold of a thin piece of paper, neatly folded into a small, flat square.

Perhaps Milena was the first person in decades to unearth this find. But for her impatience, she might have handled the delicate, thin paper with a little more care. As it was, though, her efforts to unfold it ripped it, tearing it apart at the sharp creases. It fell to pieces in her hands.

Short, quick steps and a soft jangling of bracelets announced the arrival of Aunt Borka. It was a reflex on Milena's part to cover up the damage caused by her carelessness – as she had done once before in the past when she'd brushed some crumbs of chocolate off the pages of a book and left behind a trail of ugly brown stains.

Aunt Borka stood in the open door, her hand on the handle: 'Made any progress? Did you find what you were looking for?'

'A map. Look – do you think we could get a copy of this?'

'I'll see to it. First thing tomorrow morning.' Aunt Borka came closer and looked at the clean desktop. 'Everything okay?' she asked.

'Everything's fine.' Milena zipped up her bag and smiled.

*

It was just after midnight when she closed the apartment door behind her, slid home the large bolt and the smaller one above it, and hooked up the chain. There was a narrow strip of light coming from the kitchen. Milena put her shoes on the rack, massaged her toes with one hand and quietly greeted the cat, who had emerged from somewhere or other and wrapped itself around her legs, purring loudly.

There was a plate, some cutlery, a loaf of bread and three bowls on the kitchen table with cling film stretched over them. Vera was sitting bolt upright in her chair, her folded hands resting on the table.

Milena closed her eyes for a second and asked herself what she'd forgotten to do – some promise not kept, or some wish she'd failed to satisfy. The duvet had been cleaned and picked up from the dry cleaner, and she'd told the constantly drunk caretaker of the apartment block about the water stain on the bathroom ceiling. Then it could only be the lambskin insoles she said she'd get for Vera. Or the set of guitar strings for Adam. No, on reflection it had to be about the winter provisions, the sixteen kilos of red peppers which she'd promised to get hold of last week. The next thought that crossed her mind made her go weak at the knees: 'Is something wrong with Adam?'

'The boy's asleep,' Vera said. 'Sit down.'

Milena did as she was bidden and watched as, one by one, Vera peeled the clingfilm off the bowls; she saw the drops of condensation run off the plastic and then caught the delicious smell that began to pervade the kitchen, redolent of all the loving care and attention that Vera had lavished on the preparation of the dishes: leek blanched in butter, sprinkled with pine kernels and toasted breadcrumbs; tender green beans in an oil, lemon, garlic and parsley marinade; and chicken seasoned with lovage and tarragon, crisp-fried and diced into bite-size pieces. Vera proceeded to serve Milena; she knew that whatever problem her mother confronted her with, she'd come up with a solution.

'Thanks, Mum.' Milena tried the beans while Vera wordlessly slid an old black-and-white photograph with deckled edges between the bowls and across the table to her. Milena stopped eating.

It wasn't just the full lips and nostrils, which were slightly too large. Above all, it was the expression in the man's eyes: gentle and at the same time very alert, almost impertinent. Yet this stranger seemed oddly familiar, somehow. Yes – that was it: the young man in the photograph was the spitting image of Adam, as he would look in ten or fifteen years. Out of place, though, were the swastika on the uniform cap and the SS flash on the lapel.

'Great Uncle Gottfried,' Vera said. 'Grandma Bückeburg gave Adam the photograph and told him that she always thinks of her big brother when she sees him.'

'Striking resemblance, I have to admit.'

Vera nodded grimly. 'She also told him that Gottfried died in the war, in Russia. That the Russians killed him.'

Milena cut herself a slice of bread. 'Mum, that was all a long time ago. It's Philip's family history, and that's okay. Adam's old enough now, and he's part of that German family too whether we like it or not. Believe me, it's alright.'

'No, it's not alright when Adam stands here in my kitchen and says: "When I grow up, I'll shoot all the Russians dead."'

Milena laid down her fork. So that's what this was all about. Little Adam had sounded off without realising what sensitive ground he was on. How could he? For him the Second World War was an old black-and-white movie, involving a lot of shooting and shouting, and in which good triumphs over evil in the end. For Vera, though, all it took was a few ill-chosen words and an old photograph, and her brothers were back facing the German *Wehrmacht* again.

Milena mopped up the marinade with the bread. She'd have to be diplomatic now and mediate between Bückeburg and Belgrade, between the Bruns and the Lukins. She said: 'Grandma Bückeburg didn't mean any harm. She looks at Adam and all the memories come flooding back, happy memories of her brother, and then the Russian campaign, all the horror of those years. Please give the old lady a bit of leeway.'

'Not if she incites the boy and twists the facts. We're a household of partisans, and we were never anything else. Adam's grandfather was a communist and went to prison for his beliefs. His great uncle Srećko was captured by the Germans and transported all the way to Osnabrück. Srećko met his death somewhere in the goddamn German Reich and is buried in foreign soil. So we're not about to shoot any Russians dead. We honour them. The Russians helped us to expel the Germans. They're our friends.'

'Did you say all that to Adam, in as many words?'

Vera propped herself up with both hands on the table top and got up. 'The photo of this SS lad can't stay here. Find

better words than mine, but you must explain it to the boy.'
She switched off the little light above the stove and left.
Fiona followed her pointedly.

Milena poured herself the dregs of coffee left in the pot,
went out onto the balcony and sat down on the chair between
the rotary line and the larder. She took a sip of coffee, lit a
cigarillo and stared at the grey concrete wall.

The past always found a way through, searching out little
channels and seeping into the present every bit as relent-
lessly as the bathwater of their neighbour in the upstairs flat.
And suddenly there were ugly stains on a clean white wall.
For decades the photograph had stood on the sideboard in
Bückeburg, dusted off at regular intervals and looked at not
quite so often, and everything had been fine. Now there was
a gap on the sideboard in Bückeburg and here in Belgrade
there was a photograph that did not belong, in exactly the
same way as the scraps of paper from the envelope in the
archive did not belong in her handbag. She had the option
of simply shrugging off all this stuff, recycling it with the old
newspapers and forgetting all about it. She could also send
the photograph back to Bückeburg, write a few friendly
lines explaining why this picture of the German relative in
SS uniform was inappropriate in a Belgrade home. If only
it were that simple. There was always someone who'd get
hurt and someone else to whom she owed it to deal with the
matter properly, put the pieces together again, and find an
explanation.

In her room she turned on the lamp on her desk, shifted
the pile of corrected papers into the top folder and placed
the uncorrected ones crosswise on top of the pile. She
emptied the contents of her bag onto the space she'd cleared
and sorted through them, putting things back in one by one:
her diary, her office keys, jelly bananas, a potato peeler, hair

pins, elastic bands, receipts and other assorted junk that had accumulated in there over the years. When she'd finished, all that was left on the table were a few crumbs and the little bits of paper from the archives.

Milena opened the window and fetched the ashtray from the bookshelf. Before she could close the door, Fiona darted through the narrow gap, arched her back, and meowed in complaint.

'What do you want?' Milena asked. 'You've got nothing to moan about.'

The cat jumped onto the table and settled down under the light. Milena lit another cigarillo, exhaled and put on her glasses.

The little pieces of paper were almost all the same size and had, it appeared, fallen apart exactly along the sharp creases made all those years ago. The paper had the consistency, strength and transparency of tracing paper. She randomly picked up one of the squares and held it up to the light. There was writing on it. She adjusted the lampshade. Individual block letters, written in mirror-image, and upside-down. She turned the paper around and read: 'LEDGHER'. Utterly mystifying.

She looked at the next square. There were two numbers and a cross near the bottom edge: 35×. On the next one a sequence of letters: 'GARSNAP'. Milena picked up each of the little squares individually, all forty-eight of them, reading off syllables and fragments of words, some of them linked by numbers, which in turn were often connected by a multiplication sign: MI 80×1, 15×12, NES 71×. Could they be technical specifications of some sort? She shuffled the squares about, trying to find a logical order, but nothing made any sense. Disappointed, Milena leant back. Fiona got up from her sleeping place and strolled casually across the puzzle on the desk, displaying her feline dexterity by not disturbing one single square with her paws. Milena clasped her coffee mug and stood up, disquieted by the fact that she hadn't managed to solve any of the problems she had to deal with. She had destroyed a document which might, for all she knew, be very valuable, and through her carelessness had created a riddle that might not turn out to be a riddle at all.

Great Uncle Gottfried was still lying in the kitchen. His smile was still strangely familiar. She picked up the photograph. And found herself compelled to smile back.

In the boy's room she carefully stepped over his satchel, basketball boots and magic kit and sat down on the edge of the bed. Adam was fast asleep and breathing deeply.

Carefully Milena pulled open the bottom drawer of his bedside table and hid the photograph under the paintbox there, shoving Uncle Gottfried back as far as she could.

She closed the drawer, smoothed down the duvet and kissed Adam's forehead. She had no solutions and no plan. She only had her powerlessness and this child. And she would do her utmost to prevent him becoming the victim of an idea, a system – even in the name of his Fatherland.

15

Squinting into the light, the caretaker Goran Šoć inspected the stain on the bathroom ceiling. In the corner above the bathtub was its dark brown epicentre, from which a spectrum of warm shades of gold spread out all the way up to the vent, and marbled brightly over the hot water boiler.

Next to him stood Milka Bašić, the neighbour from upstairs, in her slippers. 'I'd just leave them alone if I were you, the water stains I mean,' she said, with her hands stuck in her apron pockets, 'those little devils and their pranks up there. Eventually, they'll disappear of their own accord, you'll see.'

'So do you think it's those same little devils that are responsible for damaging the letterboxes as well?' Milena asked.

Šoć took his spectacles down from the top of his head, put them back on his fleshy nose and looked at Milena through the dirty lenses. 'We're keeping a close eye on the situation and will take appropriate action at some future date.'

After this appointment Milena drove to the market. Three sacks full of peppers, five kilos apiece, plus a sixteenth in a separate bag, which the farmer gave her free as a thank-you bonus every year. The provisions were now safely stowed in the boot of her car. She'd also ticked Adam's guitar strings off her to-do list. Her only failure had been the warm lambskin insoles. On both Zmaj-Jova Street and Macedonian Street, the shopkeepers had shrugged their shoulders regretfully: warm insoles? But summer was upon us again now, wasn't it?

When she reached her office, she hung up her denim jacket on the hook, added another potato peeler to the collection in the drawer, opened the window and loaded her e-mail. 'Philip!' she wrote. 'I know I already asked you to get Adam's Alba-Berlin baseball cap (size M) and a pair of Dr Scholl shoe insets for Aunt Borka...you probably haven't bought either yet – never mind. Could I also prevail upon you to add some lambskin insoles size 34–36 for Vera when you send the package? Eternally gratefully yours, Milena.'

Two essays stuck out of the pile of post – work that should have been handed in two weeks ago. She would correct them, and then clip the lazy buggers' ears with them. Apart from them, mailshots, an invitation to the Frankfurt Book Fair and an envelope with a cardboard stiffener in it. Sent from the Serbian Archives. If only everyone were as reliable and conscientious as Aunt Borka.

She was just running a paperknife along the edge of the envelope when her mobile rang in her bag. She pulled it out and looked at the screen. An unknown number. She pressed the green button.

A male voice: 'Am I speaking to Ms Lukin?'

'Who's calling, please?'

'Danilo Djordan.'

'Colonel.' She got up. 'Hello.'

'Please forgive this intrusion, Ms Lukin. But since we spoke I've had a few things preying on my mind. Could we meet again?'

Milena closed the window. 'What's this concerning?'

'Look, I don't want to ambush you on the phone with it right now. Sorry to be so direct, but are you free tomorrow? I know it's a bit short notice. But it's really important for me.'

'You've excited my curiosity.'

'I'll be spending the whole of tomorrow on Ada Ciganlija. I have a little houseboat there, you see. If we could meet there, that would be ideal. It's very peaceful. But only if it's not too much trouble. I'm aware it's a bit of a cheek to ask you to drive all the way out there.'

'Tomorrow, 5 pm?'

'Perfect. Just come to the marina.'

'Goodbye.'

She switched off her phone. The colonel of the Serbian elite unit wanted to tell her something. What a turn-up.

'If you want to finish your call' – Boris had popped his head through the door – 'I can come back later.'

When had this man suddenly morphed into a polite human being? Probably when he'd wanted her to bring back two bottles of *Jägermeister* for him – the large-sized ones, mind you – from Berlin with her.

'This came for you today.' He placed a letter on her desk and nervously swept his thin hair back over his balding skull. His tie was knotted so tightly that it was cutting into his plump neck and adding a third roll to his double chin.

Milena read the letterhead: 'Johnson Institute'.

'They'll arrive here on the tenth of October – that's in four weeks' time! I don't know what these people are thinking of. They're bringing a delegation of six men and we have to dance to their tune. It's always the same with these international bodies. It's outrageous, if you ask me.'

This visit didn't come as such a surprise to Milena. After all, she'd sat alongside these Johnson people at a conference in Copenhagen and had suggested they might like to take a closer look at an interesting project in Europe: the root-and-branch reform of the Serbian justice system and the establishment of an independent judiciary there.

'And guess what they want to talk to us about?' Grubač asked. 'How we're getting on with the reform of the justice system and the establishment of an independent judiciary.

Whatever made them think of us? They should go to Africa for that sort of thing.'

'Take a seat, Mr Grubač.' She extended her hand to offer him a pristinely wrapped jelly banana. 'Actually, I think it sounds like a very interesting project.'

'I knew you'd say that. But you've got it so good, working on your research and doing a bit of lecturing on the side. Do you know how lucky you are?' He squeezed the little jelly banana out of its cellophane wrapping. 'Put yourself in my shoes for a moment. I can't just tell them: "Do what you like but count me out". They're so well-connected, they know the people in the European Commission, they might even have links to the International Tribunal in The Hague.'

'The Johnson Institute is totally independent.'

'That's what they all say. And then...Ms Lukin, don't leave me in the lurch like this!'

'Try looking at it another way, Mr Grubač,' Milena leant forward and looked deep into his watery eyes. 'If you support the people from the Johnson Institute in their work, it'd be a great opportunity to further the reputation of our little institute. Did you think of that? This is a unique chance to really distinguish yourself. There could be an audience with the President in it for you.'

Grubač sucked on his jelly banana and puckered his lips. The idea of being invited to tea with the head of state and shaking his hand in front of a gaggle of photographers seemed to gel nicely with the taste of the sweet. 'All right,' he said. 'Let's look at how this could play out. What do you suggest?'

'The people from the Johnson Institute mainly need access to the ministries and executive committees.'

'I'm sure the ministries and committees will be really thrilled about that!'

'Everyone in the delegation will be assigned a liaison officer, somebody who's trustworthy and knows the institutions, who's well-connected and speaks English fluently.'

'Anything else on your wish list?' Grubač said, plucking the hair in his nostrils. 'How about a few pretty young ladies? Wouldn't that make things easier...I'm just kidding, Ms Lukin.'

'I can think of a few very capable candidates amongst my students.'

'Students? Don't you think we should convey a bit more seriousness and reliability to the Johnson Institute.'

'The image we want to get across is that we're a young democracy with dedicated young people.'

'And what else?'

'We'll organise a meeting with representatives of Democratic Awakening and a few former dissidents.'

'Hmm, not so sure about the dissidents.' Grubač loosened the knot of his tie. 'What about the Minister of Justice?'

'I consider the Permanent Secretary more appropriate.'

'A city tour? A visit to the opera, maybe?'

'I'd rather take them for dinner at the Literary Club. We should invite a representative of the Djindji-Foundation and somebody from the Helsinki Group to join us.'

'Agreed. Very good. That's how we'll do it. I think it's best if you come up with a list of suggestions for the programme. Plus some contact names.' He stood up.

She hadn't expected him to thank her.

'By the way...' he said.

She looked up.

'The German Embassy called this morning. The secretary – a total bitch, really self-important – but she wouldn't say what it was all about. I think I have the number somewhere if you want to call them.'

She put on her glasses, took out the folder with the business cards and started to leaf through them. 'How come you're only telling me this now?'

'You were out. But never mind, I know the Germans. If they want something they'll call back.'

'Thank you, Mr Grubač. I'll take care of it myself.'

Her business card collection did not yield anything. She pulled the keyboard towards her and typed 'German Embassy Belgrade telephone number' into the search engine. *Voilà.* Soon after she was connected to the switchboard. Milena gave her name and asked to speak to the ambassador, at which point she was put on hold.

She was happy that Alexander Kronburg had got in touch. And not a little curious. Maybe they'd have dinner together. She'd ask him about his projects and plans for his time in Serbia – discreetly, of course – and make the odd comment here and there, offer advice. After all, he was not yet experienced in dealing with the Serbs. She could show him the city, her favourite sites, take a stroll together one balmy night.

The secretary who picked up on the other end of the line sounded quite young and not terribly friendly. Milena cleared her throat and sought the right tone to let the girl know that the ambassador had tried to reach her and she was returning his call.

Presently, she heard the ambassador's voice; it sounded unexpectedly close. He was charming, made her laugh, and yes, it was clear he was also delighted to speak to her. Milena thought of his blue eyes and lost herself in reverie just listening to him. Suddenly, he said: 'I have a window free tomorrow.'

'A window?' she repeated.

'Exactly. From – wait a moment – from 1.15 to 2 pm. What do you say?'

'A forty-five minute window of opportunity.'

'I've got so many appointments, there are so many people I have to meet...'

'I understand,' Milena interrupted. 'Believe me. Nobody understands that better than me. But a little window like that, I'm sorry to say so, Mr Kronburg, I just can't see myself fitting into it.' And with that, she abruptly terminated their conversation.

Then she sat there and stared at her screensaver, showing the rocky coastline of Korčula.

He didn't call back.

She got up, went over to the window and breathed in the warm air. Ticket inspectors were lounging on the benches opposite the memorial, clearly identifiable from their yellow vests; they were clearly content to sit there squinting at the afternoon sun and leaving fare-dodgers to dodge their fares. A woman was throwing a stick for her dog. And the black-and-white-clad waiters from The Spring were being kept on their toes by their hungry and thirsty customers.

Milena put the kettle on and spooned coffee into her mug. She'd given her last jelly banana to her boss. A slice of Damascus Tart – that would hit the spot right now, a layer of nougat on a firm biscuit base, enriched with praline and topped with whipped egg white.

She took an extra spoonful of sugar, sat back at her desk, pulled the copy of the map from the envelope and gazed at the plan of the Topčider compound. Aunt Borka had attached a piece of paper on which she'd jotted down in her clear hand a numbered legend describing the functions of the various buildings. She'd found this information, she wrote, on the back of the original. Milena had not looked at the reverse of the map. Now the small numbers marking the buildings made perfect sense. The arsenal, the living quarters, the clothing store and the pantry. Only the dotted lines criss-crossing the whole area remained a mystery. Perhaps they were just contour lines.

Milena took off her glasses and rubbed her eyes. Tomorrow she'd meet the colonel. What could she do until then? She needed to catch up with Siniša, and it would be good if she could locate Samir. She wanted to stick the map of Topčider under the kitchen boy's nose and get him to show her precisely where he'd found the bodies. Maybe then she'd be able to pinpoint the place where the banquet had taken place. She had to be prepared, have the facts at her fingertips, and be in a position to put what the colonel told her into context. She called Siniša but only got his voicemail. She left a message for him to call her back.

She folded the map and stuck it back into the envelope. Was her theory correct? On the other hand, how could one misinterpret facts that seemed so crystal clear?

Beneath the memorial to Duke Vuk, film students who ran an art cinema downstairs were now gathering. They were arguing, smoking and taking themselves tremendously seriously. They were of Nenad and Predrag's generation, and the future belonged to them.

She picked up the phone. The ring tone barely had time to kick in before Tanja answered. 'What does the eleventh of July mean to you?' Milena asked.

'The eleventh of July?' A few seconds of silence followed. There was only static on the line. 'I can tell you exactly: the eleventh of July was the day of the massacre in Srebrenica.'

'Somewhere in Topčider that anniversary was celebrated.'

'Are you still on your case, about the two dead guard soldiers?'

'It's only a theory: Nenad and Predrag gatecrashed this secret event and saw the General. And that's why they had to be eliminated.'

'Do you have any evidence?'

'The statement of a kitchen boy.'

'Which says?'

'That a secret banquet was laid on somewhere within the barracks.'

'That's all?'

'Yes, that's the sum total, would you believe? But tell me honestly: does this all sound plausible so far?'

'Plausible? Well, if you're asking me straight out...but I'm no criminologist, mind you.'

'But you've got common sense.'

'Exactly. And that common sense tells me the idea that a war criminal with an international arrest warrant out against him could celebrate with his men in Topčider barracks is pretty absurd.'

'Wait a minute. That's not all. I've just had a call from Danilo Djordan, the colonel of the guards' regiment. He wants to meet me tomorrow, out in Ada Ciganlija, to tell me something. He hasn't told me what, but –'

'Milena.'

'Yes?'

'Just assuming your theory is correct, then you're dealing with men who are not to be trifled with. Men like the General don't mess about.'

'So what am I supposed to do, do you reckon?'

'Leave the whole matter to the police.'

Milena hated Tanja for her ability to say exactly what was objectively right, but what she did not want to hear.

'I mean it, Milena.'

'The problem is that the police won't do anything. I know it. And I can't stand it. It goes against the grain with me. I have a son myself, I...' Milena was close to tears.

'And that's why,' said Tanja. 'You are not only endangering

yourself and this kitchen boy, but your family as well. Incidentally...' – again the static on the line – 'I have another, totally different theory.'

Milena blew her nose.

'I'll tell you what I think right now, and please don't be offended if I indulge in some pop psychology. The thing is, I've got the impression that you're getting obsessed with this affair. You're about to project everything into this case, certain feelings you've always had: your discontent, your anger, your helplessness, not being able to do anything against old cliques, these nationalists who are protected from above or who the authorities just turn a blind eye to. That's dangerous. If your theory's correct, though, it'd be presumptuous and irresponsible to do what you are doing. Because you can't take on criminals of this stature.'

'You're right. Yes, I'm probably overestimating myself and what I can possibly achieve. I just thought...'

'Try to think of something else. Something nice. And I don't mean the Café Petit Prince. How about calling the ambassador?'

'That's a dead loss.'

'Really? – Shit.'

'Yes. When can I see you?'

'Sweetie, I'm on my way to the airport. The clinic, Stefanos – I've got to get away for a while. We'll talk next week, just the two of us, agreed? Are you still there?'

'You're always escaping, getting out when the going gets tough. Me, I sit everything out, stuck here on my fat arse, every bit of crap, no matter what. Why is that?'

'Listen, I've just had an idea: go this minute to Uzun-Mirko-Street –'

'What, to that ridiculously expensive boutique you go to?'

'Yeah, that's right. You'll see why. Ciao.'

Uzun-Mirko-Street, which ran from Academy Square to Paris Street, was off the main shopping strip Prince Mihailov Street. Milena was well acquainted with the shop Tanja meant, at least with its shop window, which was always tastefully decorated and not as cramped, say, as the one at 'Uppa Druppa' on Takovo Street, where Milena occasionally picked up one of her colourful bargains. In Uzun-Mirko-Street, even a bargain would have torn such a hole in Milena's bank account that it couldn't have been plugged even with a month's salary.

Milena walked to the quiet side street where she had parked her car several hours previously. In the boot of the Lada sixteen kilograms of red peppers were still simmering. The sun had just disappeared behind the tall apartment blocks.

Milena searched for her car keys in her bag while talking to Adam on the phone. 'Of course we're going swimming,' she said into the small receiver. 'Like I promised. In half an hour. You've got till then to find your trunks. Yes, exactly, ask Grandma. – See you soon, my darling.'

She put the car key in the lock.

'Are you Ms Lukin?'

She turned around.

'Your papers, please,' the policeman said. A colleague stood silently beside him.

Milena looked in her bag. 'I know I've exceeded the permitted parking period. I'm sorry, and of course I'll pay the fine.'

The uniformed officer leafed through the passport, page by page and back again. Then, instead of handing it back, he pocketed it. 'We'll have to ask you to accompany us.'

'I beg your pardon?'

The policeman opened the rear door of the squad car. 'Get in,' he ordered.

16

Pawle didn't hang around, but nor did he hurry. He walked briskly upstream along the Sava River, straight on without deviating, wearing clean jeans and an unobtrusive wind-breaker, so none of the damned joggers or any of the walkers hereabouts would have any reason to pay him any close attention. Even the old women on the riverbank basking in the sun in their petticoats and huge bras, who normally stuck their nose into anything and anybody's business, had their backs to the promenade, with their legs dangling in the cool water, and were looking over towards the city.

He was prepared; he'd eaten only a light meal and had rested, but not for too long. He didn't want to squander the chance he'd been given, so he'd invested quite some time in working out, initially using a sandbag, before adding lifts, push-ups, and sit-ups – up to one hundred at a time and more. He was fit – a thousand times fitter than the pasty-faced Belgrade boys who were doing their stretches here on the promenade. When he exercised he did it properly and, above all, alone. Nobody would witness him struggling, out of breath or sweaty.

He was in good time. The small, bothersome obstacle that had got in his way at first had been dealt with already: three trembly legs, a pink nose, a devoted doggy look in its eyes – that was how the bag of bones had suddenly appeared in front of him. He just shimmied past it, ignoring it. But it insisted on following him and when he stopped, so did the bitch; when he walked on, the cur followed, half-hop-ping, half-limping. The chunk of wood he'd found on the ground was just right for dealing with this millstone round his neck.

He had waited until the animal approached to sniff his trouser leg with its dry nose. Then he hit it with the log. The bitch fled so fast into the bushes that the second blow missed its mark. What a yelp! Die, you bitch. A good start.

On the far side of the river, the Belgrade bank, the tracks came into view, and on them some screeching passenger trains. Further north they led to the main train station. Once upon a time, he did not quite recall when, that was where he'd first arrived too. He had filled in that application back then and stuck to his guns, he'd been adamant he wanted to come here. He had no clue what a big city was like. But there was money there, he imagined, and girls, and opportunities. Just help yourself, he thought. He got infected by the others. And when, out of all of the guys, he got selected, he was the champion of course. Stupid, that was what he'd been back then – an idiot among idiots.

It was hot. Off to the right, there was a kiosk. He had enough money on him. Wondering whether to take a short detour, he hesitated, just for an instant at most, but it was still long enough. The guy at the kiosk drinking his beer stared at him like he was trying to commit every detail of him to memory. He was itching to wipe the floor with the bloke. He had stored up too much strength, after all, but he was not so stupid to let it out here.

But what if the guy was called as a witness later? Bullshit. Nobody would even think of questioning such a wimp. He just had to keep walking, keep straight on, don't slacken the pace, but don't hurry either. The bimbo teetering towards him on her stiletto heels wasn't worth a second glance. She'd taken the arm of a guy who was posturing like he was some big shot. He might have guessed: the couple turned and walked across a gangway onto a boat, a floating restaurant. Nice view, nice food. Then home to watch TV, and then, before going to sleep, a shag. Congrats. He didn't need that. What he needed was a clear head.

The sun was setting. There were trees here, but no forest. He had not seen the forest for an eternity. The forest had been his home, his playground. He let this image linger. There were others and they had built a hideout together. But in the end it was only he who ran to it, he alone; only he had run there to hide.

He was sweating. He forced himself to walk slowly. The perspiration was streaming down his back. He stumbled. Don't let up, but don't hurry either and don't tremble. Definitely don't tremble. He needed a steady hand.

He sat down in the grass and leant against a tree trunk. He was in good time, everything was going to plan. He felt the tree against his back, the knotty bark. In these calm surroundings he experienced a sensation that was new, or at least one he had forgotten existed – a feeling that was momentous and for which he could not find an expression.

At dusk he was going to cross the Sava Bridge, walk towards Belgrade on the far side and further on upstream. Darkness would swallow him, nobody would take any notice of him. He had a task, he was on a mission. He was on his way back to his old life.

17

The policeman walked half a pace behind Milena, firmly gripping her upper arm. He steered her downstairs, into a corridor, along the line of holding cells. He dictated the pace, letting her stumble but not fall. Doors slammed shut. Where there was no daylight, neon light flickered. It reeked of urine. Somebody was screaming, another crying, while a third was yelling: 'Tell Saša I'll cut his balls off!' Further to the left was a room without windows, in which all those detained sat together, criminals and traffic offenders, shoplifters and prostitutes, smugglers and blackmailers – picked up in the streets and squares, the dives and backrooms, dragged here by the men in uniform, into this cellar of an inconspicuous dirty-grey building on Sava Street, right next to the main train lines and marshalling yards, where freight trains were shunted about and passenger trains brought ever more people into the big city. Milena was confused, enraged and very afraid. 'Listen. This is all a big mistake.'

'Sit down.'

'I don't think you understand me. I don't want to sit down. I want to –'

'Sit down!'

A lanky type in a tracksuit shifted along to make room for her. The man in the uniform helped himself from the pack of cigarettes his colleague had handed to him. Mission accomplished, suspect in custody. Milena sank down onto the bench with the feeling of being a criminal.

'Caught shoplifting?' The young man nodded at her bag with his big baby face .

'I don't know what I have been caught at.' Her arm was hurting and her shaking voice frightened her. 'I've no idea why I'm here.'

'Hey, stop talking!' the policeman growled. 'Move apart. And you, take the laces out of your shoes. And the drawstring from your tracksuit bottoms. Come on, get a move on.'

The young man fumbled to undo the laces of his sneakers. While a cleaner was mopping up around their feet with a wet grey flannel he said quietly to Milena: 'If you've got plans for this evening, I'd forget it.'

'Move it!' The policeman clapped his hands.

The young man twisted his laces round his finger like a propeller and grinned before being lead off.

The woman who took his place had a hair clasp with butterflies on it and wore hooped tights like Pippi Longstocking.

'Excuse me,' Milena asked the uniformed officer. 'I need to make an urgent phone call.'

All of a sudden the door burst open. Policemen began running about, shouting orders. From inside the adjoining room came the sounds of barked orders, the police unit was clearly being prepared for a major new operation, or being reprimanded for fouling up the last one.

'Did you hear me?' Milena tried to make her voice more authoritative. 'I want to call home. I must have that right, surely?'

'I don't steal, I'm not a thief. I never took a single Dinar.' The woman next to her bent over and whimpered. 'Žarko is my witness. But ever since Dušan legged it, nobody gives a damn about Ana. You don't care how she is. But I have to look after her, you know. My Ana, my darling. She'll be sick with worry. She'll go mad with worry. I know her, my Ana. I know her like nobody else, and what you know is shit.'

'Ružica, stop being a pain,' came a voice from behind.

Hunched and with her arms crossed in front of her chest as if she was freezing, the woman turned her head and looked up to Milena. 'You believe me, don't you?' she asked quietly. On her chapped lips lingered a trace of lipstick.

Milena nodded tiredly. 'I believe everything you say, every word.'

'Sister,' the woman whispered, 'have you got a bit of change for me, maybe?'

Milena opened the zip of her bag – and immediately closed it again. Inside was the ground plan of the Topčider, or at least a copy of it. The original, the property of the National Archive, was classified and only accessible with written permission, properly signed and sealed. Of all things it had to be this piece of paper, which had been of no use so far and was in all likelihood completely worthless, which was going to get her into trouble now – and Aunt Borka with her.

'You deaf or something?' The policeman grabbed Milena's arm. 'Let's go! Come with me.'

'She's a good person,' wailed the woman whom someone had called Ružica. 'Let her go! What do you want with the little dove? She hasn't done anything, I swear it!'

The hole in which Milena was now led defied all description. Again there was no window and the contents consisted of a table, two chairs and a shelf unit, the latter crammed full of old newspapers and folders. Because of the damp down here the papers were probably completely illegible. The only interesting things were on the table: Milena's mobile, passport and a cup of coffee.

The policeman kicked the chair, dropped his cigarette butt into the mug and sat down with a soft groan. He pulled the table towards his stomach, before fishing out some form or other, placing it on the writing pad in front of him, and fastidiously straightening it up. This was obviously a bit of bureaucracy that had to be performed to the letter, and could not be got round or speeded up in any way, but which definitely could be complicated and slowed down by unnecessary questions. That was the last thing Milena wanted: to hold up a process whose conclusion surely had to be a realisation on the part of officialdom that it was all a misunderstanding, a case of mistaken identity. All she wanted now was her passport back and her phone and to get out of here, go home to her son, her mother, the cat and the bags of peppers.

'Lukin,' the policeman mumbled. 'Milena.' He copied the details from the passport into the appropriate boxes on the form, while at the same time using his thumbnail to dislodge a piece of food stuck between two teeth. 'Born...'

Milena could not hold back any longer. 'Would you be so kind as to tell me what I'm being accused of?'

'You'll learn that soon enough. Your bag.'

'I beg your pardon?'

'Your bag. Hand it over. And sit down.'

Milena obeyed. Diary, guitar strings, key ring – one by one he took out each item, studied it, moved his lips soundlessly to name it, and meticulously wrote it down on the form.

'Have you been in this job long?' Milena asked.

He pulled out Aunt Borka's envelope with the stiff back and gave Milena a questioning look.

'I mean,' – she said, trying to strike up a conversation – 'your job's not easy, is it? Day after day with so many people...'

'Don't trouble your little head about that.' At that moment the door opened.

The man who came in was wearing an open-necked shirt with a small check pattern, jeans with a belt and brown loafers. This was clearly the grand entrance of a superior officer, who usually didn't bother with the riff-raff off the street but who had somehow been moved to leave his office and make his way to this dingy cellar. He took Milena's passport, rifled through it, threw her a cursory glance and asked his colleague: 'Are you done?'

'The inventory is quite large...'

The boss made a gesture as if to say: pack up the stuff and wrap it up – then turned to Milena and said: 'Come with me.'

She helped gather up all her bits and pieces, a few sweeps of the hand and the zip was closed again. With the bag over her shoulder she felt prepared for whatever was going to be thrown at her next. The Topčider ground plan had not been taken down on record and she was going to have less of a problem dealing with this officer in his checked shirt. In his crew-cut pepper-and-salt hair, the black had almost lost its struggle against the grey, but Milena guessed that he was still not older than forty. When the lift door opened he stepped aside to let her in before him. His skin was clean-shaven and slightly tanned. The shadows under his eyes gave his face a somewhat melancholic air. Despite his slight portliness he appeared to be a sporty and agile type. He cleared his throat. 'Filipow. Inspector.'

'I find it unbelievable what's going on here,' Milena said.

'As a matter of fact my colleagues had orders to bring you straight to me.' He pushed the lift door open and went ahead. 'But it's been hell today. The game against Slovenia, you know. It can mess everything up. I do beg your pardon.'

'Pardon?' she repeated, following him out of the lift. 'You kidnap me in broad daylight, keep me locked up without telling me why, and I'm supposed to pardon that?'

He pointed at a wooden chair and walked around the desk to his seat. 'We don't kidnap anybody and we're not keeping you here for no reason. Calm down. And by the way, I'm asking the questions here.'

'Go right ahead!'

On the windowsill stood a bottle of French cognac in a gift box and, leaning against it, an English dictionary. Underneath a cupboard was a box with a picture of a set of pots and pans. Filipow leafed through a file. 'You're working at the Institute for Criminology and Forensic Science, correct?'

'Correct.'

'With Professor Boris Grubač.'

'That's right.'

'And there you are responsible for setting up...' – he read from the page in front of him: '...a task force for International Criminal Prosecution and Jurisdiction.'

Milena laid one hand on top of the other. So this was what it was all about. The arm of the military was long, obviously reaching all the way into this office, to this inspector. This whole affair was an attempt to intimidate her.

'Ms Lukin, what were you doing last Monday, 6 September, at Topčider barracks?'

She had to weigh every word very carefully now. Then again, what had she got to hide? 'I was talking to Colonel Danilo Djordan. He was kind enough to see me,' she replied.

'Were you instructed to have this meeting?'

'Instructed? By whom? What I discussed with the colonel is no secret: we talked about the guardsmen Nenad Jokić and Predrag Mrša and about the mysterious circumstances of their deaths. The media was talking about them for weeks.'

'And what has your discussion with Colonel Djordan got to do with your work at the institute?'

'Nothing. These two young men were gunned down in Topčider, the case remains unsolved. Many questions remain unanswered, and they keep multiplying. You should be investigating those rather than wasting your time with me. And now, if you have no objection...'

He picked up the piece of paper again: 'An automobile
– Lada Niva four-by-four, number plate: BG, 15–0-8–0-7,
colour: petrol blue – was spotted in the security zone of the
barracks on 6 September from 10.20 to 11.35 am, parked illegally and left unattended.' Filipow chucked the folder back
on the desk.

'You're not serious, are you?'

'Ms Lukin, the problem is that you don't appear to appreciate the seriousness of the situation! Every citizen who
enters this sensitive high-security area, especially the way
you did it, is registered and put on record. It's for our collective security.' Inspector Filipow leant forward. 'I advise you
to obey the rules.'

'Please can I have my passport back,' said Milena. 'I want
to go now.'

He handed her the document across the table. She made
to take it, but he held on to it. 'One more thing.' His brown
eyes fixed on her. 'The envelope you so hurriedly put back in
your bag – could I have a look at it, please?' He let go of her
passport.

Milena opened her bag and slipped the passport inside.
'I'm an academic. I am doing research. That's my profession.'
She handed him the envelope over the table.

Again he looked into her eyes. His lower eyelid twitched
slightly. Without taking the envelope, he said: 'You can go.'

Rather than take the lift, she walked down the four floors
to ground level, taking time as she descended the flights of
stairs to calm her breathing and collect her thoughts. But
there was nothing to collect. Just a vast emptiness, as if fear,
anger and the feeling of impotence cancelled each other
out.

The man who was running towards her, silk scarf flowing,
took two steps at a time and shovelled away the air with his

hands on both sides. He had almost passed her when he stopped and turned around.

'Milena!' He retraced a few steps and opened his arms wide. 'My old mate Vlad just called me and told me you were here.' He embraced her.

His horrible aftershave took her breath away and she could have cried with relief.

18

The little shit was a problem. He should have known. It was some kind of natural law that barracks were always the home of gypsies, in fact a ludicrous number of them, the bitches always pregnant with screaming brats in their arms or clinging to their apron strings. Just because a single rat of this pack had followed him, he had been forced to leave his chosen path just before reaching his destination and creep into the undergrowth for cover. And now he was squatting here, with the leaves in the treetops above rustling indifferently, and his time was running out.

Don't panic, he told himself. In the forest and in the darkness he had the advantage. Here he moved like a cat, not making a sound, and where others went poking around blindly he could still see everything clearly. This skill had saved his life in the past. Too bad for the rat. But it must have smelled that there was danger coming and had pissed off. Good instinct.

He retraced his path. Everything was back on track again. Everything was in order.

Crouching down he flitted over the footbridge, dived into the shadow of the wooden wall and felt his way along the boards. A fishing net, a saw and other tools were meticulously arranged in a row along the wall. He couldn't tell whether the shovel in the middle of the path was meant to be a trap. Step onto the blade, smacked in the gob by the handle and he would have been a goner. He stepped over the shovel. He wasn't some novice.

He stopped to listen. The waves quietly lapping against the wooden piles were caused by his steps. Plastic bottles drifted in the water. The business with the shovel irritated him. But if the plans had gone wrong and the target had arrived before him, he would have been informed.

The moon shone brightly. He crouched down again, waited for a cloud and then crawled across the wet planks past the tarpaulin. The cover had been weighed down with bricks. Some people favoured such tools, but they were too crude for him. His kind of instrument was in his left pocket, totally silent and quick to use – if one knew the right moves, that is. Despite his handicap he was reputed to be a dab hand with it. He couldn't honestly claim to be indifferent to such admiration, but equally he didn't know what use it was either. He just didn't care much either way.

The lie of the land had been described and sketched out for him in the following terms: a shed, containing the outside toilet, had been added onto the main building, and the entrance to it was covered by a curtain of colourful plastic streamers. On the way to the arranged meeting point the target would have to stop right in front of this curtain to retrieve a key to gain access to the building. That was the basic situation as outlined to him, and he'd been told that this was the moment when he should make his move. That was the plan. The conditions were perfect. But perfect conditions could lead to negligence. He was on the way to being rehabilitated, the first step, and had to be extra careful. Under no circumstances should he give them cause to reject him again. He tried hard to suppress the memory of the idiotic grins on the faces of some of his comrades. No matter how this turned out, he'd make sure he wiped them off for good, anyhow.

Shoulder first, he slipped through the curtain, causing the plastic strips to move only as much as a gentle breeze wafting through them. Inside he climbed on top of a box, a move that not only made him more invisible but would also lend greater impetus to his thrust forward, not that he thought that would be necessary.

It was cramped behind the curtain. He looked straight ahead into the darkness. He registered every sound, reduced his breathing to the bare minimum, every muscle taut.

The constriction. The curtain. The silence. He had no image for his memories, only sounds, rushing towards him with gathering speed like his ear was resting on a train track. He could do nothing. The screaming and shouting swept over him. With all his might he wedged himself between the walls to his left and right, pressed his eyes shut, and clenched his teeth to stop himself from screaming. He must not scream.

And then suddenly it was all over. Footsteps were approaching in the hush. A keyring jingled. The moon bathed the figure on the far side of the curtain in white light. It stood there, motionless, just like Pawle.

He must stop panting. He must act. He clutched the knife with his left hand. He was holding it so tightly that the blood in the veins of his fingers stopped circulating. In slow motion the figure outside turned towards him. In the next moment he would push aside the plastic strips and discover him.

Pawle thought of the spider. Instead of acting, moving, it had perished in its web. This thought only flashed through Pawle's head for one second – a second that might cost him his life.

19

A gentleman like Siniša not only escorted Milena from the police station to her car, which was still parked on Gračanica Street, but also drove her home in it. He lugged the three bags of red peppers into the lift and through the flat onto the balcony. And he complimented Vera on her radiant appearance, her beautiful home and her cookery, in this case mackerel, carefully skinned and boned, served cold with potato salad and an oil and vinegar dressing with a garnish of cornichons and red onions.

Siniša took off his jacket when Vera put the *Rakija* on the table, the good one with the anise roots added, which old Jelisveta still insisted on digging out of her Montenegrin home soil with her bare hands, despite the fact she could barely crawl by now.

Fiona sat enthroned on Siniša's lap and with closed eyes allowed him to stroke her thick fur. Next to him stood Adam with his eyes glued on Siniša, intent on hearing every word that came from his lips. Siniša ranted and raved against despotism, against corrupt officials, against all the misery that stifled progress in Serbia. 'But this inspector,' Siniša vowed, 'this...'

'Filipow,' Milena said.

'...this Filipow will curse the day he arrested you, I swear it.'

'Curse?' Adam asked.

Siniša finished his glass of *Rakija*, putting it down on the table in such a way as to underline what he had just said.

Milena was tired. 'Look, nobody's cursing, nobody's cursed, not even this inspector. He's probably just following orders. Like you're about to now, Adam. Off to bed with you, you hear?'

Siniša held up his index finger in front of the boy's face. 'Don't worry. As long as us two – you and me – look after your mum, nothing's going to happen to her.'

Vera was sorting through various plastic bowls and a heap of lids she'd got down from the cupboard, eventually choosing the largest one.

Holding this bowl, now containing an extra-large portion of potato salad, Milena accompanied her friend to the lift in the hallway. Only here did she tell him about Colonel Djordan's call. 'You won't believe it,' she said. 'Djordan wants to talk.'

Siniša knotted his scarf with the delicate paisley pattern. 'I wouldn't get your hopes up if I were you,' he told Milena. 'Why would Djordan crap in the nest where he's so comfortably ensconced? I know these kind of men. They're all incredibly vain. At best he just wants to leave you with a better impression of him than you had after your last conversation.' He took the bowl with the potato salad from her. 'In any case, this whole enterprise is really dangerous. I'll let you go and speak to him on one condition, Milena.'

'Let me guess – that you come with me, or at least hang around nearby while I'm talking to him?'

'Exactly.' He patted her arm.

They agreed to drive to Ada Ciganlija together and to take Siniša's silver-grey Renault rather than the petrol-blue Lada, which the authorities were too familiar with by now.

After Siniša had disappeared into the lift and she'd locked the flat door behind her, she went into Adam's room. It was past midnight. She picked up the hoodie from the floor, hung it over the chair, collected his slippers and put them next to the bed so he could slip straight into them in the morning.

Through the Desert and Wilderness was the title on the dust jacket of the book he was reading. Milena, too, had eagerly devoured this adventure novel by Henryk Sienkiewicz when she'd been Adam's age. 'Not a bad story, is it?' she asked, sitting down on the edge of his bed.

He gave a barely perceptible nod and turned a page.

'Have you reached the bit where Staš works in Khartoum for a whole day to earn enough to buy twelve dates for Nelly?'

'Yeah, they're in Baobab now and Staš has lied to Nelly, telling her he's already had something to eat.'

'And he bites his lips to hide the fact that he's incredibly hungry from her – Staš is cool, isn't he?'

'No,' Adam said. 'He's just in love. We men are like that when we're in love. To be honest, I like Nelly better.'

Milena looked at her boy, who now counted himself a man. 'What do you like about her?' she asked.

'I like that she's so sincere and graceful. And that she's blonde. I like blondes, I've got that in common with Dad.'

Sometimes she did not recognise her little son. His pupils raced across the lines and she could have gazed at him forever. But when he turned another page she softly took the book from his hands and put a bookmark between the pages.

'I'm sorry, darling, that we didn't manage to go swimming today.' She closed the book and put it on the night table. 'We'll make it up on the weekend, promise.'

'What was it like to drive in a police car?' Adam folded his arms behind his head. 'Did they have the siren on?'

'Oh right, that would really have made my day!'

'Were you frightened?'

'Frightened?' She stroked his hair gently. 'It was more liked a mixture of feelings: I was afraid, but I was angry too. And I felt helpless. Luckily I knew I'd done nothing wrong.'

'And you still went along with the policemen. That was very brave.'

'Brave? I had no choice.'

'Did they handcuff you?'

Milena shook her head. 'No, they were quite friendly, all in all.' She straightened his blanket and tucked him in tightly. She thought of the young woman with Pippi longstockings – Ružica. Where would she be now? At home with her child as well?

'I did something really funny today,' Adam said.

'And did you remember to do your homework too?'

He nodded.

'And practise the guitar?'

'Shall I show you quickly what I did?'

'No, best go to sleep now.' She kissed him and switched off the bedside light. 'And tomorrow I'll make you rice pudding with dates.'

'Mum,' he said.

'Yes?'

'We won 3–1 against Slovenia.'

'Very nice. Now go to sleep and dream of something nice.'

'Mum?'

'Adam, please!'

'Siniša should be your role model.'

'Why?'

'Because he doesn't smoke.'

She had to kiss him again. 'Alright, my sweets. I'll make sure of that.'

He flung his arms around her neck and whispered, half-asleep already, 'I love you, Mum, forever and ever.'

'I love you too.' She felt his small, cold nose in her hair, breathed in his childlike warm smell and wished a fervent wish that, whatever else happened, she'd be able protect him from all the evil lurking outside.

In the kitchen she took a spoon from the sink, scraped the remaining potato salad from the bowl, picked at a few grapes, cleared the bottle of *Rakija* off the table and turned off the small light over the stove. She put the *Rakija* next to the bottle of cognac in the living room, and slipped the TV listings magazine into the newspaper rack. The rug had migrated again along the polished parquet floor. She bent down and pulled it back to its proper place.

The light was still on at her desk. Obviously Adam had badgered his grandmother until she'd given in and let him play his beloved computer games on the internet. There were just two rules that had to be observed. Rule number one ('half an hour max – that's it!') he broke regularly. But he had always followed rule number two ('don't touch anything on my desk!'). Today, though, things seemed different. The pile of corrected essays had been shoved aside and piled up with all the other stuff on a heap between the scented candle and the filing trays. 'Oh Adam,' murmured Milena in disbelief and sank on her rotary chair, 'what have you done.'

He had used the cleared space to do a jigsaw, all the pieces of which were virtually the same size, almost square and with the consistency and transparency of tracing paper.

She adjusted the lampshade. 'LEDGHER' formed part of the words 'pickled gherkins', and 'GARSNAP' part of 'sugar snaps'. Four commodities and their respective quantities had come to light in Adam's puzzle:

Pickled gherkins 35×12
Sugar snaps 71×12
Tinned sardines 115×12
Salami 80×12

All the letters were neatly written, but the list had been jotted down all over the place. It was a curious mix of order and disorder.

Milena bent over the paper. Only the words 'sugar snaps' had a thin border drawn round it. For some reason this little box was distinct from the other entries.

Milena got up and fetched the ashtray from the shelf. Why had somebody, decades ago, gone to the trouble of carefully fashioning the inner sleeve within the outer envelope only to put such a mundane message inside?

She lit a cigarillo and opened the window. Every package insert, every enclosed label either contained indications of risks and side effects, or instructions and directions on use. How did this list fit into that scheme of things?

Fiona sat like a beautiful sculpture under the lamp and stared at Milena. Again Milena was unsure whether her eyes were simply like beautiful glass or more like big, mysterious marbles.

'Stop looking like that,' Milena told the cat. 'Why don't you help me instead? Tell me, what does this leaflet mean? Is it significant or not? Am I missing something?'

The cat remained enigmatically silent.

Maybe she was just thinking too much. Perhaps there was no secret hidden on this piece of paper and it was just an ordinary shopping list or inventory of some sort. Thanks to Adam she now knew what it was all about and could file away the list and the map. The whole affair had cost her a lot of time, she'd become obsessed by it, these things could happen. But it was over and done with now, she could put the puzzle away. She didn't want to destroy it, though; she'd keep the individual parts all safely together so they could be reassembled if necessary.

Adam had thought of everything; on the reverse side, he'd stuck the pieces of paper together with sellotape.

She turned on the light on her bedside table and switched off the desk lamp. Adam had earned himself a huge reward.

Not just an ice cream, but something special. Maybe a weekend in the country with Aunt Isidora and Uncle Miodrag. He could see how much their little calf had grown, help Uncle Miodrag get the treehouse ready for winter and bake a chocolate and walnut cake with Aunt Isidora. She fiddled with the tiny clasp of her necklace. She was spending far too little time with her son. There was the editorial she was supposed to write for a German weekly magazine, plus attending to her students and Grubač's extra tasks – all this on top of what she already had on her plate. It was just too much. If only that jumped-up, petty bureaucrat, that clerk in Bonn, that Blechschmidt bloke would keep his word and finally get back to her to let her know where she stood with her contract!

Poor Adam. No wonder he couldn't wait for the autumn holidays with his father in Hamburg. There he was the centre of attention, and was allowed to be a child and a boy, and go sailing with his father and rock-climbing with this Jutta woman. And what about herself? She kept postponing the swimming lesson and couldn't come up with anything more exciting than sending the boy to Aunt Isidora and Uncle Miodrag.

She fluffed up the pillow. She couldn't hope to compete with Philip on his terms. But if he was responsible for sport, then she should take responsibility for Adam's cultural education. After all, he mustn't be allowed to become another Philip Bruns. He should see other cities, hear other languages spoken. French, for example. Paris.

She pulled back the duvet cover. The scent of freshly washed laundry wafted over her. Why not? She'd take Adam to the Louvre, show him the Mona Lisa and explain to him what was so special about this woman – even though she wasn't a blonde. And she'd book a lovely hotel in the Marais district, in the Rue Vieille du Temple, for example, which she loved so much.

She turned off the light. Fiona lay on the duvet like a stone.

Milena dreamed of the Tuileries, the Jardin du Luxembourg, of Adam on top of the Eiffel Tower and of a boat tour on the Seine. The next morning she felt refreshed and rested in a way she hadn't for a long time.

She put on her robe, knocked on the bathroom door, called out 'hurry up' and walked into the kitchen. Vera was sitting at the table reading the newspaper. Sunlight was streaming through the sparkling windows, a fruit salad was waiting, fresh white bread and jam made with fruit from Uncle Miodrag's garden. Up in the corner the television was on, silently showing the breakfast programme of Studio Belgrade.

'Did you sleep well?' Vera rustled the paper, Adam slammed the bathroom door, Milena drank her coffee, black and strong, and experienced a moment of profound happiness.

'Mum?' Adam flung his satchel onto the chair. 'I've got to ask you something. It's really important. Are you listening?'

Milena was spreading four-berry jam with the spoon. 'Of course, I'm listening.'

'Can I have an advance on my pocket money?'

Vera chuckled and shook her head without looking up from her paper.

'Please, Mum!'

'You always get your way, don't you, mister?' She put her jam sandwich down on her plate. 'Look, you did me a huge favour when you glued together those bits of paper yesterday.'

'Bits of paper?' Vera asked, looking over her glasses and putting the paper aside.

'Sugar snaps, tins of sardines, salami and pickled gherkins,' Adam recited. 'So can I have my advance? Twenty Euros, say?'

'You'll get it. Do you want to go travelling or something?'

'No, I'd like to take Katinka to a film.'

Vera poured tea into his cup and exchanged glances with Milena.

'I want to take Katinka to the afternoon show and afterwards go to 'Roggenart'. Or not 'Roggenart', maybe somewhere else. And I don't want you two spying on me.'

'Well that's made that clear,' Vera said and tied up her apron.

Milena observed her son. Saw how he bit into his jam sandwich, how he drank his tea, how he chewed. And how, in his thoughts, he was with Katinka. How quickly all this had happened. Wasn't it only yesterday he'd learned how to walk?

'Adam,' Vera reminded him. 'Your tram.'

He picked up his satchel. 'Agreed?'

'Agreed,' Milena answered and shook on it.

'Ciao!' A moment later, the front door of the apartment slammed shut.

Vera cut the red pepper into strips.

'Who's this girl, then?' asked Milena, 'this Katinka?'

'She's pretty.' Vera looked up at the television and Milena followed her gaze. There was a reporter and a big, fluffy microphone. A cordoned-off area, policemen and children trying to get themselves into the camera shot. Vera picked up the remote and turned up the volume.

'...*took off last night and cost him his life.*' Although the reporter was trying to sound matter-of-fact, his voice betrayed his excitement. '*How this could have happened is something that hopefully Inspector Jovan Dežulović, who is leading the investigation, can explain.*' A bald-headed man in a short leather jacket came into view. '*Mr Dežulović, what happened?*'

'*The forensic team hasn't finished its investigation yet and I don't want to jump to any conclusions. I must ask for your patience.*'

'*So is this a crime scene?*'

'*At this point in the investigation, we must assume we're dealing with a tragic accident.*'

'*Can you give us any details about the identity of the victim? Who was the man, and what was he doing out here?*'

'*I'm sure you'll appreciate that I can't give any details at this point out of consideration for the next of kin.*'

'*Thank you, Mr Dežulović.*' The reporter turned, smiled haplessly into the camera and said: '*Now I'm handing you back...*'

'That looks,' Vera said as she put the remote back down, 'like Ada Ciganlija.'

'It was Ada Ciganlija,' replied Milena.

Her mobile rang, the screen showed Siniša's number. He also sounded agitated. 'Have you seen the news?' he shouted.

'We were just watching *Studio Belgrade*, but –'

'I guess our little excursion this afternoon's off now.'

'Why? Oh no, you're not saying...'

'I am. They've claimed their next victim. They've taken out Danilo Djordan. The colonel's dead.'

20

Milena stood on King Alexander Boulevard, not far from the Law School, and looked towards Nikola Pašić Square. Despite the fact that rush hour had not properly started yet, the streets were already jammed. Even at a distance, though, she recognised the Renault, not so much from its colour – a silver grey – as from the style of driving: abruptly switching lanes, overtaking on the wrong side, cutting in a bit too tight in front of a van, approaching the kerb fast and screeching to a halt right in front of her. She only had to bend down, open the passenger door and get in.

'Chop chop, girl,' Siniša said, 'we're running late.'

Their route took them into Crown Street, the narrow but splendid avenue that ran parallel to the big King Alexander Boulevard and ended at the rear entrance to the castle, where the king and his court once resided and where the president now lived. Many houses along the Crown Street had alcoves, curved loggia and wide staircases in the Secessionist style, the southern European variant of Art Nouveau so characteristic of Belgrade. Here one was reminded of the influence of the Habsburg Empire, but also of the Turks, who had brought their culture and way of life from the East. Ordinary people had never lived in these houses. In former times, they had been the preserve of the upper middle class: the Jewish merchants and industrialists; later Communist Party functionaries had moved in and now they were the haunts of the *nouveau-riche* and government officials and civil servants with good connections. Siniša found a parking space round the corner, in Queen Zorka Street.

The previous Friday he had called the colonel's widow and asked to meet her. At first, Mrs Djordan had been hesitant, but then yesterday – Monday – she'd contacted Siniša's chambers and agreed to a meeting. It was only natural that Milena, in her role as an employee of the Institute for Criminology and Forensic Science, should accompany him. Especially as the official and final report of the military investigation commission had been released on the Monday. The television channels and newspapers had reported it extensively in their regional editions and quoted the salient passages. According to the report, Danilo Djordan, Colonel of the Honour Guard, had been alone on his houseboat in Ada Ciganlija and decided to clean his weapons, namely his shotgun. During this operation, the gun had accidentally discharged and killed him. The death of the colonel had been a tragic accident, caused by his own carelessness, and no one else had been involved. Only the left-wing newspaper *Vreme* discussed a possible connection between the death of the colonel and that of the two guardsmen two months earlier, but no other organ of the press followed its lead. The next day, coverage of the case had already been relegated to the back pages and today, four days after the tragedy, there had been no mention of it at all.

They rang the bell at Number 20, waited for the buzzer to sound and then ascended a broad, carpeted staircase to the elegant first floor.

The woman waiting for them at the door to the apartment wore a headscarf, a knitted jacket, a skirt and woollen stockings. Her grief was not only evident in her black mourning garb; her red eyes, sunken cheeks and pale complexion also suggested that she hadn't slept much in the past few days but had cried a lot. Milena and Siniša expressed their sympathies.

'Come in,' the woman whispered. 'Nevenka will be here shortly. I'm Danilo's inconsolable sister. God bless him, my beloved brother.' She crossed herself, limped ahead, one leg thicker than the other – it was probably bandaged beneath the black stocking. From somewhere behind one of the dark panelled doors, an aged, querulous voice could be heard. Its hectoring tone clearly had the potential to rise rapidly to screaming pitch if the wishes it expressed weren't fulfilled. Before they reached the far end of a long hallway filled with cupboards, the old woman opened a door.

In the room beyond stood an oval table with a polished surface of exotic wood and six matching chairs, their backs and seats covered in dark red velvet. There was a tall cupboard with glass-panelled doors filled with long rows of books with gold-leaf blocking on their spines, many of them sets of complete works. This and the rest of the décor, including an oil painting of a romantic landscape in a heavy gilt frame on the far wall of the room, failed to convey any sense of homeliness. The yellowed curtains hanging in front of the tall windows were tied in swags, but even so only let in a little light, meaning that the room had to be lit by the lamps on the heavy chandelier even during the day. In this parlour, guests were received and probably always served tea in dainty cups from the little teapot that stood on a warmer, and offered a bowl with a selection of dried fruit. 'Sit down. Take a seat,' Djordan's sister instructed them.

In the corner, a grandfather clock ticked, while from outside came the constant roar of traffic. The old woman slumped down onto a chair at the far end of the table.

Siniša cleared his throat. 'We are truly sorry about what happened.'

'He always did his duty, he was always there when his country needed him – fought in the war, trained the young men. And now he's even spared his country from paying him a pension.' She dabbed her sore nostrils with her little fist, which clearly contained a handkerchief. 'Life isn't fair. Look at Nevenka's father. If he died, it would be a relief. Instead God has taken my little brother.' She beat her chest with her fist and whimpered. 'I'm an old woman, I don't expect anything from life anymore, but even the little that's left has been taken from me. Why is God punishing me like this? God's will is cruel, but that's how it is.' She reached for the white handkerchief Siniša handed her and blew her nose loudly into it. 'You're a lawyer, aren't you?' She was breathing heavily. 'Why should Nevenka need a lawyer? Danilo's dead, and you won't bring him back to life. Excuse me, Mr...'

'Stojković. And may I introduce Ms Lukin...'

'My name is Ivanka Lutovac. I came here the day before yesterday from Split.' She started crying again.

Siniša focused on the dried fruit, raising his eyebrows as he hovered over pieces of apple and pear, and finally picked an apricot ring from the small dish. Milena followed his example.

'Yes, I've come from Croatia, I married a Croatian, from the coast as it happens, my Boran – I converted to Catholicism for his sake. Don't think badly of me. I'm a Serb, just like you. And back then nobody imagined there'd be a war. As God is my witness: I tried everything to get Boran and Danilo to sit down together and bury the hatchet. So help me God, I couldn't manage it and my strength is all spent now. Danilo and I – we didn't part on good terms and I'll carry that with me now forever. And he never forgave me for marrying a Catholic or for having the children brought up as Catholics. Proud Croatians they became, they drive German cars and earn good money now, so should I have stopped that? But despite all that, I achieved what his precious

Nevenka couldn't: I gave my husband three children, two of them boys. Danilo would have given anything to have experienced the happiness, worries and pain that your own children bring you. Well, the marriage to Nevenka was his fate, as my marriage to Boran was mine. But this life, here in this flat with his father-in-law, he hated that.'

'That's enough, Ivanka.' The woman standing in the door had bright red hair, which she wore in a topknot, making her seem even taller than she actually was. A knee-length skirt and dark patterned blouse clung tightly to her body, accentuating her curves. Her cleavage was decorated with a grey precious stone, probably a smoky topaz, in a gold setting. Siniša rose from his seat to greet her.

'If you could leave us now...'

The person she had addressed held her ground.

'Ivanka, please.'

The old woman stood up like she wasn't just carrying the weight of her own body, but lifting the burden of the whole world's cares and lugging it out of the room. As she hobbled out, she hunched herself over and looked up reproachfully at her sister-in-law.

Nevenka Djordan shut the door firmly behind her. 'I do apologise,' she said, pouring out cups of tea. The hand holding the saucer trembled and made the porcelain tinkle.

Sitting almost motionless, she accepted the condolences that Siniša expressed on his own and Milena's behalf. In the meantime, he had settled back on his chair and begun verbosely to expand upon his doubts about the official report. Nevenka sat with her back straight, nodding politely, but the way she blinked repeatedly betrayed a silent impatience. She had almond-shaped eyes which slightly shifted the proportions of her face in an intriguing way. Nevenka Djordan was a handsome woman and must have been a real beauty in her day.

'Anyway,' Siniša concluded, 'the theory of a tragic accident and the claim that while inexpertly cleaning his weapon – '

'Mr Stojković,' the widow interrupted him. 'I've been thinking since we spoke on the telephone. On the one hand, I totally agree with you. I can't imagine this was an accident either. I simply cannot accept that he could have been so careless with a shotgun. On the other hand one has to take the report seriously, I suppose. The military employs proper experts after all, not any old amateurs. And that's why I'm not clear at the moment where you want to begin and where you want to take things.'

'Please don't concern yourself on that score.' Siniša smiled. 'You should know that I'm personally acquainted with the investigating judge, this Dežulović fellow. I – '

'I'm sorry, Siniša,' Milena cut in. 'Just one question, Mrs Djordan: If you trust the military experts, why are you finding it hard to accept that this was an accident?'

'There are inconsistencies, things don't add up.'

'For example?'

'To start with, Danilo never went to the houseboat on Thursdays. He went there on Fridays, after coming off duty, and stayed the weekend. That's how it always was – I can't honestly remember an exception to this rule.'

'But that he went there on Thursday is a fact, is it not?'

'That's beyond dispute, yes. But his fishing tackle's still here – all ready for Ada Ciganlija. And so is his uniform, which he would have needed for the next day. It must have been a pretty spontaneous decision.'

'You mean, he dropped everything...'

'...and went there just to clean his gun?' Nevenka Djordan shook her head. 'It doesn't make sense.'

'I completely agree with you,' Siniša said. 'I think the accident with the shotgun is a fairytale. Now, what I think happened is as follows...'

'Wait a minute, Siniša,' Milena chimed in. 'Did he take a phone call on Thursday evening before he left?'

'I assume so. One has to entertain such thoughts, I suppose. Maybe it was some madman who lured him out there?'

'Are you thinking of anybody in particular?'

'Madmen are everywhere, aren't they? You only have to read the papers.'

Milena nodded. 'But you couldn't say for certain whether there was a call before he left, could you?'

'I didn't hear anything. He withdrew to his study after supper, like he always did.'

'And he didn't tell you that anyone had called or where he was going?'

'No.'

'And you didn't ask him?'

She shook her head and pressed her lips together tightly.

'Mrs Djordan,' Milena said quietly, 'we want to find out what happened. You should speak totally frankly.'

'Well it's no secret and there isn't much to tell in any case. It just happened. We shared one life but he lived another, totally separate one. The shared one dwindled over the years and in the end, I'm afraid, it amounted to nothing more than having supper together. And we each kept out of the other's personal life. I respected that.'

'What impression did your husband give that evening?'

Her eyes flitted round the room. 'Now you mention it – it was a bit odd: he was in a good mood, better than he had been for a long while. Laid-back, almost relaxed. Well, the weekend was just around the corner. Even so, in the light of what happened...' She took a deep breath, looked at the ceiling and said: 'Looking back I would say, he was unusually cheerful.'

'Do you think he was planning on meeting another woman?'

Nevenka Djordan smiled patronisingly. 'Even if there had been affairs, that wouldn't have changed anything between us. We loved each other. And a separation – if that's what you mean – was never on the agenda.'

Siniša pulled a little notebook from the inside pocket of his suit jacket. 'If your husband was in such an upbeat mood that evening it means, by implication, that he'd been in a bad frame of mind over the previous weeks.'

'You could say that.'

'You know that there were two deaths in his elite unit a couple of months ago.'

She placed her hands on top of each other and closed her eyes for a moment. Milena and Siniša exchanged a brief glance. 'What are you thinking?' Siniša asked.

'That it all might be connected to the death of those two guardsmen. But I thought these two young men were the victims of some sect or other.'

Siniša jotted something down in his notebook. 'That's the official version, at least.'

'Which you clearly don't believe?'

'The question is,' Milena said, 'what your husband believed. Whether he ultimately took any steps to investigate the case himself?'

'Why should he have done that? The case was closed, wasn't it? The fact that the death of those two young men affected him deeply is another matter.'

'Did he ever talk to you about them?'

'He didn't talk about it. He settled these things within himself. But believe me, I knew Danilo. For him those guardsmen weren't just soldiers he had trained. They were his pupils, and with many of them he even knew their families personally. He wanted to pass something on to these young men: values, bearing. Think about it: this wasn't just any old unit, this was the elite. Danilo loved his men, the same way he loved his country. Even if this might sound a bit pathetic to you – to train this elite and to see his country blossom, that was his life's goal. And then suddenly, out of nowhere, these two young lads kill themselves – in a secure zone, almost in front of his eyes. It was gruesome. Danilo was an honest, well-meaning, good person.' Her eyes filled with tears.

Milena thought she heard a muffled thud somewhere in the flat.

Nevenka Djordan leant forward. 'I want to say goodbye to my husband. I want to see him. But they won't let me, they say it's impossible.' She looked at Siniša, then at Milena and then back again. 'Why?'

'Look.' Siniša edged forward on his chair, as if trying to get emotionally closer to the widow that way. 'The military authorities are dealing with your husband's case the same way they dealt with that of Guardsmen Jokić and Mrša. The bodies were locked in sealed coffins and so removed from any further investigation. Nobody will get to see your husband again.'

'But I'm not asking for the impossible! Mr Stojković, you're a lawyer, you have some influence, surely. I want you to raise objections, to intervene – whatever it takes. Could you do that for me?'

'I'm afraid you'll have to come to terms with the inevitable. And – please don't take this the wrong way – maybe it's for the best. Remember your husband as you last saw him.'

'But what's behind this? I don't understand.'

'Could we take a look at his study?' Siniša asked.

'What? – Yes, of course. But you won't find anything except the furniture. The military police took everything. Papers, files, photographs, his telephone – everything and anything. I was told it's normal procedure when somebody with access to classified information dies.'

Siniša closed his notebook.

'What do you know, Mr Stojković? I get the feeling you're keeping something from me. I was totally open with you, so now I expect the same frankness from you.'

Siniša wiped his face with his hand, leant back and began: 'Ms Lukin and I have been looking into the case of Jokić and Mrša quite closely in recent weeks and have discovered several inconsistencies. For example: manipulated reports, frightened men in the barracks and corrupt officials who are trying to scare us off. To put it another way, we're digging up a lot of dirt. And in the course of these investigations we've uncovered papers which suggest that Jokić and Mrša were murdered, that is to say: that they were executed on the spot. In the case of your husband, I must admit, we don't know anything yet.'

Nevenka Djordan seemed to look straight through Siniša. 'What has all that got to do with my husband?'

'Maybe he knew something. Maybe some system he wanted out of.'

'If, as you say, he wanted out, then he must have been part of the system he wanted to quit.'

'That's a possibility,' Siniša said.

Nevenka Djordan touched the teaspoon with her fingertips. Her mouth twitched, but she did not say a word. She sat there, completely motionless.

'Mrs Djordan?' Milena enquired quietly.

'It seems pretty far-fetched to me.' She looked at the floor.

'Will you allow me one more question?' asked Milena.

Nevenka Djordan endeavoured to smile politely.

'Your husband called me on the afternoon of the day he died and arranged a meeting. He wanted to see me on Friday to tell me something. Do you have any idea what that might have been?'

Nevenka Djordan shook her head. 'I wish I could help you.' She got up. 'Please excuse me, but I'd like to be alone now.'

'As to your husband's personal effects, I'll see to it that you get them back as soon as possible.' Siniša put away his notebook.

'That's very kind, thank you.'

Milena pushed back her chair from the table. 'The fishing tackle you mentioned – you said he'd got that ready for Friday – did the police confiscate that as well?'

They walked into the darkened hallway. Nevenka Djordan switched on the light. 'His fishing bag? No, that should still be hanging on the hall-stand.'

'May we have a look inside? Maybe there's something that...' From somewhere in the house came a clanking sound, followed immediately by a loud scream. Startled, Milena spun round.

Nevenka Djordan opened a door. An old man with an emaciated face and a bib around his neck was sitting at a table. His hands angrily clasped a spoon, while the old woman, Ivanka Lutovac, breathing heavily, was bending down to retrieve a tin plate from the floor.

'What do you think you're doing?' Nevenka Djordan prised the spoon from the old man's hand and started cleaning his mouth and messy hands with the bib. 'You're supposed to eat, Dad.'

Chuckling, the old man clutched at her hands, her nose, her ears and then suddenly, startled, let go. Nevenka Djordan had slumped down, her back shaking and her shoulders heaving. She was crying. The old man flung his arms around her neck and began crying himself.

Ivanka, the sister-in-law, stood behind Milena. 'Come with me. I'll show you out.'

Milena laid her hand gently on Nevenka's shoulder. 'I promise you,' she said softly, 'we'll do everything we can to find out what really happened on that houseboat.'

On the way to the door the old woman said: 'Did you know that her father was once director of state television? Such a powerful man – and look what's left of him now. She always wanted a child, even their marriage failed because of it. And now she's got one.' Her hand was already resting on the door handle when she added: 'Who can tell what's sent to try us and what to punish? Whatever it is, it's God's will.'

Siniša put the key in the ignition without starting the engine. They sat silently next to one another, staring at the windscreen. Milena closed her eyes. Cornflower blue had been the only colour in Danilo Djordan's life – at least that's how it seemed to her. Apart from that, nothing but grey and black and loneliness.

'For you.' Siniša held out an envelope.

Puzzled she took it, turned it over and looked at it. No address, no sender.

'It was in his bag,' said Siniša.

'You mean...'

'Yes, it was hanging on the hall-stand. Don't look at me like that. We asked to have a look inside and Nevenka Djordan didn't explicitly say we couldn't. This envelope was the only thing that didn't really belong in there, I mean, not particularly. Let's just say, he obviously didn't carry this envelope around with him like his shaving kit. I'm certain it was meant for you.'

'You have to give it back to his widow, this instant.'

'Milena, we're investigating a murder here, the third in quick succession. And can I remind you that you secretly, in the archives – '

'What if this is a suicide note?'

'A suicide note?'

'After everything we've seen and heard up there in the flat, I believe this was a man at the end of his tether. The Honour Guard was no longer *his* Honour Guard, and his marriage, his family life – all that was in pieces. And he – drives out to his houseboat and takes his pistol –'

'You mean his shotgun.'

'And the military covers up the suicide as an accident. So no one can say that he has ended his life dishonourably.'

Siniša raised his black eyebrows as far as he could towards his white hairline. 'So why does he arrange to see you and then a few hours later blow his head off with a shotgun? Okay – something just snapped. Well, that's all sorted then, isn't it?' Shaking his head he took back the envelope.

From it he extracted a piece of paper, unfolded it and stared at it without letting his face betray anything. Milena took the sheet from his hands.

It wasn't a letter. It was a drawing. Showing the church of St Peter and St Paul, the intersection, which these days was a roundabout. The gates to the barracks, the main building, where she had met Colonel Danilo Djordan, and the other buildings. And the dotted lines criss-crossing the compound.

'Can you make head or tail of this?' Siniša closed his eyes, as if trying to block out anything that might interrupt his thoughts. 'Was he murdered because he was planning to give you this map? Is that what happened? And if so, what did he want to show you on this plan? The location where the bodies were found? Why?'

Milena shoved the piece of paper back in the envelope.

'Where are you off to?'

'To do some thinking.' She opened the passenger door. 'I'll call you.'

She walked in the direction of Njegoš Street and crossed Mackenzie Street. She wandered for three blocks until she came to the extension of King Milan Street, which for this short stretch was called 'Street of the Holy Sava' and led uphill to the church of the same name.

She hadn't been up here for quite some time. It was enough for her to catch sight of this colossus of a church every day when she was in town and happened to glance up the straight boulevards. It had only been here for a few years and Milena had still not got used to the sight: a huge cylindrical building with two towers of different heights, and a half-moon added on either side. The church had been clad in polished marble, which sufficiently concealed the many tons of concrete used to construct the colossus in the space of just a few years. On the towers were copper-green roofs like hoods surmounted by golden crosses that looked somehow like ostentatious handles. When this house of God shone in the bright sunlight, it seemed to resemble a fat, rather too garishly made-up cousin who had pushed herself forward as the favourite relative and had got herself the nicest room to boot. The Church and government officials who had championed this gigantic project had wheeled out every justification for building it in this location: the Turks had allegedly burned the bones of St Sava up here and in 1806 Karađorđe, also known as 'Black George', had led the Serbs to their first victory against the Ottomans on this hill. The foundation stone had been laid as early as the 1930s, but construction work had come to a halt when the Germans invaded in 1941. And then came Marshal Tito, in whose Socialist Yugoslavia there had been no plans to resume the building work. Now, after the Balkan War, after defeats, humiliations and traumatic losses of lives, territory and state, nothing less than the biggest church on the European mainland would have sufficed for Serbia – and it would have been just that if the Russians hadn't beaten Serbia to the punch with the building of the gigantic Redeemer Church in Moscow.

Milena weaved her way through the hordes of tourists who were using the church as a backdrop for their holiday snaps. By local standards the dimensions of St Sava Church were still immense. Also, it had ended up costing far more of the taxpayers' money than anticipated, so much so that there was apparently nothing left to help desperate Serbian refugees from Kosovo. But no one cared about that. Just as no one cared that in the course of the construction the adjacent university library, an elegant building from the 1960s, subsided and precious books sank into the groundwater – for Milena a sign that the Church's megalomania had finally triumphed over the human intellect.

She walked over to the benches set prettily between low hedgerows, symmetrically cut bushes and dainty lanterns. Children jumped over the flat basin of the fountain here, screaming as they ran their outstretched hands through the flowing water, and pensioners rummaged through the bread bags they had brought for crumbs to scatter on the wide stone slabs – attracting not only bickering gaggles of hungry pigeons but also stray dogs, the mangy mongrels that roamed Belgrade in packs and were forever fighting, biting or mounting each other.

Milena let the strap of her bag slip off her shoulder and sat down. Clouds were piling up in the sky, forming cotton-wool mountains, and the sun warmed her face. She tipped her head back and closed her eyes, while her hand strayed into her bag and touched first her purse, then her thick appointment diary and finally the envelope with the map of Topčider, which she had filed at home, though another copy had resurfaced posthumously thanks to the colonel of all people. She delved down further until she encountered rustling cellophane.

As the sweetness spread across her tongue her brain began working slowly and methodically. She saw the system that liquidated people and claimed, without fear of contradiction, that they had died in tragic accidents. A system whose arm had a long reach, into the police apparatus and probably further still. She saw the colonel, who had decided to do something against this clique, to reveal something important about what he knew to Milena, and who had paid for this decision with his life. She opened her eyes again. She had an uneasy feeling she was being watched.

The eyes staring at her were bloodshot and would have looked dangerous had it not been for the legs the poor cur was standing on; three trembling sticks that were barely able to support the few kilos of its body weight. The animal's coat was so mangy that its patchy skin showed through, skin that shone piggy-pink only at the tip of its pointed nose.

Milena bent forward and stretched out her hand so the dog could sniff it and reassure itself she meant it no harm. But the animal flinched like she was about to hit it, and bolted away as quickly as its three legs would allow, dashing around the square in a wide arc before hopping towards the benches again from the other side of the fountain.

Milena pulled her bag over her shoulder and got up. She didn't know what to do next. She only knew that she'd lost an important, perhaps an absolutely key informer, that she had to consider every step and that she had to be doubly careful. Maybe she just needed to behave like this dog, which stubbornly followed its own path despite its handicap. As if on an invisible lead, it trailed after a passer-by who, instead of taking the prescribed path and turning at right angles, climbed over the hedge, ran across the lawn and made off as fast as he could. Following the man, the dog vanished into the shadow of the magnificent church, which in truth was nothing but a huge, ugly bin of a building.

21

Milena had the receiver jammed between her ear and shoulder; a piece of white paper lay in front of her on the desk. On it were written the names 'Nenad Jokić/Predrag Mrša', 'Danilo Djordan' and 'Samir the kitchen boy'. Milena was busy drawing circles round the names when Tanja asked from the other end of the line, 'are you actually listening to me?'

'Of course, I'm hanging on every word you're saying.' Milena completed the circle around 'Danilo Djordan' and repeated back to her friend: 'Your lover Stefanos wants to come to Belgrade and you're shit-scared.'

She could hear Tanja light a cigarette and exhale. 'How can I explain to the guy that I love him madly, but not madly enough for him to buy himself a ticket with an open return?' Tanja launched into her lecture on female independence and Milena used the time to reread and complete her notes on the list.

Nenad Jokić/Predrag Mrša – born in the Bosnian town of Bratunac, guards in the Serbian elite unit, on guard duty on the night of the eleventh to the twelfth of July. The entry angle of the bullets indicate that a third party must have shot them.

Samir the kitchen boy – reports the special order (lamb) received by the barracks' canteen from the very top, but not from the colonel.

'Are you still there?' asked Tanja.

Milena put the pen aside and sighed. 'I see these circles, but I can't make sense of them, you know? The colonel, for example. What did he want to show me on the map of the barracks? Where the party took place that night? Where the bodies were discovered? Or something completely different that I don't yet know about?'

'Sweetheart, you'll never find out now the colonel's dead and I for one thank the Lord that you're still in one piece. I hope you realise what could have happened to you.'

'The only one I can still ask is the kitchen boy – in theory at least. In practice, though, I'd be putting him in mortal danger if I did. And if I waited for him at the bus stop and tried to talk to him again – without really knowing whether he can tell me anything more – that'd be so dangerous for the poor guy, and completely irresponsible! Tanja, I'm totally stumped.'

'Stay well away from this case, if you ask me, and tell me how I can take your mind off it.'

Milena doodled a big question mark on the paper.

'Look, it's Friday,' Tanja said. 'Shall we go to the movies?'

Milena looked at her watch. It was just after five. 'Now, don't get mad at me, but...'

Tanja chuckled quietly. 'Sacrosanct Friday – I know, it's all right. Do your homework, but look after yourself, you hear? I'll call you – at the very latest once I've heard from Stefanos again.'

Feeling across the floor with her feet, Milena pulled her shoes towards her and used a finger to ease her heels into them. So many tasks had already mounted up again that the best thing she could do now was to prioritise. She put the sheet with the names and the question mark with the other dog-eared bits of paper, arranged the books into stable towers and the students' essays into a neat pile. Before reaching for the telephone once more, she combed her hair back.

It rang three times. 'This is Nikolaus Blechschmidt's extension. I'm not at my desk, but if you leave a message I'll call you back as soon as possible.'

The silence after the beep invited her to speak. Milena took a deep breath – and hung up.

She pushed the chair back and opened the window. A young couple was leaning against the monument. The girl had stuck her hand into her boyfriend's back pocket as he gently stroked her face.

Milena breathed in the fresh air. One day she'd be able to face the beautiful aspects of life again. And if her lover flew in from, say, Boston, Berlin or Budapest without having booked a return, she wouldn't complain.

She made circular movements with her shoulders, gripped her neck with one hand and massaged her tense muscles. Above all, she should complete her thesis – that was the most pressing task, so she could quit the institute on a high. Then some renowned institute or maybe a university would roll out the red carpet for her, for sure. But for this beautiful dream to become a reality, she really needed to secure her funding for the next year.

She shut the window, sat down and pressed the 'Redial' button.

'Extension Blechschmidt...'

'Hello?' she answered.

'Mr Blechschmidt isn't here right now.'

'Who am I talking to, please?'

'The intern.'

'I'm Milena Lukin. From Belgrade. I have a message for your colleague. So I suggest we hang up and I'll call back and leave it on his answering machine.'

'You can tell me what's it about and I'll pass on the message.'

'And your name is?'

'Holger.'

'Well, Holger, please tell Mr Blechschmidt that Milena

Lukin called. And that I'll call back on Monday. That isn't a threat, by the way, but something pretty close.'

'Okay. Milena Lukin. From Belgrade. Your case came up a few days ago.'

She gripped the edge of her desk. 'Oh really? Maybe you could let me know how things stand, then.'

'I'd love to, but as I said, I'm afraid I'm only the...'

'So it's bad news?'

'Honestly, I don't know what the outcome was in your case. But I promise I'll leave him a message that you called.'

'Thank you.'

'Have a nice weekend.'

Milena hung up. Her legs were freezing. She crawled under the desk, switched on the electric heater and, deciding she needed a cup of coffee first, promptly switched it off again.

Clasping the steaming mug and with warmth radiating from below, she stared at the rocky coast of Korčula and tried to clear her mind of all thoughts – an impossible task that only made her head ache.

As she moved her mouse, the Croatian island vanished from the screen and at the same time the parquet floor in the hallway began to groan and creak. It was Boris Grubač's step. Then came the all-too familiar squeak of the wooden boards, and the next instant the door opened.

The head of the institute had already reached a level of alcoholic intake that would enable him to float, as lightly as a feather borne on a cloud, into the weekend. Even so, there was something different about him today. It wasn't the greasy stain on his tie, which by now had blended in almost perfectly with the speckled pattern. No, it was his nostrils. In the round caverns from which great tufts of hair normally sprouted, there was now gaping holes. The change subtly altered the appearance of his round, rubicund face.

'Just wanted to tell you: the programme, Ms Lukin – just excellent!' He was sucking his end-of-the-working-day-peppermint. 'Especially your idea with the committee meeting.'

'Seriously?'

'Of course. We'll give our colleagues from the ministry some tips on how to prepare for the meeting, and the guys from the Johnson Institute can be flies on the wall. Then we can relax and don't have to fear any nasty surprises.'

'I hadn't looked at it that way,' Milena muttered.

'You're a real gem, you know? Have you got the thumbs-up yet from the Minister of Justice?'

She moved the mouse and gazed at the bright screen. 'I'll take care of it.'

'Are you okay?'

'I'm fine.' To prove it, she made a quarter-turn on her chair and smiled at the head of the institute. This gave her another opportunity to study those nostrils. Maybe he'd got himself a girlfriend. 'If there's nothing else, Mr Grubač, I suggest we speak again next week.'

The door had barely closed behind him when it opened again. 'Did the German Embassy get back to you?'

'Should they have?'

'Not really, but that's just it: most things sort themselves eventually. It's a good lesson for the future.'

She pressed her thumb and index finger against the bridge of her nose and waited with closed eyes until the sound of his footsteps had receded down the hallway. Then she opened the word processing programme, clicked on the file 'thesis' and then on the document 'bibliography'.

Scrolling through the alphabetically arranged list of authors felt like running down a line of old friends and giving each of them a high-five. She added two nice new papers, highly topical studies that had been drawn to her attention by a colleague from Brussels, and which she had immediately ordered from the Berlin State Library on an inter-library loan.

She pulled one of the two books from the pile, opened it, skimmed the contents page, looked through the index, picked up a pad and a pen and made a note, opened the document called 'chapter 4' in the thesis file and started typing: *Is a system of collective security based on legality ever possible?* She hammered down on the keys as though trying to add emphasis to her words. When she next looked up, she had written a long paragraph.

She went back to the beginning, muttering to herself, correcting the odd phrase, amending a thought here and there, and in the process generated another paragraph. In the distance, she registered the hubbub that always arose when the audience streamed out of the arthouse cinema downstairs, discussing the film they'd just watched. Then a stillness descended, allowing her to focus on the question uppermost in her mind: what role can an international tribunal play in the critical reappraisal of macro crimes?

Her keyboard clattered away, papers rustled and the desk lamp illuminated just enough of the page for her to immediately locate the passage supporting her thesis and to expand on her idea.

It was almost half-past eleven when she looked up and gave a sudden start, as she unexpectedly caught sight of her own pale reflection in the black windowpane. But had she heard something too? She focussed on a spot on the floor and listened intently, holding her breath.

Someone was coming along the hallway. The squeak of the floorboards was louder than usual. For a brief moment there was silence, then the parquet creaked. Silence again, followed by more creaking. As if the person was reading the names on the doors.

Milena gripped the plastic armrests of her chair and stared at the door handle. She had to do something. But the only thing moving was her heart, thumping away madly.

A noise. Now someone was outside her door. The handle didn't move.

Again came the groan of the floorboards. It took her a few seconds to realise that the steps were receding. Why had someone come all the way to her door only to walk away again? She pushed her chair back, took three large steps and boldly flung open the door.

'Hello?'

The hallway was empty.

Steps on the stairs, but no reply.

Milena ran down the corridor past closed doors, turned the corner and leant over the balustrade. 'Hello!' she screamed. 'Hey, you there, wait!'

She saw a flash of a grey trench coat as the front door shut behind it.

As silence returned, Milena stayed there gripping the balustrade. Her heart was still pounding. Had this person been looking for something and not found it, or just lost his way?

Light streamed from the open door of her room, the last but one, into the corridor. She walked back and, with her hand already on the handle, was just about to close the door behind her, maybe even bolt it, when she suddenly realised she'd caught a glimpse of something outside the door, at eye level. She stepped back and looked round the corner.

There, stuck into the thin metal frame of the sign bearing her name was a piece of paper. A little card. '*Tchaikovsky. Manfred Symphony in B-minor, Op. 58*. Row 38, seat 2.'

Her first thought: Alexander Kronburg. He wanted to invite her to spend the evening with him at this concert to apologise for his gaffe with the 'brief window'. But why tiptoe through the institute at night for that?

She inspected the card more closely. No, the German Ambassador definitely had nothing to do with this concert. The Serbian State Military Orchestra was playing. The Military Orchestra came under the Ministry of Defence and was part of the Serbian Honour Guard.

'Thursday, 23 September. Veterans' Home, Vasa Čarapić Street.'

She turned the ticket over. There was an ad for the public transport system, and three words in the margin. The letters were in pencil, a bit crooked but written in a firm hand: 'Please come. Important.'

22

From behind he was well protected by the big rubbish skips, while ahead he had a clear field of vision through the wire-mesh fence. And if he lay flat on his stomach up here, he'd be almost invisible from down below. But with all the racket going on down there he could have performed cartwheels and the people below wouldn't notice a thing. He was lucky that the bathing cap was the only one with rubber flowers on. He'd be a complete idiot to lose sight of that.

As instructed, he'd parked the car on the street below. Yesterday it had been a 1982 Zastava, but today he'd got lucky and been given a 1994 Golf, with five gears and a cassette player.

A driving licence was vital for this job; ever since he had been ordered to do the Erdelj run, they'd been aware he had a valid one. He'd had orders to collect the fresh meat in a minibus and drive it right across the Puszta into the camp on the Hungarian border. Week after week the same route. It had been the perfect job for him. Always alone at the wheel, and in the back these guys – real fighting machines – but on that trip they were shitting themselves. It was well known at that time that the boot camp was no walk in the park.

On the return journey, just past Subotica, he would occasionally stop at a roadside service area – not to use the services of the whores in their trailers, but for a Coke and a sandwich, though he never reported these breaks. He had no idea what possessed him. He'd been young, cocky and a bit stupid back then. The transfer to the depot had come out of the blue and was a real shock. To this day he had no idea who'd ratted on him. But that was eons ago now, and nobody gave a flying fuck anymore.

Pawle took out a pad and pen from his back pocket, looked at his watch and noted under the date, 'Sunday, 19 September': *16.20 municipal swimming pool.* Every time, every place, every bit of shit had to be recorded. He was not used to this paperwork, or to working without any proper procedure or timetable. He never knew what would happen next, where the trip would take him. Was this mission remotely important? – he had no idea. He hadn't received any instructions or special training for it. So there couldn't have been a lot riding on this, but on the other hand you never knew how things would pan out. And although not a word had been uttered about it, he suspected this was somehow connected to the previous mission, although he didn't know how. As always, he didn't ask any questions. If Momčilo was to be believed, the only important thing was to stick to the highway code – every morning the same instructions when he handed over the keys. One day he'd really lay into that sack of shit and deflate him. So what if he risked being hanged? At least then Momčilo could take his highway code and shove it. Arsehole bookkeeper.

Yesterday, after he'd worked his arse off out in the cold, when it had been pissing down with rain and he'd been accosted by some tramps, he briefly fell to thinking that his old job had had certain advantages. Mopping the floor with soapy water and occasionally changing a light bulb...okay, that job was really low-rent – but had it really been so shitty that they needed to choose that clubfooted cripple, of all people, to succeed him? No idea what hole they'd dug him up from. It was like a hundred years had passed since they'd last clapped eyes on one another, but suddenly that zombie was standing in front of him again. With that fishy, flabby fin of a hand and those murky, watery eyes. Pawle hated the clubfoot's whining, his disabled veteran's attitude and all his old stories, which had got on Pawle's nerves even back in the day. And on top of all that, he'd made out like he was his long-lost pal; it looked like he was about to hug him, for Christ's sake, before Pawle put a stop to that, sharpish.

He took the camera from his trouser pocket and searched for a suitable diamond in the mesh to poke the lens through. Yes, indeed, he had to pay attention, mustn't get too uppity, mustn't make any mistakes, even when things seemed to be a piece of piss: he, Pawle Widak, was back in the big league. The success of the last mission had been a huge step forward. He'd even got a bonus, though he'd passed that on to Momčilo to use as he wanted: concert, cinema, brothel – Momčilo's choice. But the main thing was that in return, that arsehole of a bookkeeper now owed him a favour. And with the good connections he had upstairs that was no bad thing, right?

The camera was so small that he could operate the zoom with his right hand. He zoomed in as tight as possible on the target, getting a really close view of the plump woman – saw how she was standing on the ladder in the pool and blocking the way for everyone else with her big bum. What a bathing suit! What thighs! Now she'd turned around, shoved out her fat arse, stepped backwards into the pool and – what a wave! Suddenly this kid shot forward like a torpedo and jumped on top of her. Both went under, spluttering and laughing.

He missed pressing the shutter release in time. He had no picture, just a sensation – a sharp pain that hit him without warning and bored into him. What was happening to him? With the fingers of his crippled hand he wiped away a tear from his face.

He hated this disabled veteran's attitude and this whining. He hated this job and this woman. And he hated this kid.

23

'Did you see that dog, Mum?' Adam screamed. The green tram rounded the corner with a screech of metal, its bell clanging insistently.

'What dog?' Milena was carrying her bag over her shoulder, clutching three flat pizza boxes under her arm and holding her son's hand. On Sunday evening the traffic was not so bad and they didn't need to take the detour via the traffic lights.

'Thin as a rake and starving and only three legs!' Adam pressed the bag containing his wet swimming trunks to his chest. 'Shall we give him some of our pizza?'

'Fatty food's bad for animals.'

'Not for humans?'

'Oh sure, it's bad for humans as well.' She leant against the security glass, pushed the door open and let Adam go ahead. She had got used to the broken post boxes. But now the light was also out of order; Milena couldn't see a thing. 'Adam?' she called. The boy had suddenly disappeared. 'Don't mess about, Adam!'

'Boo!' His scream was so piercing she almost dropped the pizzas.

'Stop it, right now!' she yelled.

The lift door opened. All of a sudden Adam was standing there in the light cast by the lift, grinning from ear to ear and blocking the path of their upstairs neighbour Milka Bašić, as she stepped out of the cabin in her slippers. 'Listen, little man,' she said to him, 'there's a package for you upstairs; I've had it since yesterday.'

'From Hamburg?'

'Pick it up and you'll see, won't you? In ten minutes. I've got to go to the shop across the street first.'

'Thank you, Mrs Bašić.' Milena shoved Adam into the lift. 'It's bound to be my new baseball cap,' he called out and pressed the button with the rubbed-away number. Instantly the door closed and the lift began to ascend.

Before they'd even reached the flat, Milena told him: 'Wash your hands. And please hang up your swimming trunks.' Fiona scampered wildly from the hallway into the living room like she'd taken leave of her senses.

Once Vera began washing, preparing and slicing red peppers, cauliflower, courgettes, celery and carrots, it was a sign that summer was definitively over. The vegetables were placed in a salt-and-vinegar-brine together with beet-root, white grapes and green tomatoes, and peppercorns, mustard seeds, bay leaves and vine leaves were added, and, last but not least, a dried cherry-tree twig. Milena loved *Turšija*, the Serbian version of mixed pickles, especially when eaten with cornbread and goats' cheese, but only the really hard sort.

Over the rim of her spectacles Vera cast a critical eye over the toppings on the pizza: tinned pineapples, tinned mush-rooms, processed ham.

'I know,' said Milena, 'you need the stone. I'll get it from downstairs in a mo.'

'Thanks.'

The stone in the cellar was, Vera maintained, the only really effective implement for pressing down the pickled fruit and vegetables, before the barrel was sealed and stored and left alone for at least four weeks.

Adam burst through the front door and banged the package down on the table. He cut through the sellotape with the kitchen scissors and impatiently tore off the wrapping paper.

The package contained the Alba-Berlin baseball cap, size M, the Dr Scholl shoe inserts, and bars and bars of chocolate. Plus a brochure with a yellow Post-it note attached. 'Are you up for this?' Philip had written on it in his peculiarly ornate handwriting.

Adam leafed through the brochure. Milena could see from his wide eyes how taken he was with its colourful pictures. This wasn't just Paris, this was way better: Disneyland, the wonderful world of Shrek, Bambi and all the familiar characters from books, comics and the movies. The prospect of meeting them all in his autumn holidays, in the company of his father, filled the boy with such delight that it choked Milena.

While he was excitedly calling Hamburg, Milena put the cold pizza onto a plate and broke off a large corner of the chocolate. She noticed there were no lambskin insoles in the box.

All thoughts of practising his guitar or learning his vocabulary had evaporated, and it took quite some time to get his school satchel packed, his teeth brushed and the Pavlović Ointment applied to his eczema. But eventually the baseball cap was hanging off his bedpost and Milena was giving him the tea that Vera had prepared from lime blossom, lavender seeds, camomile and balm, which was meant to send him off into a healthy and deep sleep. To make it taste nicer, she'd added a spoonful of the acacia honey from the Mlava Valley in north-eastern Serbia that Vera got from Uncle Miodrag.

Milena watched Adam drink the tea and stroked his hair. 'You'll see the Eiffel Tower,' she said.

'And the café where Sartre sat?'

'Maybe. But if you don't it's no big deal. There's always next time.'

'But then it'll only be with you.'

'Of course. And, if we can manage to persuade her, Grandma too.'

'Okay, I'll work on her.'

'It's a deal, then.' She kissed her son. 'Sweet dreams.'

'Mum?'

'Yes?'

'Shall we adopt the dog?'

'What dog?'

'The one outside our door. With the three legs.'

'The dog doesn't want to be adopted, chook. It's used to roaming around outside. That's his life. Now go to sleep.' She left the door slightly ajar as she left.

Back in her room she took the ashtray down from the bookshelf, opened the window and lit a cigarillo. She smoked and stared at the grey concrete wall opposite.

Once again Philip had presented her with a *fait accompli* and was now officially the Superdad, and, yet again, she was pissed off and jealous. Then again, it was just a short trip. It was okay. End of. Even the fact that the blonde Jutta with her big boobs was going to be part of the Disneyland Paris jaunt was okay with her.

Would Philip remember to send on the warm lambskin insoles, she wondered?

She was just stubbing out the cigarillo and closing the window when Vera came in. She was balancing a big mug on a saucer.

Smiling, Milena gratefully accepted the black coffee as Fiona jumped onto the desk. 'Mum, you're such an angel.' She drank the coffee in small sips and noticed how good the hot drink felt. Vera sat down on the edge of the bed.

'You know,' Milena said, sitting down at the desk, 'I wanted to show him the Mona Lisa and the old men playing *boules* in the Jardin du Luxembourg.'

'The Mona Lisa and the old men won't run away, will they?' Vera had got up again and fluffed up Milena's pillow. 'This trip's important for Adam. He needs the time with his father. He needs a male role model.' She came over to the desk and laid her hand on Milena's shoulder. 'What's that?'

'A map, or rather: two of them. And some sort of instructions for use. But I can't get the two to marry together.'

Vera stroked Milena's hair and Milena shut her eyes for just a moment.

'Don't forget,' said Vera, 'to get me that stone from the cellar.'

Vera pulled the door shut behind her and Milena looked into Fiona's speckled eyes. 'So, what's up?' She adjusted the direction of the desk lamp. 'Got something to say to me, eh? Are you pondering something or just sulking again? Is that it?' In front of her lay the two maps – one from the archives, the other from the colonel's bag, both showing the Topčider military compound. She tried to concentrate. Their scales looked identical.

She compared every square centimetre. The Church of St Peter and St Paul, the intersection, the gate, the main building. And those dotted lines, which she had traced with her fingers so many times. Everything on these maps seemed identical down to the last detail. And on the instructions these four terms:

Picked gherkins 35×12

Sugar snaps 71×12

Tinned sardines 115×12

Salami 80×12

All the letters had been meticulously written down, and 'sugar snaps' framed with a fine line.

She leant back. Fiona lay beneath the lamp, purring and blinking and with her long whiskers occasionally twitching.

Why was there no explanation on the tracing paper, which had been put so deliberately with the ground plan, no useful pointers, nothing of the usual paraphernalia of such sets of instructions?

With a sigh she laid the maps on top of one another and the semi-transparent paper on top of them. And suddenly she noticed something she hadn't seen before.

Sugar snaps 71×12: the little frame around it exactly matched the outline of the weapons store on the map.

She placed the tracing paper over the map so that the two boxes aligned, flattened the sheets and looked at the ground plan one more time, but this time through the tracing paper.

The picture that emerged revealed something totally new. Suddenly the words on the paper became completely irrelevant. Even the numbers didn't matter anymore.

The door handle turned. Adam was standing in the doorway, his eyes little slits. 'Mum?' he asked in a high-pitched voice, 'can I sleep in your bed tonight?'

She turned off the light on the desk. 'Come here, you.'

A little while later his head was resting in her elbow and she was pushing her nose into his soft hair. He was breathing deeply and calmly.

'You know,' she whispered, 'the way you put that puzzle together the other day, that was brilliant.'

24

Today the wind was gusting from all directions, blowing through the canyons between the buildings and creating such a vortex that dry leaves danced pirouettes and startled crows flung themselves into dramatic nosedives, swooping low and then soaring up again, and Milena's hair was wildly tousled. Only Duke Vuk, looking down on it all with a stony face, stood aloof from the whole circus.

Passing beneath his rifle, Milena hurried across the square, reached Toplica Venac Street on the other side and ran down the hill. It took her less than fifteen minutes to get from the institute to Siniša Stojković's chambers; using the car for such a short distance and risking having to search for a parking space just wasn't worth it, even in this weather.

Number 30 had been built in a time when Kosmaj Street was still called Marshall Birjusow Street, after the victorious commander of Soviet forces on the Southern front. In the entrance was a huge mural depicting the Socialist youth of the multi-ethnic state of Yugoslavia advancing towards a brilliant future full of beauty, strength and confidence. That was a long time ago. Now there was nothing left of that confidence, or of the multi-ethnic state, and the mural was just a historical curiosity, whose colourful mosaic stones had lost much of their brilliance.

Siniša's chambers were situated on the fourth floor and the lift had long since stopped working. The stairs were covered with bits of rubble, crumbling plaster and mortar, and the smell of toilets wafted through the hallway on the cold draught. The entrances to the lower floors had been screened off, but this didn't signify that restoration work was going on behind, it was just a way of keeping people out of those areas. In fact the only thing that anyone had done here since Tito's day was raise the question of who owned the building; in the absence of any clear answer a state of post-socialist limbo had set in, which suited Siniša down to the ground. So for years there had been no land agent or account to pay the office rent to. And if it hadn't been for Siniša, no one would have bothered renting out the third and fifth floors, which were still in a reasonable state of repair. And as long as the old socialist cables kept supplying free electricity, the inhabitants didn't mind the fact that only the toilets on the fourth floor were working – though even there the flush curiously ran more or less permanently. But Siniša wasn't asking an exorbitant rent, just enough to pay his two assistants Alisa Raićević and Velika Pudar.

Pushing open the rickety glass doors, Milena entered the foyer, where a brightly backlit glass wall stood. 'Justitia' was etched into the frosted glass – not strictly speaking the name of Siniša's chambers but of the NGO he had invented to evade the clutches of the Serbian tax authorities. Alisa, the secretary, sat behind the wall. Her desk doubled up as a kind of reception area. From the way she sat hunched over her keyboard it was clear that typing was not her forte. 'You can go straight through,' she told Milena. 'The Doctor's expecting you.'

Milena knocked on the mahogany door with the brass plate proudly marking it as the office of 'Doctor Siniša Stojković'.

'The gentlemen should have got off their fat arses sooner, then.' The dark silhouette in front of the window beckoned Milena to enter. 'No, not one centimetre! No way! They can do headstands for all I care.'

Siniša loved these kind of telephone calls, all the more so when he had an audience. And better than that an appearance in court or – this was the tops, of course – in front of the TV cameras. By contrast he detested methodical paper work. He hated flickering computer screens and preferred to have Alisa take dictation.

'What did you say?' He laughed out loud, before shouting scathingly down the phone: 'Listen here: no more pussyfooting. In this matter, we'll be shooting from both barrels.'

Milena sat down at the oval conference table strewn with newspapers, books, catalogues, chocolate wrappers and CDs. Next to a bottle of Scotch stood another containing French aftershave. The chairs – like all the other furniture in the room – had belonged to the previous tenant. Throwbacks to Socialist times that had clearly played host to many an apparatchik's arse.

She always positioned herself so she didn't have to look at the giant mural; a dark portrayal of the Kalemegdan Fortress in the seventeenth century – if the fantasy of an untalented artist was to be believed. Milena preferred looking at the huge bookshelf, where the law books did not form serried ranks but stood isolated or in small clusters amongst novels by Balzac, Tolstoy and Goethe; guidebooks to California, Florence and Wales; and dictionaries and textbooks such as *Learning English in 100 Lessons*.

The shelf at eye level contained a row of framed photographs: Siniša with prominent Serbian politicians at a champagne reception, Siniša at a panel debate, and Siniša waving a scarf at the head of a protest march, with his eyes fixed ahead bravely and determinedly. Then there was his certificate of appointment as permanent secretary. No sign, though, of the certificate of dismissal, which he had been handed after barely six months in office.

'I'm sorry, my dear, that wasn't very polite of me.' Siniša said, putting on his jacket. 'But that had to be sorted out.' He circumnavigated his desk, stopped suddenly and looked at her pensively. 'The way you're sitting there, sunk in your own serious thoughts – and here am I kicking up such a racket.' Shaking his head he sat down, fiddled with his cufflinks and smiled at her. 'Milena, you're not only beautiful, you're also very special. And one day, I truly believe you'll be my destiny.'

She unfolded the silver frame of her spectacles, brushed back a strand of hair from her forehead and put the glasses on her nose. 'Right. To the matter in hand.'

'Topčider.'

She shook the papers from the stiffened envelope.

The door opened. In a whisper, Alisa apologised and placed two cups of coffee and a small dish of linseed cookies on the table.

'Thank you, Alisa,' Siniša said. 'No more calls now. We don't want to be disturbed.'

As Milena sipped her coffee, which as usual was as weak as tea, Siniša shoved the papers on the table aside to make room and began examining the documents. 'What have we here?' he exclaimed. 'Two maps of the compound. One from the Serbian Archives, the other from Colonel Djordan.'

'The plans are completely identical.'

'And this list, which nobody can make any sense of.'

'It's the instruction leaflet.'

'What?'

She laid the tracing paper on the desk. 'You know, every instruction leaflet must have its use, and that's why I couldn't leave this list alone. Take a look. What do you see?'

He bent forward and read: 'Sugar snaps 71×12.'

'And what else?'

'There's a line around it.'

'The frame' – she placed the map in front of Siniša – 'precisely matches the outline of the arsenal.'

With screwed up eyes he watched as Milena aligned the tracing paper with the map so that the little box around 'sugar snaps' exactly overlaid the outline of the weapons store. 'Now take another look at the crosses, the 'x's, in the quantities.'

One 'x' lay close to the main building, one immediately beside to the arsenal and the other two in the middle of the compound. But what was striking was that all of them, irrespective of their location, were situated on dotted lines.

Milena pointed at the marking in the middle of the compound, below the main building, half-way to the Sava River. 'That could be the place where the kitchen boy found the bodies.'

Siniša shifted closer to the edge of his seat. 'Curious,' he muttered, 'but I don't understand. Why are all the crosses on the dotted lines?'

Milena took her cigarettes out of her pocket. 'The key question is: What do the dotted lines mean? And what do these crosses mark? Why were Nenad and Predrag killed near one of these marks?' She pushed a strand of hair behind her ear. 'Our theory had always been that Nenad Jokić and Predrag Mrša had to die because they happened upon a celebration of the greatest massacre of European history. In the middle of Topčider, the criminals felt so secure that they even ordered a lamb from the barracks' kitchen for their banquet.'

'Yeah, we came to that conclusion already.'

'Sure, but we never asked ourselves where exactly the banquet might have been held. In the open air? Unthinkable. Somewhere inside the barracks, in a room or a hall? But then how come the kitchen boy found the two guardsmen in the middle of the compound?'

'You mean...'

'What if these broken lines mark underground passageways and our two guardsmen discovered the secret entrance, one of four indicated by the crosses on the map?' Milena lit a cigarette and blew the smoke straight up.

Siniša nodded, reflecting on what she'd just said, as he reached for the packet and took out a cigarette for himself. 'A bolthole, then. In the middle of Topčider, in the lion's den so to speak.'

Milena gave him a light. She couldn't recall ever having seen Siniša smoke.

'Maybe the guards passed it on their sentry rounds.' He smoked, studied the map and spoke very softly. 'And if there is a secret entrance to some subterranean vault, it must have been guarded. People went in and out. These criminals, they must have felt totally safe. And our boys, completely unsuspecting, saw or heard something down there. Or they strayed off their normal route without permission. Maybe they just wanted to look at the river at night.'

Milena flicked her ash into the saucer. 'Who are the men hiding out there, celebrating their atrocities? Are these the old generals and war criminals, who are still dreaming of a Greater Serbian Empire?' She stubbed out her cigarette. 'And the colonel – was he one of them? If he wanted to meet up and show me this map – then he probably wanted to tell me about that secret meeting too. Why, though? What did he have do with all of this?'

Siniša watched the smoke from his cigarette. 'The colonel must have known there was a secret cabal within the military. This group entertains high-level contacts with the ruling elite, all the way up to the presidential guards. Djordan was part of that system. Presumably he turned a blind eye to everything that went on there.'

'Until suddenly two of his guardsmen fetched up dead.'

'Maybe you rattled him with your questions and set him thinking.' Siniša put out his cigarette, though he'd only smoked half of it. 'Where do we go from here? Viewing the crime scene's out of the question, I suppose.'

'Shall we inform the police?' Milena asked.

'Why don't you call Dežulović, I'm sure he'd be delighted.'

'The media?'

Siniša shook his head. 'I can just see us calling a press conference and telling journalists about sugar snaps and little crosses on tracing paper.'

'Why not? Don't forget we still have the report from Ludwigshafen with the information about the angle of the entry wounds. All this taken together presents a picture that's absolutely convincing. We know enough already, we just have to go public with it.'

Siniša leant back, crossed his arms in front of his chest, and looked pensive.

Milena sighed. 'I know my theory of the underground tunnels is a bit far-fetched, and going public with it is quite dangerous, but I don't see any other way.'

Siniša rubbed his face. When he looked at Milena again, he suddenly appeared very tired. 'What you say is right and it's compelling too. But it's not the right time to start publicising it.'

Milena got up and walked over to the window. On the other side of the street was Zeleni Venac, the fruit and veg market. Dirty tents and colourful awnings were flapping in the wind. Next to it was her old primary school. And there was the little wall still, which she had balanced on, holding her mother's hand. Back there was the spot where her father had waited for her every Friday.

She turned back to Siniša. 'We don't know where these men live, what they do all day or where they're hiding. The

perpetrators have no faces; they're invisible. How are we supposed to get to these guys, with the means at our disposal, if
they're protected by an entire military apparatus?'

Siniša had stood up and was pacing in circles around his
office. 'Right, from the top again and let's take it one step at a
time: there's this night of the eleventh to the twelfth of July.
A group of people has gathered in this subterranean vault,
while up above two guards are routinely doing their rounds.
They unwittingly stumble upon the entrance to the vault
and the group is almost rumbled. The worst-case scenario is
averted at the last minute, albeit at a high cost: two bodies
and a massive public outcry. A disaster. What happens next?
Instead of things calming down, a woman marches into
the barracks and, to make matters worse, is received by the
colonel in person. That's enough to place him under surveillance. Then the colonel decides to meet up with the woman
again. Shortly afterwards he turns up dead as well.' Siniša
stopped and looked at Milena. 'I don't know how you see
this, my dear, but I reckon we know more than enough.
These men are utterly ruthless...'

'...and they're losing their nerve.'

'...but they have eyes and ears everywhere.'

'That's our opportunity. If they're getting nervous, they'll
make mistakes.'

'Milena, are you listening to me? We have to assume that
they've got you in their sights now, too.'

She slowly returned to her seat. 'What do you mean?' She
sat down. 'Do you mean we should just give in?'

'Yeah, that would be the best thing to do in the circumstances. There's another way though, one that doesn't entail
risking our lives and losing the small advantage we've gained.
Look, they don't know as yet that we've got the maps and
have figured out what a nice little hideout they've built

themselves in the middle of Topčider. So let's just let them calm down. We'll wait until the next anniversary, the next eleventh of July. Maybe the time will be right then and, who knows, maybe we'll manage to catch them red-handed in their lair.'

Milena gathered up the papers and put them back in the envelope. 'Right, let's wait for fairer weather. Let's wait for the eleventh of July.'

'Where are you going?'

'Home.'

'And the papers?'

'I'm taking them with me. Why?'

Shaking his head, Siniša took the envelope from her hand and walked to the door with it. 'You can't go carrying around such sensitive material with you anymore,' he told her. 'And you definitely can't keep it in the flat where not only you, but also your son and your mother, live.'

In Alisa's reception area the computer had been covered up and the chair neatly pushed under the desk. Siniša hung his jacket over the backrest and walked over to the refrigerator, a huge, ancient appliance in the corner by the window. Alisa was forever complaining that it turned everything to ice.

Siniša grasped the smooth sides of the fridge, as if he was embracing the behemoth, and inched the fridge out of the corner. In the wall behind it, a medium-height door with a metal wheel came into view – a safe.

Siniša loosened his tie, opened the top button of his shirt and pulled out a key hanging on a leather strap, which was too big to carry around in his trouser pocket. He stuck the key in the keyhole and turned the wheel first in the one direction and then the other. Silently, the big steel door opened. In the dark square lay a few bundles of grey-green dollar bills and a small pile of papers.

Milena stashed the envelope with the papers: two maps – one from the Serbian Archives, the other from the bag of the dead colonel – and one piece of tracing paper, which Adam had pieced together from the little snippets, stuck together with sellotape.

'Seventy-one dozen sugar snaps,' Siniša wheezed as he manoeuvred the fridge back into place – 'did Tito's partisans think that up, or is it from the time of the Turkish occupation?'

25

The yellow anorak, which was always to hand on the first hook in the hallway, had been a bargain Milena had picked up during her student days in Berlin. How many times had she worn this jacket, riding her bike between the lecture theatre, the language lab and her job at the bar? This thing would last forever, it seemed. Back then, she'd bought it for its striking yellow colour, but nowadays she loved it for the outside pockets which, if pushed, could hold a jam-jar or a pound of coffee.

Milena buttoned up the anorak, put her purse and keys in the pocket and shouted out: 'I'll be back in a bit!' It was Tuesday, 21 September, late afternoon. She should have gone to a service station before heading out of town. But the cheap autogas she needed since the Lada had been converted wasn't available just anywhere. It was annoying that she had to keep clear of the filling station on Sava Square because of a demonstration that was taking place there. It was the most conveniently placed for her, but the demonstrators – workers at a local car plant – deserved her support: for the sum of just one Euro, the whole plant was about to be flogged off to an Austrian investor and the workers, who hadn't been paid for months, were threatened with losing all their back pay and most likely their jobs too. Milena rapped on the fuel gauge on the dashboard with her knuckles; the needle moved up a bit.

To her right the large road signs came into view: Budapest – 374 kilometres, Athens – 970 kilometres, Zagreb – 429. A low-slung sports car cut in sharply in front of her, showing her its fat exhaust, steeply raked spoiler and two bright brake lights. She changed lane and swept under the motorway bridge into an area called 'Greater Belgrade'. The area adjacent to the motorway was sectioned off into different lots with tall corrugated-iron sheets and barbed wire, which if need be could easily be extended in any direction. Used cars were on sale here, along with tyres, washing machines, Italian handbags, toilet seats, coffee machines and a host of other goods generally considered useful, practical or beautiful.

A few kilometres further south another world began: salmon-pink houses with cute dormer windows and gables and attached garages; a housing development for the new upper middle class built with funding from Canadian investors. Alongside these, dotted around the landscape, stood buildings that had been cobbled together – an extra floor here and an extension there – according to how much money was available at any one time, in most cases earned by a younger generation that had gone abroad while their parents stayed behind, living on the building site and hanging their washing on lines strung between scaffolding poles. These gradually petered out into fields and wild meadows. In the rear-view mirror purple-black clouds were massing, while ahead the late evening sun's by-now almost horizontal rays lit up the grass and potato fields and bathed the poplars in a silvery glow. Behind the trees lay the Sava River and the island of Ada Ciganlija.

Milena indicated and turned into a small road that ran past a parking area and large advertising hoardings and ended at a barrier with a little ticket booth. She rolled down the window, handed over her money and was given a small piece of paper in return. Slowly Milena drove her car onto the little bridge.

Ada Ciganlija – most Belgraders associated this name with water skiing, picnics in the open and campfires. Whenever

Milena set foot on the island, she recalled her school sports days, which were held here every year. Ada Ciganlija – for her it meant sweaty sports kit, competitions she'd messed up, and the gazes of spotty boys eyeing up Milena's naked, white legs. But these innocent images had lately been eclipsed by the crime committed here ten days ago.

Milena followed the small road that ran across the top of the meadow, passing upturned rowing boats. Some youths were standing around a brick fireplace barbecuing. Milena pulled up in front of a wooden chalet decorated with club pennants and flags, switched off the engine and got out. The air was full of the smell of barbecued sausages. Somewhere a radio was blaring. 'Excuse me!' Milena shouted above the noise. 'Could you tell me how to get to the houseboats?'

One of the boys, sitting on crate, pointed his beer can in the direction of a small wooded area.

'Will I find Danilo Djordan's boat there, too?'

The youths looked at each other and shrugged their shoulders.

The trail led through beeches, low spruces and ferns, through various bits of flotsam: a petrol can, newspapers, condoms and other litter, partly covered by ivy. After a few minutes' walk, a group of small wooden huts came into view through the trees, looking from a distance like pergolas in the middle of allotments. Landing nets, brooms and other tools were neatly lined up, and in the flowerpots on the windowsills the geraniums were in bloom. Plastic bottles were bobbing in the dark water and little waves lapped against the thick boards. Narrow footbridges led to each of the houseboats, but one was cordoned off with red-and-white plastic tape.

Milena dug her hands deeper into her pockets and imagined the murderer lurking there between the water butts, under the cover of darkness. He'd probably come to the island on foot to avoid drawing attention to himself at the barrier. Perhaps he'd taken the same trail as her, making his way through the undergrowth. Turning around to look at the route she'd taken, she got the shock of her life .

A figure was standing there, leaning motionless against a tree and looking at her; she got the impression he'd been there quite a while. It was a small figure, a boy, not even Adam's height, barefoot, wearing knee-length shorts and a shirt that was much too small. Maybe the boy belonged to the Roma, who had set up a cardboard and corrugated-iron shanty town where the adventure playground had once been.

'Hello.' Milena took a step towards him. 'Do you live here?'

He looked at her challengingly. 'Have you got a cigarette?' His dark eyes glinted.

'What's your name? Do you often hang around here near the boats?' Milena took out her purse and gave him a coin. 'Do you know the guy who owned the houseboat over there? He was here almost every weekend.' The boy's eyes followed her finger, then he glanced at the coin she'd put in his hand and wiped his nose on his sleeve.

'Do you understand what I asked you?' The boy didn't respond. Milena wondered whether she should just ignore the tape and go and have a look around the houseboat. She'd be committing a criminal offence, and what did she hope to find anyway? An answer as to why the colonel had asked her to come here and what he'd wanted to tell her? Probably not. Big drops of rain started falling, making rings in the water. She buttoned up her raincoat, tightened the drawstring at the hem and decided to take the long way back along the riverbank. It was dusk by now, and the woods seemed forbiddingly gloomy. She took a few steps forward, turned around and noticed that the little boy was following her.

'I saw a man,' he suddenly said.

Milena stopped in her tracks. 'Where?'

He pointed at the woods.

'And what did the man look like?'

He gave her a sly little look and held out his hand again.

'When did you see this man?' Milena asked.

No answer.

'Did you stalk him – like you've just done with me?'

He nodded.

'What did the man do?' She got out her purse again. The boy took the coin. 'He hid.'

'From you? Why? Was he afraid?'

He nodded.

Milena gave a sigh. 'Look here,' she said, 'don't tell tales.'

'He hid,' the boy insisted. 'There.' Again he pointed at the woods.

It had probably been an innocent walker who'd needed to relieve himself. She shoved the purse back in her coat pocket. 'Did you notice anything about the man? Was he tall or short? Fat or thin?'

Little wrinkles formed above the bridge of his nose. Either he was searching for words to describe what he had seen or he was about to let his imagination run riot because there was nothing to describe.

'Go home.' Milena told him, pulling the hood up over her head. 'Haven't you got any shoes? Or a jumper?' Adam's wardrobe was full to bursting and needed a good clear-out. Milena decided to return soon with a bag full of clothing. 'Now, run on home,' she said to him, 'otherwise you'll get soaked to the skin.'

He put out his hand to her once more, but this time it wasn't to ask for more money or even to wave her goodbye. Instead, he'd made something like a little fist, with his index and middle fingers firmly clasping his thumb, and his ring finger and little finger extended.

Sitting back in the car, Milena tried replicating what he'd done, but couldn't manage it. You probably needed a child's hands to perform such contortions. He'd obviously meant to tell or show her something with the gesture, something she didn't understand.

The closer she got to the city the harder the rain started coming down and soon turned into a deluge. Though the wipers were going full-tilt and she was crawling along, she could still barely make out the carriageway through the curtain of water. An SUV barrelled past her, doing at least 80 kilometres per hour, buffeting her aside with its bow-wave. It took all her strength to prevent her car from swerving; she reduced her speed still further. Then another lunatic appeared. The guy behind her was driving on a single headlight; at first glance, she'd thought it was a motorcycle. She urgently rapped the plastic cover of the fuel gauge.

Sava Square was still cordoned off, blocking the direct route to the filling station. Milena cursed. She had no choice but to turn into Karadjordjeva Street, wondering where she should turn next to get to where she wanted. The guy with the broken headlight dogged her every move. Was he tailing her? She pulled over as far as she could to the right to let him pass. The needle on the fuel gauge looked like it had been nailed to zero. And now she'd missed her turning and found herself on Duke Bojović Boulevard, which would take her in a wide arc beneath the fortress and lead her out of town again. She needed to turn around as soon as she could and get back into the centre. She checked her rear view mirror nervously. Her pursuer was sticking to her like glue, constantly maintaining the same distance.

At the next junction, the lights were already on amber.

Milena made up her mind in an instant, gunning the engine and shooting across the intersection as they turned red. Glancing up at her rear-view mirror, she could see her pursuer's headlight growing ever smaller.

She was sweating. She turned down the heater and tried to get her bearings. The area she was now driving through was unfamiliar to her. Low houses all around and dark entranceways. Out-of-service buses were parked along the side of the road, and the only street lighting hereabouts, apart from a red neon heart flashing in an otherwise black window, came from the light cast by brand-new billboards showing huge pictures of tights and sandy beaches. The snack bar was boarded up, the railway track was disused and the street was full of potholes. No, it was actually the engine which was stuttering. She gripped the steering wheel, pressed the clutch, then the accelerator and prayed that the Lada wasn't about to give up on her now. Too late – the engine stalled and the only thing she could do was use the last bit of forward momentum to steer the car to the kerb. Even so, it finally came to a halt blocking the access to a side road.

All her attempts to restart the engine failed. She would normally have called Siniša by now. But the phone was in her handbag and that was hanging on a hook in the hallway at home.

In the silence, the rain was drumming on the roof. From behind, a light suddenly appeared. Milena stared into the rear-view mirror. Her heart was pounding faster. The car with the broken headlight was approaching again at a crawl, closer and closer until she could see the black silhouette of the driver behind the windscreen.

26

He stopped the car about twenty-five metres behind the Lada. He didn't get it. First the long schlepp through the city, then suddenly out to Ada Ciganlija. The conversation with that rat of a gypsy. Then another marathon drive back and now this stop near the harbour. What was this woman up to?

The broken headlight had given him away. Because that arsehole of a bookkeeper had given him this heap of junk in the first place, and because the guys in the garage had been asleep on the job, he'd been rumbled. But who'd be held responsible when the mission failed? Observe, note, take photographs – those had been his orders. He could only follow them properly if he remained invisible. Pawle made a fist with his left hand and blew into it.

The woman got out of her car, and looked over at him. He pressed himself down into the seat. What if she came over, to his window, looked in his face, saw his hands? He counted to ten, fast. Then he forced himself to count again, this time more slowly. They hadn't briefed him for this eventuality, but he'd be left carrying the can all on his tod, so he had to weigh up all the likely outcomes. In the headlights the woman blurred into a bright, yellow spot. He had to act, now. Pressing down the clutch, he put the car into gear.

With a squeal of tyres, he raced forward into empty space, slammed on the brakes and spun around, coming to a stop across the road. He saw how she began to run down the side road. Her damned Lada was blocking the entrance to it. He flung open his door. Rain lashed into his face.

She had a head start – only a hundred metres, not even a block. He slipped on the wet cobblestones. But he was fit, so the old bitch wouldn't stand a chance. The mud on the wet cobbles made them extra-slippery and he fell again, grazing his hands. He cursed; the pain made him wild. He ran, a sprint of around twenty, thirty seconds. Puffing, he stopped at the corner, pressing his hands to his hips.

There wasn't a car parked anywhere nor anyone in sight. The wet pavement shone in the glare of the street lights. He heard the patter of the rain, a dripping and gurgling sound, and spun around. If something had moved, he'd have noticed it.

He kicked the lamp post – once, twice, again and again, until finally the light went out. Under the cover of darkness he crossed the street in the direction of the open gateway.

27

Somebody came running across the courtyard in the rain. The steps echoed in the entranceway, then grew slower before stopping altogether. Milena sat hunched behind the rubbish bins, on top of a pile of pallets, trying to catch her breath and not daring to move. Her chest hurt and the back of her feet had chafed in the sneakers. She'd run down streets and through backyards, rattled gates and doors secured by metal padlocks and, after eventually finding an exit, had dashed along a parallel street and through even more courtyards. By now, she was utterly exhausted.

The stranger had to be very close. She couldn't see him, only hear him: the click of his lighter, then the silence before he exhaled. She tried to breathe calmly. Was her heart really pounding so audibly? Terrified, she looked up.

The face which appeared above the rubbish bins was clean-shaven, with a scar clearly visible above the chin. The dirty-white jacket was made from a tough, coarse material and the hair under the cap, which was shaped like a little boat and perched slightly skewiff on his head, was cut so short that the skin shimmered through.

'Can I help you?' The man bent down towards her. 'Is there something wrong? Are you hurt?'

'I'm...' She smiled, and tried to conceal the quaver in her voice. It was just some harmless guy in a chef's outfit. 'It's nothing,' she said. 'Everything's alright. But could I use your phone?'

Squinting at her, he inhaled one last time, threw the butt of his cigarette into the street, where it landed in a puddle, and replied: 'You'll have to go round the front. The entrance is round the corner.'

His steps receded across the courtyard, an iron door slammed shut. Then silence again, and the patter of the rain. Milena walked hesitantly out of the gateway. It was less than ten metres to the next corner. Cast-iron street lamps emitted a warm glow. On an oval sign she read the name 'Jevrem', in old-fashioned lettering. The stairway to the entrance had a canopy over it and was decorated with pretty flowerpots and little lanterns. As Milena climbed the steps, she noticed that her jeans were clinging to her legs. The yellow nylon fabric of her anorak was soaked by the rain, and the terry lining had sucked up all the moisture like a flannel. Summoning up what seemed like her last ounce of strength, she leant against the door and pushed it open.

The waiter in his long apron who immediately came rushing towards her paid her no attention whatsoever. Balancing several plates in his hands, he swung around a large ornamental palm, with his head held haughtily high, and disappeared from view.

Milena followed the voices and the sound of a popping cork. Through the leaves of the palm tree, she could see tables laid with white tablecloths and elegant people engaged in civilised conversation, candles everywhere and the glitter of cut glass. Mirrors hung on dark panelled walls, and somewhere in the room, laughter was sparkling like bubbles in a glass of champagne. Every gesture, every look seemed to obey a set of clear rules and came together to form a harmonious whole, in which only a single element jarred: a pair of eyes at the far end of the room staring over at her.

Startled, Milena took a step back and bumped into a lectern with an large open guestbook. She suddenly noticed the small puddle of water that had gathered at her feet and a woman in a black suit, most likely the manageress, who asked her unsmilingly: 'Do you have a reservation?'

Milena brushed a wet strand of hair from her forehead. 'My car broke down. Would you be so kind as to call me a taxi? I'll wait outside. Thank you.' She hurried towards the door.

'Ms Lukin – wait!' A tall, slim figure approached her with long strides. 'What brings you here?' the surprised Alexander Kronburg enquired. 'Has something happened? Why, you're wet through!' His hair was swept back and his well-polished shoes shone. He pulled a finely woven handkerchief from the breast pocket of his jacket for her to wipe the raindrops off her face. As she was doing so, the ambassador helped her out of her jacket as if it were a fur coat, handing the dripping garment to the employee with the words: 'Could you please get us a towel?'

'Of course, your Excellency.'

Milena pressed the thin material of the hankie in her hand. She was uncomfortable with the whole situation. She didn't want a towel or to be treated like a countess. Thoroughly embarrassed at having to stand like a drowned rat in front of the German ambassador, she hissed: 'My taxi's waiting. I must get home.'

'You have to warm yourself up first.' All of a sudden, the concerned furrow in his brow was replaced by a faint smile. 'Can I order you some tea, or would you rather have hot broth?'

'Look, I'm in a real rush, Mr Kronburg.'

The furrow reappeared. 'I'm sorry, but I can't let you go back out on the street again like that.'

The woman in the black suit beckoned to the waiter.

Shortly afterwards Milena found herself in the ladies' cloakroom, crouching under the hand dryer and attempting to dry her hair, until her back started to hurt. The woman who stared back at her from the mirror looked dishevelled, with pale cheeks and an unattrative hard set to her mouth, something she hadn't noticed before. No, it hadn't all been a dream. The dark silhouette behind the windscreen, the guy who had chased her up the hill – who the hell was this man, stalking her across the entire city? Shouldn't she call the police this instant?

Milena sighed. She was supposed to make small talk now and be witty, and she didn't even have a lipstick on her.

As one waiter laid an extra place, another served her tea with lemon and poured her a glass of red wine. Alexander pulled out her chair for her and introduced her to the rest of his guests: representatives of banks from several countries, associations and organisations; a secretary at the embassy; a cultural attaché; and all their assorted spouses. Far too many names for her to remember all at once. And how they all looked at her! For these people she was a woman in jeans and a jumper, with no make-up and straggly hair, who had suddenly breezed in from the street and been invited to join their party by the ambassador, who introduced her as a 'member of the Institute for Criminology and Forensic Science'.

'Dr Lukin,' Alexander added, 'is currently engaged in setting up a department for International Criminal Prosecution and Jurisdiction, isn't that right?'

Milena waved it aside and hoped that would be the end of that matter.

'Interesting!' A lady wearing a blouse with a flower pattern looked at her with wide eyes. 'So that means you have to deal with real war crimes, right?'

'Theoretically, yes,' Milena said. 'But in practice, only indirectly.'

'Do tell.'

Milena was tired. She didn't feel up to explaining what was so international, interdisciplinary and new about her work. Nor was she in the mood to talk about bureaucratic hurdles, which usually made for wonderful anecdotes and were the perfect topic to sound off about if she'd only been in a better state of mind. 'Well...,' was all she could muster.

Alexander came to her rescue. 'Above all Ms Lukin is an academic who deals with the critical reappraisal of war crimes.'

'So we don't need to worry, then?' A woman in a burgundy-coloured blouse sitting to one side of Milena – with an American accent and dimples in her cheeks – pushed back a strand of hair behind her ear and smiled at her.

'Worry?'

'You don't have to go around with a bodyguard?'

'Samantha!' Alexander laughed. 'Ms Lukin is in academia, not the secret service.'

'You'd imagine so,' murmured Milena.

'Where are you from, may I ask?' a gentleman with a full head of grey hair, sitting two seats away from her, enquired.

'I was born in Belgrade,' replied Milena.

'So you're a Serb.'

'Right.' Milena put her tea glass back down on the saucer. 'And you? Which country are you from.'

'I'm half-Greek, half-Turkish.'

'That's not exactly straightforward, then, either.'

'You can say that again.'

'I grew up in the former Yugoslavia,' said Milena feeling the warmth slowly spreading all the way down to the tips of her toes. 'My cousin is a Croat, my mother's from Montenegro, my father from Voivodina. In my family, we combine half the Balkans, so to speak.'

Milena politely took a sip of her red wine.

'One thing interests me.' The woman with the dimples

– Samantha – placed her hands flat on the table as if she was studying the emerald ring on her finger. 'If you're developing a course in international criminology, then you're working in a field where Serbia in particular has a lot to answer for, aren't you? Is your nationality a disadvantage or is it a precondition for getting your job?'

'Ms Lukin,' Alexander chipped in, 'is also a German citizen, however.' He laid a hand on her arm. 'In this project she is acting, in a way, as a representative of the German academic world.'

'Okay.' Samantha nodded. 'That makes things easier.'

'And the German passport must have come in handy when you applied for the post, I'll bet.' The grey-haired fellow winked at her. 'You can live well in Belgrade on that kind of money, can't you?'

That was the last straw. Being a Serb was a stigma, whereas owning a German passport was a privilege – it was always the same. 'I can assure you,' she said, making no attempt to hide her irritation, 'that simply owning a German passport isn't enough to secure the job I'm doing. You need some other qualifications too.'

'But of course!' The pin-striped guy held up his hands defensively.

A man with wire-rimmed glasses, who hadn't spoken before, leant forward. 'Your work and your commitment do you credit, Ms Lukin,' he said. 'There's no doubt that the war criminals will be arrested and put on trial.'

Everyone nodded.

'But it's quite another question,' he continued, 'whether Serbian civil society is prepared to make a clean break with the past. You can't order such a thing from on high. It has to be willed by the people. And – I'm sorry to say – I don't see any evidence of such a will in Serbia.'

'That's because you're not looking closely enough!' Milena shook her head. 'Most Serbs, and not just the young, feel themselves part of Europe. They took to the streets against a dictator and threw him out, don't forget. But these same people now need some prospects, like those the Federal Republic of Germany was presented with after the Second World War, incidentally. And the urge to break with the past didn't come about overnight there either, unless I'm very much mistaken.'

Milena saw a look of mild consternation pass across Alexander Kronburg's face and got up. 'I'm sorry, it wasn't my intention to spoil your evening. I apologise. I'll take my leave now.'

He followed her to the cloakroom, bringing back memories for Milena of their first meeting at the reception in the German embassy.

'So I still don't know how you pitched up here totally drenched, Milena,' he said softly. 'For a moment I got the impression you might be running away from someone or something. Is there a problem?'

Milena gave him a tired smile. 'Do you believe that some day this country will turn out fine?'

He gazed at her with his blue eyes and answered: 'As long as there are people like you I'm not worried about this country. But what about you? Who's looking after you?' He took off his jacket, draped it over her shoulders and held the door open for her.

A few stars had finally broken through the clouds, and it had stopped raining. Alexander walked her down the steps past the lanterns and flowerpots. 'Please tell me if I can be of assistance to you in any shape or form.'

'With German diplomacy? – Please call me a cab.'

He raised his hand and made a sign. 'My driver will take you home.'

A black limousine rolled forward and stopped directly in front of them. Alexander opened the back door. 'I was serious with my offer. And...' He took her hand. 'Please don't do anything rash. I'd really like to see you again.' He moved her fingers to his lips.

She got in and told the driver her address. The door closed and Alexander disappeared from sight.

She sat back in the soft seat, felt the blister on her heel and the spot on the back of her hand where he'd kissed it. The lights of the passing city suddenly seemed dim to her through the tinted windows. Everything she had experienced seemed slightly unreal.

The limousine stopped in front of her house. Milena laid the ambassador's jacket neatly on the back seat, thanked the chauffeur and got out without asking him to wait until she was safely in the building. Now it was too late, but it was only a few metres anyhow.

In the dim light cast by the street lamps she scurried between parked cars along the deserted pavement, unlocked the front door and pulled it shut behind her. The caretaker still hadn't fixed the light in the hallway.

In the darkness she walked to the lift, which she had to call by pressing the button. It creaked and groaned in the lift shaft. Milena grabbed the door handle and waited motionless.

When she reached the door to the apartment she noticed that yet again her beloved family had only double-locked the lowest of the Yales. Once inside she locked all three. She wasn't hysterical by any means, but she still felt compelled to look in on her son even before taking off her shoes and jacket.

Adam was breathing regularly, deeply and calmly. Milena straightened his blanket, gently stroked his hair and gave him a kiss. He stretched in his sleep, pulled a face and for a moment seemed to smile.

As she was pulling the door to, she turned around and suddenly found herself confronted by a dark, slender figure.

'Child, where on earth have you been?' Vera was wearing a nightgown with a little lace collar; the only things missing were a nightcap and a candle. 'And what a sight you look!' With an anxious expression she stroked her hair and cheek. 'Has something happened?'

Milena shook her head, closed her eyes for a moment and tried to smile. 'Everything's fine.'

'We can't go on like this,' Vera said. 'We'll have to get out the winter duvets tomorrow. Otherwise the boy'll get cold at night.'

Milena kissed her mother on the cheek. 'Will do. But go to sleep now.'

A pot of cold coffee was standing on the stove and there was a plate on the table with foil stretched over it. Fiona twisted her warm fur around Milena's leg. Everything was normal – and yet nothing was the same anymore.

She pressed her hand to her mouth. The realisation hit her with full force: if she was a target, then so were her mother and her child. She sank onto the kitchen chair. All the fear, despair and helplessness that had built up inside her, now came flooding out. And Fiona, perched on the windowsill, observed this outburst with her customary sense of serene detachment.

28

Pawle heard the keys in the keyhole – once, twice. The door slammed against the wall. Clubfoot jingled the key ring and gestured with his head: report, chop chop. Pawle obeyed.

Clubfoot hobbled ahead, knocked on Momčilo's door, saluted and yelled in his high-pitched voice: 'Beg to report...' Pawle entered.

Momčilo was sitting with his elbows propped up on the desk, hammering his fingertips together rhythmically. As Pawle entered, Momčilo gave him such a hard stare that Pawle instantly forgot the speech he'd prepared. He was afflicted by a complete mental block. His back and his temples started to sweat. Pawle hated himself for that.

'Stand to attention, man!' Momčilo screamed at him.

Hastily Pawle mopped his brow with his sleeve and straightened his back. He put his hands on the seams of his trousers and lowered his eyes.

'And look at me when I'm talking to you!' Momčilo seemed to fix his gaze on the sweat running down the ridge of Pawle's nose. When the drop reached the end and hung there, Momčilo turned away and looked at the small report sheets, arranged systematically on the desk in front of him. Eventually he selected one from the lowest row and leant back: 'Wednesday, 22 September,' he read out loud. '20.00 hours: return from Ada Ciganlija to Belgrade.'

Pawle's report from yesterday, the day when everything had gone wrong.

'Correct?' Momčilo looked at him.

His throat was dry. 'Correct,' Pawle confirmed.

'I can't hear you. You'll have to speak up.'

'Correct!'

It was so quiet that the hum of traffic could be heard from far off. Outside the door the floorboards creaked.

'20.35,' Momčilo continued. 'Target goes home.' He put the piece of paper back in its allotted space, and asked very quietly: 'Correct?'

Pawle kept his back straight and tried to hold Momčilo's gaze. 'Not entirely...' His voice broke.

'Not entirely!?' Momčilo screamed. 'It's a pack of lies – every word of it! You're a damned liar.' Again the fingertips hammered against each other. 'You think you're something better, don't you? You always thought that. But in actual fact you're shit. You're stupid. Whatever move you make, I'll hear about it. I know everything. I know what you think. You think: good old Momčilo owes me a favour, am I right? He has had a good time at my expense, with my bonus. He'll let this one pass.' He nodded. 'I understand, comrade, I understand. But good old Momčilo won't be able to do anything for you. You've abused his trust. He doesn't know whose side you're on anymore. It doesn't look good for you.' He placed each piece of paper on top of each other and straightened the pile. 'Dismissed!' he barked.

The second Pawle turned he heard his name again.

He turned back and looked into Momčilo's face.

'Have you got anything to say to me?'

Pawle moved his fingers as if he was kneading the air. He wanted to say that he couldn't stand the uncertainty again, that he'd rather be demoted or thrown out than locked up across the hallway one more time, where he couldn't see the moon, and where the images haunted him and robbed him of his sanity. But not a single word passed his lips.

'Come here,' Momčilo said.

Pawle stepped forward.

'Closer.' Momčilo did a quarter-turn in his chair. 'Come right up close. That's it, come over to me.' While sitting down Momčilo's trousers had moved up his leg, exposing his grey socks and part of his white calf. Keeping his eyes fixed on Pawle, he pointed down and whispered: 'Sort this out for me.'

Pawle knelt on the floor and bent over Momčilo's boots and loose laces.

Catching hold of the flecked bootlace with his left hand was no problem. The difficulty came with the right. Grasping, threading, looping and pulling tight only worked if the fingers of his left hand took over functions which the stump on the right could no longer perform. The fact that he couldn't stop shaking, and that Momčilo kept watching him silently from above, did not make things any easier. He made a number of attempts; several times he had to start from the beginning again. Finally, using the five fingers of his left hand and the ring finger and little finger of his right, he managed to tie a double knot with a proper bow on top.

The laces had soaked up the sweat of his palms and fingertips and were wet, and drops of perspiration from his forehead and nose had dripped onto Momčilo's boots. Hurriedly, Pawle polished the leather with his sleeve, removing both dust and sweat. Then he got up and stood to attention.

Momčilo moved his foot, tested whether everything was tight enough and finally announced: 'You're still under arrest.' He turned back to the desk. 'Dismissed!'

Pawle crossed the hallway back to his room. Clubfoot followed and locked up behind him – once, twice.

He listened to the darkness. There was no moon, no solace, not even the sound of the dog, who after being unleashed to roam free had ceased its yapping and howling.

He crouched down on the floor and leant back against the wall. The U-bend below the sink was at eye level. There, right in the bend, was where the spider had lived. She had spun her web in the stupidest of all places and no one had even noticed her die there.

29

The shoes were made from red leather, hand-stitched and soft as a glove. They made her legs look longer, completely altered her posture and cost three times as much as a Serbian pensioner who had worked all his life received in a month. These were the shoes that Milena had dreamt of all her life. The shop assistant smiled as she wrapped them in tissue paper, laid them in their shiny gold box and closed the lid. Milena picked up the bag with the elegant logo of the boutique in Uzun Mirko Street and looped the long, soft cords over her shoulder. 'I don't know what to say,' she said, 'you're mad.'

Tanja put away her credit card. 'Just do me a favour and wear them as often as you can. They look fantastic on you.'

Milena took her friend's arm and kissed her.

They strolled along Count Mihailov Street, passing from one shop window to the next and commenting on whatever they encountered: the autumn collection displayed on the dummies, the shop assistants behind the showcases, the women teetering on their high heels ahead of them – too boring, too emaciated, too dressed up to the nines, too timorous and tasteless was their verdict. They behaved like they were still the silly little airheads they'd been as teenagers, who'd been convinced they knew it all, except that back then they'd never have thought it possible that they could ever be put wise.

When they'd sat down at one of the street cafés and Tanja had plunged her fork into a 'Diplomat's Torte', made of pure chocolate and iced raspberries, she asked: 'So when are you going to see him again, your ambassador?'

'Darling, he's not *my* ambassador.'

Tanja sighed. 'Come off it – a count who kisses your hand as he says goodbye and has you whisked home from the ball in his diplomatic carriage? – ah, how is it *I* always fall in love with idiots?'

'I'm not in love.'

'Of course not.'

'He's married with two children.'

'So why aren't they with him – his wife and children?'

'There was also this American woman, Samantha, very intelligent and beautiful. She was sitting rather close to him.'

As Tanja lit a cigarette, exhaled and started to explain why – in her opinion – Alexander Kronburg must be smitten with Milena Lukin and no other woman, Milena noticed how the young men in the café on the opposite side of the street kept stealing glances across at them. The guy leaning against the wall behind the popcorn booth and incessantly texting on his smartphone was doing the same. And what about the would-be bigshot with his sunglasses sitting two tables away from them? Milena put the fork down on her plate. It wasn't just the dates and the nuts in the Esterhazy Torte that were lying heavily on her stomach.

'Just take my word for it,' Tanja concluded. 'I've got a gut instinct for these things.'

Milena nodded and looked at her watch. 'I think it's time. Shall we go?'

They walked across Republic Square, past the equestrian statue of Mihajlo Obrenović, on whose helmet a pigeon had settled, and turned into Vasa Čarapić Street just behind the National Theatre. Taxis were drawing up there in front of a grey-fronted building whose slim windows looked like embrasures, creating a traffic jam. Across a red carpet, people in evening dress were making for the entrance, mingling as they did so with a group of school children, whose laughter and chatter echoed beneath the arcades.

Tanja grabbed Milena's arm and insisted: 'If something goes wrong, if you can't find a taxi – anything – you call me, understood?' She hugged her friend. 'Good luck!'

Milena got out her ticket: Tchaikovsky. *Manfred Symphony in B-flat, op. 58.* The doorman tore off a corner and handed it back to her – the ticket on which a stranger had written three words on the back: 'Please come. Important.'

She walked through the grey marble vestibule illuminated by heavy brass chandeliers and remembered the butterflies she'd experienced on her last visit here. That had been a long time ago, one 25 May, Tito's birthday. Then she'd been sporting the red neckerchief of the young Communist pioneers, and as the school's star pupil had been chosen to recite a poem on stage in honour of the great Marshal. Vera sat in the front row and silently mouthed every word her daughter spoke: '*Down at the foot of the hill, Comrade Tito rides at the head of a column of partisans...*'

Milena checked the bag into the cloakroom, rearranged her silk scarf and straightened out the black velvet jacket in front of the mirror. '*Up on high, the monster with blood-shot eyes. But Comrade Tito looks up at it without fear...*'

The man coming towards her on the stairs was slightly tanned and had dark shadows under his eyes, which lent him an air of melancholy. The sheer effrontery of the man, the way the Inspector tried his damnedest to look straight through her, was unfathomable: 'Good evening, Mr Filipow,' Milena said pointedly.

'Good evening.' With his arm around the waist of his companion – a young, pregnant woman – he pushed past Milena, who smiled affably and stepped aside.

The foyer's high ceilings had yellowed panelling, peeling

gold stucco and faded curtains. In the centre, underneath the huge chandelier, the evening's hosts had assembled: guardsmen in high boots, with gold braid down the seam of their trousers and medals on their chests. Though these military men exuded an air of dignity and confidence in their own strength, especially in this setting they appeared to Milena to be more like extras in an operetta, chocolate soldiers waiting to be fêted by their audience. The ladies – almost all wearing ball gowns and freshly made-up – toyed with their pearl necklaces while the gentlemen queued at the bar for glasses of champagne. Some of their suits looked like they'd spent a long time in wardrobes before being brushed off and deemed good enough to pass muster one last time. Milena inspected each one closely, her thoughts wandering back to the grey trench coat, which she'd just glimpsed the corner of that night at the institute. It was pointless. Milena decided to go into the concert hall, take her seat and wait and see what happened. All of a sudden, there was a commotion in the hall.

A lady in a long black dress had appeared in the middle of the three entrances from the foyer; she was wearing her red hair pinned up in an artful topknot which made her look even taller than she already was. With a smile, Nevenka Djordan filed past the soldiers, graciously acknowledging the respect they paid her – holding their caps in front of their chests and clicking their heels. She shook a hand here, and exchanged a word there as she made her way towards Milena down a narrow path the men cleared for her.

'How nice to see you,' Nevenka Djordan greeted Milena when she finally reached her. 'Did you get my message?'

'I most certainly did.' Milena's handshake was brief. 'This is a surprise.'

Nevenka smiled, but seemed a little irritated. 'A surprise?'

'Why this big production?' Milena tried to lower her voice.

Nevenka shot her an inquiring look. 'I needed to speak to you one more time. Maybe I should have called you at home rather than contact you at the institute. But I didn't have your number. I'm sorry.'

'Come on.' Milena took her arm and led her to one of the booths. She didn't want to discuss the matter within earshot of Inspector Filipow and all the others. The guardsmen kept their eyes fixed on them the whole time – not that the widow seemed to mind, even assuming she noticed it at all. But then Milena's nerves were shredded after yesterday's events. 'Please excuse me,' she said.

Nevenka smiled back. 'I could have contacted Mr Stojković too,' she said, 'but I thought it might be best to talk to you first. Please don't misunderstand me: Mr Stojković supports me whenever he can. And if anyone's able to get my husband's private archive back then it'll be him, am I right?' They sat down.

'So what did you want to talk to me about?' Milena asked.

Nevenka Djordan straightened her dress and crossed her legs. A pair of high-heeled silver slingbacks peeped out from under the hem of her skirt. 'I've had a lot of time to think over these past days and weeks,' she said. 'I keep thinking I should make contact with the families, the Jokićs and the Mršas. But there's something that stops me.' She twisted her wedding ring nervously round her finger.

'What do you mean?'

'What you said in our last conversation: that my husband was "part of a system". That he might not have behaved as correctly as I might have expected of him. Do you remember?'

'Mrs Djordan,' said Milena, 'this is all pure speculation. We can't prove a thing. We're still fumbling round in the dark.'

'So, you mean your accusation...'

'Accusation?'

'...alright then, your supposition that my husband might not have been squeaky clean could turn out to be completely untrue?'

Milena kept quiet. Should she tell her that she'd been out to the houseboat, been followed and had to run for her life? That this incident was yet more evidence of a system within a system, and of the colonel clearly having had a hand in it? Why else did he have to die? But all this was complicated, Milena couldn't prove any of it and the grey, cat-like eyes of Nevenka Djordan were looking for a simple answer.

'Whatever happens,' Milena said, 'I know in my heart of hearts your husband was a good soldier.'

It seemed to take a while for Nevenka to take in her words. 'He certainly was.' She rummaged around in her evening bag for a tissue. 'I'm sorry.' She blew her nose.

'What's your plan now?' asked Milena.

'Well, I thought...' Nevenka dabbed at her nose. 'Maybe the families need support, advice or some money. It might sound strange but I feel responsible for them somehow – now that Danilo's gone. I'm sure it's what he would have wanted me to do.'

'I understand.' Milena pressed her palms together. She didn't want to say the wrong thing. 'This plan does you credit, and in principle it's absolutely right. But if you approach the families, you should be prepared for the fact they might see it differently.'

Nevenka nodded. 'I know what you're driving at.'

'After what's happened, the Jokićs and Mršas won't have much time for the Honour Guards. So they might not welcome you with open arms, that's all I'm saying. That might not have anything to do with your husband as a person.'

'I don't want to push myself on them. I just thought...'

'To put it another way: you have to be prepared for them to slam the door in your face.'

With an indulgent smile Nevenka shook her head. 'With all due respect, Ms Lukin – you've got the wrong impression of these people. For these families, it's an honour and a privilege for their sons to wear the uniform of the guards – and that'll be the case for generations, believe me.'

'You fail to appreciate the situation.' Milena had to take care not to speak too loudly. 'The circumstances of Nenad Jokić and Predrag Mrša's deaths are still unexplained. These parents curse the day when their sons were accepted into the guards.'

Red flushes had appeared on Nevenka Djordan's cheeks.

'On the other hand,' Milena went on in a more conciliatory tone, 'I'd imagine they'd be honoured if the colonel's widow made contact.'

'Do you think?' Nevenka crumpled up her handkerchief in her hand. 'This is really important to me. Could you help me make contact?'

The bell rang. The performance was about to start in a few minutes. The two women got up.

'How well did your husband know the families?' Milena asked.

'You mean – personally? I've no idea. They came from Bratunac, that was enough for Danilo.' Nevenka adjusted the thin material over her shoulders. 'You know Danilo was once stationed near Bratunac? He was traumatised that he wasn't able to do anything to help his fellow countrymen down there in Bosnia; it was a running sore with him, right up to the end. You understand what I'm talking about.'

'If you mean what our soldiers did there...'

'...and the terrible chain reaction that sparked! Danilo was one of those who rang the alarm bells over Bratunac, but that's all he could do. He couldn't save these people. Only stand and watch them flee. No, "flee" isn't the right word. Watch them run for their lives.'

The bell rang a second time. Apart from a few latecomers, who dashed past Nevenka and Milena, there was no one left in the foyer now. Again, Nevenka searched around in her little evening purse. 'He almost never spoke about that time and when he did, it was only hints. But there was always a bond with those people. Right up to his death.'

'I'll try to put you in touch with the Jokićs and Mršas,' Milena said.

'Thank you.' Nevenka smiled. 'I knew it was right to talk to you.'

'And next time you want to talk,' said Milena, 'just give me a call.'

'Of course. What else?' Nevenka looked at her with astonishment.

Milena stopped. 'Well, I mean this whole rigmarole with the concert ticket and the cryptic message...'

'Concert ticket?'

'Then it wasn't you who sent it?'

'The message on your voicemail at the institute from this afternoon – that was from me.'

Milena was dumbfounded; she watched as the widow showed her ticket at the doorway to the auditorium, was directed to turn right and disappeared.

'Madam?' The usher asked, bolting the left wing of the door. 'Are you in or out?'

In the dark, Milena searched for her seat, row forty-eight, the last in the auditorium. Two seats on the aisle were still empty. Milena slipped into her seat, number two, just as the conductor raised his baton.

The overture opened softly with violins and clarinets.

Then the flutes joined in. Milena loved Tchaikovsky, and the Serbian State Military Orchestra was considered one of the best in the country. But she found she couldn't concentrate. A feeling of powerlessness forced tears to her eyes. She'd been made a fool of and she didn't even know by whom. Who was pulling her strings like this?

The light above the emergency exit was dimly lit. To her left sat an old couple and she could only just make out the silhouettes of the people in the row in front. Kettle drums set in. Milena let herself be carried away by the music, closed her eyes and saw Adam splashing about in the sea, the drops of water on his hair glistening in the sun. She saw the blue ocean, the sky, wheatfields brushed by the wind, and suddenly felt a draught and a light knock against her seat.

Milena opened her eyes. A stranger had sat down next to her. She didn't dare move. Out of the corner of her eye she saw the glint of a ring and some well-groomed nails, then somebody leant over to her. She felt warm breath next to her ear and heard hastily spoken words. By the time she'd sorted the syllables and understood what they meant, the person had already got up again and disappeared in the dark.

'After the second movement,' the strange woman had whispered. 'Ladies' cloakroom.'

30

He lay flat on his back, hands on his stomach with his fingers tightly clenched. His body was as narrow as his hiding place, the space under the floorboards, which had stopped bending above him. After all the ranting and raving, the silence was even more horrible. It took an eternity for each muscle to wake from its paralysis. His brain started functioning again and coordinated the movements, his fingers loosened their tense grip and he found he was able to press his palms, in slow motion, up against the boards.

First he felt a draught of air, then he could see a gap. When he was able to lift his head and his eyes had adjusted to the low level of light, he could make out faint outlines: furniture turned over, smashed objects. Lifeless bodies in clothes that were familiar to him. He felt his way out of his hiding place, crawled over dolls, feeling something sticky and then broken glass. The low whimper coming from somewhere, maybe even from himself, was the soundtrack to something unspeakable.

Suddenly there was a hand, huge, holding his mouth shut. He lost his footing, flying through the air like he was on a carousel. Male voices roared around him, he lost his bearings, only saw the axe come crashing down and bright colours. Pawle screamed.

He was lying hunched up under the sink, drenched with sweat and pressing the stump of his right hand to his mouth. It had returned: the nightmare and the pain, which was a phantom pain. When he had caught his breath, he dragged himself across the floor towards the door. Back then, he had somehow just got to his feet and started running. Now he banged his hand against the wood that was barring his exit, harder and harder. There was only one way out.

'For Christ's sake!' Clubfoot yelled on the other side. 'Have you lost your mind?'

'Open up.' Pawle wheezed. 'Open the door!'

'The door? No way – go and piss in the sink!'

'Open it,' said Pawle.

Silence.

Pawle screamed: 'Can you hear me?'

'Are you hurt?' Clubfoot sounded concerned. 'Have you harmed yourself?'

'You've got to help me.' The fear and pain had vanished, his brain was functioning, his thoughts were crystal-clear now. Pawle spoke through the door like Clubfoot was standing right in front of him. 'Comrades stick together. Or aren't we comrades? You sure are to me, always have been. No matter what happened to you – I stood by you and always will. We're there for one another and help each other.'

It was quiet for several seconds, then he heard the jingling of the keys. Pawle pressed himself against the wall. In the shaft of light that penetrated his cell now, the shadow of a figure became visible. Clubfoot took a step into the room. 'Comrade?' he asked, before the side of a hand chopped down violently on his neck.

Pawle stepped aside so the heavy body did not sink onto his feet. Next to its limp hand lay the key ring. He bent down, picked it up, stepped over the man-mountain and walked through the door without looking back.

31

'The ladies' cloakroom?' The usher made a gesture like she was swatting a fly. 'And then turn right.'

'Thank you.' Milena hurried through the foyer, which was deserted except for the barmaids. Their muffled chatter and the clink of glasses mingled with the music, which drifted through the closed doors. In the corridor both sounds died away until all she could hear were her own footsteps. To the right the corridor led along the upper side of the vestibule to the far side of the foyer, but Milena kept walking straight along the well-trodden carpet. She encountered no one. Guardsmen, policemen and civilians alike had stayed behind in the auditorium and nobody would notice that a conspiratorial meeting was taking place outside.

Beyond the landing the pattern of the yellowed silk wallpaper changed. The left of two doors here was marked 'Ladies'. Milena was about to grasp the brass handle when it was pushed down from inside and the door suddenly opened. Two dark, kohl-lined eyes looked at Milena.

'After you.' The young woman with the long catering apron stepped aside, and, with her foot, politely held the door open for Milena while tying her hair back with a clasp.

An abundance of paper towels bulging out of the waste paper bins and lying scrunched up on the ledge near the soap dispensers indicated that this room had been much in demand before the performance. In the next room all the cubicles were empty, doors wide open or left ajar. Perhaps the catering girl had unwittingly scared away the person who was planning to meet her.

Milena hesitated, but then noticed that the last cubicle door was shut.

'Hello?' she asked quietly. No answer. The silence sounded like someone was holding her breath. The door was unlocked. Milena screwed up her courage and pushed down the handle.

The toilet seat was missing its cover, and on the cistern stood a crumpled-up extra loo roll. Milena exhaled audibly. What she was up to here – sneaking along deserted hallways, poking around public lavatories – was not only undignified but, after all she'd been through yesterday, far too risky. She'd better get out of here.

In the ante-room a door opened. Milena did not move.

Through the narrow gap of the cubicle door she saw a petite woman, wearing a black sheath dress and carrying a small handbag; she was blonde, with chin-length hair and a round, almost chubby face. Her small mouth wore light pink lipstick, and her eyes, searching around restlessly, were blue and expressed something Milena couldn't quite put her finger on. As she was still trying to make up her mind whether it was clarity or coolness, their eyes met.

'Ms Lukin?' The strange woman stepped towards her.

Milena had been determined to conduct this meeting from a position of authority. And now here she was, stepping out from behind a toilet door like she'd been caught doing something naughty. The stranger came towards her without saying another word, walked past her and quickly checked every cubicle. 'My apologies,' she said, 'this whole game of hide-and-seek – it's just a precaution. I'm not very well versed in this.' Then she shook hands with Milena; her hand felt cold and humid. 'Thank you for coming.'

'Who are you?' Milena cleared her throat to find her voice. 'And what's this all about?'

'I work for the military tribunal, in the forensic science department.' She hesitated, as if suddenly scared by the situation she'd brought upon herself. 'I've seen the colonel,' the woman blurted out.

'Danilo Djordan?'

'His carotid artery had been severed. A cut below the Adam's apple. He didn't stand a chance.'

'My God...,' gasped Milena. She grabbed hold of the sink to steady herself.

'The perp worked quickly and efficiently, a real pro. – Are you alright?'

Milena pressed her thumb and index finger against the bridge of her nose. She'd always known that the colonel had been murdered, but to hear it now spoken out loud...And his widow, who had no idea, just a few metres away among all the guardsmen.

'A professional,' Milena repeated. 'What does that mean? That we're dealing with a killer? A hitman? Who ordered the hit?'

'I can't tell you anything on that score,' the woman replied. 'All I can give you are the medical facts.'

'And what am I supposed to do with those facts? Go to the police? The press?'

The woman glanced in the direction of the door. 'That's your decision. I don't want anything to do with that.'

Milena looked at her pink lips, her small ruby ring, her manicured fingernails and asked: 'What's your name? Have we met somewhere before?'

'My name wouldn't mean anything to you. That's why it's better I don't tell you. I just wanted you to know what really happened.'

'If you don't trust me, in all honesty I don't know why you wanted to meet me at all.'

The woman nervously brushed back a strain of her hair from her face. 'Okay. My name is Nataša Tošić, but you won't have heard of me.'

'Why did you sneak into my institute at night? Why are we meeting here, among all the guardsmen?'

'I sent someone else to deliver the ticket, my cleaning lady to be precise. I thought about it for a long time. Maybe one of us was being watched. So it seemed safer here among all these people.'

Milena nodded. 'And why bring this information to me of all people?'

'You were recommended to me.'

'By who?'

'That doesn't matter. I promised I wouldn't involve him.'

'Who was it?'

The woman called Nataša Tošić closed her eyes and said: 'Zoran Filipow.'

'The inspector?' Milena leant against the sink, crossed her arms in front of her chest and asked: 'Anything else I should know?'

'You already know more than I take responsibility for.' Nervously she opened her handbag and closed it again. 'As I said: the cut was made with great precision, but there's one small anomaly: the termination is on the left-hand side.'

'The termination?'

'The point where the knife is pulled out.'

'So what does that mean?'

'That we're dealing with a left-handed perp. Maybe you'll find that information useful.'

Milena smiled. 'I appreciate your trust and I'm grateful for this information. But honestly: how could this information be useful to me?'

Nataša Tošić looked at her in surprise. 'In your investigations, of course.'

'In my investigations.' Milena nodded. 'I think you may have got the wrong impression about my "investigations". I'm working with a lawyer, Siniša Stojković, we have no assistants, no funds, and apart from the grieving relatives nobody's supporting us. Quite the contrary. We are being followed, threatened and intimidated by Mr Filipow among others, at least that was certainly the case two weeks ago.'

Nataša Tošić stuck her little handbag under her arm. 'Please remember: you didn't hear the name from me. This meeting never took place. And if we ever meet again anywhere, we don't know one another.'

'Please wait!'

Nataša Tošić stood still.

'Please don't misunderstand me,' Milena said. 'We rely on people like you, brave people who give us information which we wouldn't get otherwise. I want to thank you expressly for that.'

The forensic scientist smiled meekly. Two more steps and she'd be out of the door and gone forever. It was Milena's last chance: 'Look, if you really want to do something against these criminals, then we need evidence.'

'I'm afraid I can't do anything more for you.'

'I think you can.'

The woman turned away.

'Get us the autopsy report.'

After a long pause, Nataša Tošić responded quietly without looking at Milena: 'Maybe it was a mistake to meet you in person.'

'No, it was the right thing to do. We now know who we're dealing with. And that we can trust each other. If we could get hold of the confidential autopsy report, we'd finally have something concrete.'

Nataša Tošić turned around. Her eyes were red-rimmed. 'I'm not like you. I'm not brave.'

'You arranged this meeting. You came here. Now let's take the next step. Please try.'

'I'm sorry.'

'Please think about it.'

The woman turned her back and the door closed behind her.

32

He needed to walk to avoid drawing attention to himself. Heading for somewhere without having a clear goal. That was his mission. And this mission was too much for him.

The situation was confused. Countless entrances, gateways and side streets. People everywhere, crawling out of these crannies like cockroaches, running along the pathways like ants. There was always somebody behind him.

It was vital that he didn't turn round, press himself against a wall, or stop, or do anything obtrusive; above all he had to avoid being seen in the same place twice. After covering one street, he moved on to the next. When he did stop it was only for a moment and always somewhere with a lot of through traffic – near snack bars or beer stands. Here there were no pleasantries, no fuss, no charades. Goods in exchange for money, that's all. He ate, drank and pretended not to see anything, but in reality he was constantly on the lookout.

The people who stared at him one instant but in the next – when he stared back – pretended he was made of thin air, pissed him off. Behind his back they laughed at him, especially the men in front of their bitches. Bitches, the likes of which he'd never seen before except in the movies.

These suits, these babyfaces and pen-pushers, could all take a hike as far as he was concerned. They were all as harmless as the homeless, tramps and all the other riff-raff fighting over returned empties, booze and places to crash for the night. The only guys who were really dangerous were those who could tell at first glance that he did not belong here.

Something about these guys was strangely familiar. How they looked, moved, appeared and suddenly disappeared again. At the same time they spooked him. Maybe Momčilo had put a price on his head. Maybe they were after that reward. He kept a tight grip on the knife in his pocket. He had to keep walking. He had to blend into the crowd.

No sooner had he found a place to kip for the night and settled down there quietly than the images came flooding back. They had no soundtrack, nor any set sequence. Fishes in shallow water. The fat woman and the thin child. Plastic bottles in the water. Girls with plates and flower-pattern dresses. Clubfoot, standing to attention. A tarpaulin weighed down with bricks. These images clung to him, like the shaggy dog who warmed his cold feet at night.

Purposefully, he walked down the street and then the next one. He suspected he was going round in circles and would probably end up back where he started. He needed a mission, an order and an objective. Thus far, he only knew one thing: he hated the streets, and didn't belong here.

33

It required patience to remove the peel from the flesh, bit by bit. Milena forced herself to summon up that patience. She had promised Adam she'd make rice pudding with dates, a sweet he really loved because of the orange sauce that went with it. It took 200 millilitres of juice and the carefully peeled rind of three oranges. Milena worked away at it, talking all the while on the phone wedged between her ear and her shoulder.

Five days had passed since her trip out to Ada Ciganlija and the pursuit, four days since her conspiratorial conversation at the concert with Nataša Tošić. Since then she'd had her car towed back from where she'd abandoned it, filled it up, and had also drafted the programme for the upcoming visit of the people from the Johnson Institute. She'd also made lots of telephone calls. The only person she hadn't managed to reach, on any of his numbers, was Siniša. It was only now, on the Monday, that she'd finally managed to get hold of him and found out that he had been 'madly busy,' which might just as easily mean that he had a new girlfriend. Milena decided not to quiz him, but reported what she had been told by the forensic scientist in the ladies toilet. 'Are you still there?' she asked when she'd finished.

'So that's how the colonel was killed.' Siniša sighed. 'It's a butcher's technique: sit on the pig's back, grab its neck from behind, pull it back and slit its throat with your free hand.'

Milena put her knife to one side and sat down.

'Way back, we learnt this method from the Turks. The Croatian fascists used to butcher partisans like that during the Second World War, and Serbian nationalists used it against Albanians in Kosovo.'

'There seems to be no end to butchering in the Balkans.'

'The cut this guy used is like a fingerprint,' Siniša said.

'Who does it point to, then?'

'Former soldiers work like that, the drifters, the ones who are way down the pecking order in paramilitary units, the guys who have to do all the dirty work: they threaten, blackmail, kidnap and kill on the order of men who continue to fantasise about power and a Greater Serbia. And I'll tell you something else: these men are in our midst. I bet you most of them are leading a completely respectable life under an assumed name, some might even have responsible positions in public life.'

Milena put the pan on the stove. 'The guardsmen were shot, the colonel had his throat cut. To me this looks like perps with totally different M.O's.'

'They're all part of the same gang, I'm certain of it. Once we have the results from the autopsy, plus the report from Ludwigshafen, we'll have enough evidence. Then we'll be able to force them to open an inquiry, especially now I've met this young public prosecutor – a very intelligent woman, incidentally. We can count on her support. Then it's all in the bag. These criminals will be subpoenaed to appear in front of the committee, the whole lot of them: the minister of defence, that Judge Dežulović who lead the initial enquiry, all those highly decorated gentlemen soldiers, right up to...'

'...up to Filipow and the forensic scientist?'

'Yes, maybe.'

'Now listen here.' Milena poured sugar into the hot pan. 'I don't know what you've been up to over the past few days, but I've been chased across half of Belgrade by a madman. I know that the woman I met isn't only risking her life and her career but is as good as dead if her name is mentioned in any paper or if she has to appear in front of an enquiry and give evidence. She's not about to show herself in public and she's not going to get us the autopsy report either. There's nothing you can do about it.'

'Okay...' She thought she could hear Siniša sigh again. 'You're right. So what do we do instead? I suggest we go through Filipow. I still don't buy it that he's on our side all of a sudden, though it's worth a shot. If you've no objection to this idea, I'll take care of this guy.'

Milena stirred the sugar, which was starting to caramelise, and slowly added the juice. A sweet, fruity aroma spread through the kitchen and made her more mellow, but that did not alter the facts. 'Filipow would rather jump out of the window than work with us, believe me. If you went to him now, he'd clam up or even start actively working against us.' She added the orange segments. 'Are you still there?'

'So we do nothing?'

'For now.'

'And then?'

'I don't know yet.'

'Milena...'

'Give me a little time. I'll call you.' She pressed the red button, put the phone down, placed the lid on the pan and reduced the flame. The rice pudding, seasoned with cardamom, cinnamon and orange peel, was steeping under the duvet cover on her bed. The pitted dates were ready, but it was too soon to put them in. They would only be stirred in at the very last minute.

Milena looked at her watch. Vera was at the chiropodist, and Adam was in school for his afternoon classes. Before she did anything else, she had to take care of something very urgent.

She poured herself some coffee, took the cup and went into her room, sat down at the desk and began browsing the internet.

Flights. Belgrade–Paris. All airlines. Departing 8 October. Coming back on the sixteenth. Milena scrolled through all the offers. Serbian sites were ninety Euros cheaper than the French, no contest. But Milena still couldn't help but have misgivings about this trip. She typed in Adam's name and his birth date, put in her bank details, confirmed and clicked to send.

Fiona was sitting next to the screen looking like a stuffed animal and staring at her. 'I know,' Milena said to her, 'a week's a long time. But what am I supposed to do? Tie him down?'

She opened her email inbox – the booking confirmation had already arrived – and started typing: 'Philip, I've booked the flights: Adam arrives on 8 October at 19.40 on a plane from Belgrade, Air France 7310, flight to Charles de Gaulle. Please be on time at the airport for your son. Don't let him hang around unnecessarily, after all, Charles de Gaulle is a hotbed of international smugglers and traffickers...'

Fiona closed her sleepy eyes. Milena sighed, hit the delete button until all the letters of the final sentence had disappeared and wrote instead: 'More to follow. Milena.'

She got up, pulled back the duvet cover and took the rice-pudding pot from the bed. A wave of deep melancholy swept over her. Her son was looking forward to seeing his dad and going to Paris with him, and all she had to offer was milk rice pudding with dates and an orange sauce.

She went out to the kitchen, fished the cardamom, cinnamon and orange peel out of the rice, folded in the dates and washed up the dishes, cleaned the work surface and hung up the tea towel. Then she picked up paper and a pen, went out onto the balcony and sat down on the chair between the clothes horse and the barrel of *Turšija*.

She lit a cigarette, inhaled and looked at the grey concrete wall opposite. She had to concentrate, examine the facts, sort them and try to make connections. She took some notes to help her order her thoughts.

On the night of the eleventh to twelfth of July, the anniversary of the massacre in Srebrenica, two guardsmen are on routine night watch duty and are doing their rounds in the military compound at Topčider. What do they stumble across? A subterranean system of tunnels, men from paramilitary units, war criminals, maybe even the General. The guardsmen see something they aren't supposed to and are shot because of it. The crime is hushed up by the military authorities.

The memorial service for the dead guardsmen. Colonel Djordan shows up as the only representative of the elite unit. Why? The guardsmen were his trainees. They came from Bratunac, an area in eastern Bosnia where the colonel was stationed during the war. In the neighbouring towns Muslim men and youths had been rounded up by Bosnian Serb forces and shot. The indigenous Serb minority, which the Jokićs and Mršas belong to, feared Muslim reprisals and fled across the border. The war ends. The perpetrators, troops of the Serbian army and their commanders, chief among them the General, are protected by influential groups and never called to account. In the meantime Danilo Djordan, now promoted to the rank of Colonel of the Honour Guard, makes it his mission to train a new cadre of more responsible recruits. The shame brought upon the army by the actions of former Serb soldiers is supposed to be a thing of the past. Then two of his star pupils turn up dead. Did the colonel conduct his own investigations and make enquiries without realising that he himself was already under surveillance?

He decides to meet the woman who'd surprised him with her visit to the barracks and confronted him with her suspicions and accusations and maybe awakened doubts he had himself, for another conversation, this time conspiratorial. Before this meeting can take place, he's murdered as well. By a 'professional' as Nataša Tošić put it, judging by the killer's speed and efficiency; Siniša talks about paramilitary units and 'fingerprints' he believes he's identified. Did the colonel fatally underestimate his adversary?

The apartment door slammed, keys jingled and a bag dropped to the floor. Vera's voice could be heard – deep and quiet – and Adam's – bright and noisy. Milena put out her cigarette, pushed the ashtray behind the little basket of clothes pegs, took out her mobile and scrolled through her contacts.

Maybe it was simply out of the question to mix facts and assumptions in the way she had. Maybe it was causing her to miss seeing the bigger picture.

Behind her pot lids clattered. 'Milk rice pudding with dates!' she heard Adam yell. 'And orange sauce!'

Vera: 'Go and wash your hands.'

'Hello Mrs Jokić,' Milena pressed the receiver against her ear and pulled the balcony door closed behind her. 'It's Milena Lukin here. I'd like to come and visit you if I may. Would sometime this week be convenient?'

34

He couldn't remember ever having passed this wall made of dirty yellow breeze blocks and dark bricks. The massive iron gate stood open; he walked through it without expecting to find anything special behind it.

What he saw next was a revelation: dead-straight pathways with intersections at regular intervals. Grid squares extending over a vast area, with clearly defined borders and sealed off against the outside world. Trees, birds chirping, and people who represented no danger or threat. If somebody did happen to look at him, then that glance was always accompanied by a nod and a sense of respect he had not encountered before. It was as if he'd been initiated into the group of people who looked after those whom this place was all about: Ksenija Marković, 1890–1964. Dragoljub Tirk, 1947–2009. Maja Vidaković, 1954–1998.

Now Pawle came to the cemetery every day, turning off this way from the main path one day, and another the next, and making calculations his mission: Ksenija – seventy-four, Dragoljub – sixty-two, Maja – forty-four years of age. Once he'd calculated one grid, his task was done. It gave the day a purpose, a structure and an order, so creating a space for doing what he'd never done before, because somebody else had always done it for him: namely, to think about what he should do next. Time was pressing. The cold, which made him shiver at night, was growing more intense during the day now, too. He needed a plan, a winter plan.

However he turned it over in his mind, he always arrived at the same conclusion: he wanted to go back. Not crawling on his knees, but as a hero. He'd have to perform a great deed, something that would give his escape some meaning and turn it into a plan that had been carefully devised and boldly executed.

That was where he ran aground, though. Because whatever that deed was going to be – he hadn't been given an order to do it. And to act without an order was as fatal an error as not following an order. He couldn't escape this bind. Or maybe only if his deed was so great and unique that the General would generously overlook everything else. He had no experience of that, nor had he ever heard of any such thing happening in the past. But if anyone was capable of performing such a great and unique deed then it was he, Pawle Widak.

It was a fantasy, a dream. The fact was, he'd acted rashly and had painted himself into a hopeless, inescapable corner. He was at a dead-end. He'd lost, and he hated losers.

He only glimpsed the wooden crosses in passing, caught sight of the letters and numbers from the corner of his eye. He stopped and went back, moving his lips silently as he read: Nenad Jokić. Predrag Mrša.

In the dizziness that overcame him, and the darkness that enveloped him, he saw two figures. They came closer, approached him directly. The order was clear. 'Hello?' he heard a voice say. 'Are you okay?'

The outlines gradually melted away to form a face. Pawle saw dark eyebrows and a defiantly curved upper lip. The guy was getting dangerously close. Pawle clenched his fist around the knife in his pocket.

'Do you come here a lot? Did you know Nenad and Predrag?' A hand was being extended towards him. 'I'm Dragan. Who are you?'

35

Bajaderas were barefoot dancers with long eyelashes, long hair spilling down over their shoulders, and slightly blushing cheeks – in Milena's mind's eye, at least; and indeed, just such an image was shown on the lid of the box of *Bajadera* nougat from Kraš. Confectionery from the town of Kraš, named after Josip Kraš, the Croatian communist and partisan, was simply the best. Milena recalled family celebrations, significant birthdays and baptisms, conjured up memories of gold foil and solemn faces passing round these sweets. And she also remembered the time when suddenly, overnight, chocolates from Kraš became a product from abroad, with an import ban imposed on them after Croatia declared its independence at the beginning of the nineties. Going to the black market and eating *Bajadera* nougat changed from being just a question of taste into a political statement. Milena handed over the box she'd brought, along with half a pound of coffee.

Sonja Jokić accepted both with a smile; shaking her head, she said: 'There was really no need, Ms Lukin!'

How important Milena's visit was to her was clear from the heap of homemade sweets she'd arranged on a plate in the living room: *Lokum* – the Turkish word for 'bite-size' or 'morsel' – was a sweet, sticky speciality made from syrup, gelatinised cornflour, sugar and pistachio resin. Added lemon or orange juice, rosewater or pureed apricots gave the sweet a pastel colour and a unique tang. Once it had set, *Lokum* was cut into little squares and dusted with sugar, then served with strong coffee and a glass of water. Milena tasted the sweets with closed eyes and expressed her especial delight at the ones with pureed apricot and finely chopped nuts. Those had been Nenad's favourites, too, and Milena felt sure that his mother would be setting aside a few pieces to take to the boy's grave later on, if she hadn't done so already.

Two and a half months had passed since Nenad's death. The two photographs with the black ribbons, which had stood on the little table in the hallway, had been separated and Nenad's portrait now stood next to a candle on the sideboard amid dark red roses and white lilies. From his elevated position the boy with the finely arched eyebrows looked down gravely on what was going on in the living room. Milena could not escape his gaze as she asked after the family and the Mršas, and discovered that Mrs Mrša had gone to the country several weeks before to calm her strained nerves, and that the men, who together ran a small taxi business, were now working even harder, sometimes around the clock.

'What about Dragan?' Milena asked.

Mrs Jokić sighed. She hardly saw the boy from one day to the next, she said reproachfully. Take now, for instance – she didn't have the faintest idea where he was, let alone what was going on in his head. Everyone in the family seemed to shut the rest out from their grief, to want to be alone with their pain.

'And you?' asked Milena. 'How are you?'

'Oh, my,' said Mrs Jokić and gave a shrug with her slender shoulders that spoke volumes. Evidently, things were very difficult. 'Colonel Djordan's suicide,' she added after a pause, 'might have been an admission of guilt, but it won't bring our boys back.'

Milena nodded. Siniša hadn't told the families that the 'suicide' of Danilo Djordan was a pack of lies. Ignorance was their protection.

'I spoke to his widow a little while ago,' said Milena. 'Nevenka Djordan. She'd like to get to know you.'

Mrs Jokić looked up, startled: 'Why?'

'She feels a connection to you. She'd dearly love to meet you.'

Sonja Jokić smoothed down her skirt. 'Please pass on our condolences and our sincere sympathies. But we cannot grieve together. She mustn't think badly of us, though.'

Milena took a sip of water. 'Did you know Danilo Djordan? I mean, did you ever meet him in person – apart from at the memorial service that is? In the war he was stationed near Bratunac.'

'We had nothing to do with the military then and I wish it had stayed that way.' Sonja Jokić adjusted her black hairband, tightening her blond hair; the effect was to make her face look even paler, her expression even sterner. 'I sometimes ask myself whether Nenad would have joined the military if we'd been allowed to stay in Bratunac. Or whether he'd have taken over the garden centre.' She cast a tender look over at the lilies, the roses and the photograph. 'Probably not. He was always crazy about flying.'

'You had a garden centre in Bratunac?'

Sonja Jokić's expression, her whole demeanour, suddenly lightened. 'Three big greenhouses,' she said. 'Twelve employees, fruit and veg were just part of it. My husband, you know, was particularly famous for his roses.'

Milena nodded and smiled. 'And Predrag's father – what did he do?'

'The Mršas owned a bus company, a fleet of six huge coaches, they took tours right across Europe. And now look at us: between us, we own two old taxis that constantly need repairs. The life we once led has gone forever and none of its beauty and ease can be reclaimed. Like there wasn't enough room for it in the luggage we managed to take with us.'

'You started a new life here,' Milena said. 'Your son was born here.'

'Of course. Dragan is our great joy, the only good thing that's happened to us since then. He's our comfort. If it wasn't for him...' She lowered her gaze and stared at her hands with the little liver spots. The afternoon sun glared through the window, revealing that Sonja's blonde hair was about to turn snow-white.

'Back then, when we fled, we thought we had no choice. But that's not right. You always have a choice.'

'Please excuse me, Mrs Jokić,' said Milena, pushing aside her plate. 'But when the army starts rounding up people and killing them, you have no choice. You've got to flee.'

'But one of us made that decision and stayed. "There are no human beings where you're going," he said. "Do you want to die as beggars in a foreign country?" Back then we thought Stefan was mad, today I can understand him and sometimes I even think that pig-headed so-and-so made the right call. – I know it must sound wicked to say that.' She took out a handkerchief and blew her nose. 'After all, what's so wonderful about deciding to die before your time and taking your family with you to the grave? Stefan was such a talented man, a carpenter with magic in his hands. And Liljana, his wife, you should have seen her, she was so beautiful, and Angelina, the oldest, she was her spitting image. And they had two boys – the younger one, Boris, was a playmate of Nenad and Predrag. What a trio, always up to no good. In the autumn after we left, they'd have all started school together.' She gave a deep sigh.

'And did they all die?' asked Milena quietly.

'What could we have done? Force him to come with us? Kidnap his wife and children from him? Sure, that's what we should have done. But we were only thinking about ourselves and how to save our own skin.' She pushed the handkerchief back into her sleeve. 'Nenad and Predrag always said they'd go back and erect a stone for the Widaks. It wasn't to be.'

A stone for the Widaks. For Stefan, his wife Liljana, their daughter Angelina, and little Boris.

'The old stories – you shouldn't rattle old skeltons.'

'What was the name of the other one, the older son?' Milena asked.

Around Sonja Jokić's eyes the thin red line appeared once more, so thin it could have been drawn with a eyeliner pencil.

'Pawle,' she said. 'That was Pawle Widak.'

*

Milena still had the sweet taste of syrup on her tongue and the heavy aroma of lilies and roses in her nostrils as she descended the stairs, holding on to the rail. She felt like she'd just crawled out from under a dark glass dome, weighed down by all the sorrows of the people of Bosnia throughout the centuries. Where Orthodox Serbs, Catholics and Muslims lived cheek-by-jowl, relations between communities and families were a powder-keg, and it only took somebody to come along and light a match to blow everything sky-high. That was what had occurred in the 1990s. Politicians and generals had played with fire, using nationalist slogans to stir up neighbours against one another. Thousands had been killed, and hundreds of thousands forced to flee. Back then, Milena had met some of these displaced people in Berlin: refugees who had lost everything, who were dependent on authorities, translators, officials and their discretionary powers, and with no home or a state that would defend their rights.

Stefan Widak hadn't wanted to live like that. But hadn't he realised that the Bosnian state and its institutions had already collapsed? That nobody was going to protect him and that he now had to go in fear of his fellow countrymen, the Muslims? He'd effectively been declared an outlaw in his own country. Along with him more than a thousand civilians were killed, Bratunac and countless villages in its immediate vicinity destroyed, burned and razed to the ground. Many of these crimes were never prosecuted, and many of those who committed them were still at large. Milena felt helpless and impotent, just as she had back then, and that made her angry and sad.

She didn't use the front entrance onto the street, but instead went out the back, past the door that was still wedged against the floor to keep it open. It was six weeks ago, after the memorial service, forty days after Nenad and Predrag's deaths, that she'd wandered around this courtyard looking for Dragan. The table and the chairs were still there, on the carpet of verdigris and moss, and across the way the old fridge leaning against the wall. Now there was also a small cupboard with a door and its back panel missing, and two dishcloths rather than one were drying on the line.

Milena carefully tried the cellar door, to avoid the racket the battered birdcage had made when she last opened it.

'Hello?' She felt her way down the steep staircase into the darkness. 'Are you there? It's me, Milena Lukin.'

At the bottom of the stairs, she had barely taken a single step forward when the tip of her shoe knocked into something, causing an almighty clatter and rattle which seemed to go on forever. Startled, she tried to regain her balance by clutching at a pillar. Dragan had installed another security cordon made up of empty bottles.

Milena stepped over the bottles and walked through the cellar vaults. She smelt something – not cigarette smoke this time, but the smoke of a candle that had just been extinguished. 'Dragan?' she called out, pushing aside an old buggy. She knew he was there. 'I just wanted to say hello and find out how you are.'

At the place where the room behind the wooden slats had been carefully hidden from strangers' eyes, the door was ajar. Dragan was probably lying on the mattress listening to music and shutting out the world outside with his headphones. What were the security cordons for then? 'Am I disturbing you?' She didn't want to startle him again. Carefully she pressed the flat of her hand against the slat door.

The light from the small window was so dim that it barely formed a clear rectangle on the floor. It took a few seconds for Milena to get her bearings. There was the upturned orange crate with a candle on top and next to it the mattress. No sign of Dragan, though.

Milena bent down to feel whether the wax around the wick was soft. Midway through stooping down she froze. She could hear the sound of breathing, very close.

She slowly turned her head to one side and found herself looking into two bloodshot eyes. Yellowed teeth flashed beneath bared gums. The dog was snarling and lowering its head in a threatening way. Milena knew it would lunge forward in the next second. She spun around, felt its body bump against her leg, but no pain. The dog dashed headlong past her and ran down the aisle between the partitioned storage rooms.

Her heart was thumping as she watched it disappear. The dog was not so much running as hopping! It was the mongrel she'd seen in front of the Church of St Sava that time, and later in front of her house – the stray with three legs, which had been spotted round the neighbourhood a lot recently. Why had Dragan locked up this dog in his cellar? And why hadn't it taken this opportunity to make a break for it, out into the open? In the middle of the cellar it stopped, barked and howled, turned around its own axis as if it was trapped or had lost its bearings. The piercing bark echoed back from the cellar walls. She just wanted to get out of there, but the animal was blocking her path.

'Good boy – shush now,' she said softly, trying to placate the stray dog. 'Quiet now.' She advanced slowly towards it. The dog pinned back its ears. Three more steps and she'd be past it. Carefully she inched forward. Again the dog barked and snapped at the air.

Milena held her breath. She noticed that the stray was looking down one of the side corridors and turning up its ears, as if expecting a command to come from there. And suddenly Milena realised that someone was hiding behind the buggy and that it definitely wasn't Dragan.

'Hello?' Milena said quietly.

Panting and with quivering flews, the mongrel looked at her, then at the buggy and back again.

'Is anybody there?' asked Milena. 'Who are you?' She was standing too far back to be able to look around the corner. She was also afraid of what she might find there. 'I'm not going to hurt you.' Her voice was trembling. 'You don't need to hide from me.'

Suddenly the buggy shot out from the corridor. Milena screamed, and the dog yelped. It hit her like a bullet. As she fell, she could just make out the dog disappear in pursuit of a shadow.

Milena cursed. Her arm was hurting, but it had softened the force of the impact. She extricated herself from the buggy and got to her feet with some difficulty. After brushing down her clothes, she moved her injured arm gingerly and found she'd got off with just a nasty bruise. It was too late to take up the pursuit – which would have been pointless in her condition anyhow. Who was the guy? How did he know about

Dragan's cellar and why was that damned dog with him? In the circumstances it was legitimate to have a look around. Hesitantly, she went back into Dragan's cellar room.

The old newspapers had been piled up neatly in the corner, the rubbish swept up into a small cardboard box and set aside. The overturned orange crate stood at right angles to the mattress, the candle was stuck on a little dish, and at the foot of the mattress lay a blanket.

Milena bent down. The blanket hadn't just been folded up. It had been done with great care, edge to edge, with no overlap and no creases. Whoever had been here had performed this little task with a painstaking precision and efficiency that went beyond any simple wish to keep the place tidy and leave no trace of his presence; rather, it was as if he'd been drilled to do nothing else.

36

It was Friday 1 October, Milena's first day of work without a contract, though that probably wasn't the reason why she'd been summoned to a meeting with the head of the institute so close to the start of a weekend. In his tower room, the light of the evening sun streamed in through the narrow old windows and illuminated Boris Grubač's ears from behind, casting his face into shadow and making it difficult to judge his mood. He was giving off a pungent smell, as though he'd just splashed aftershave on his face. He was fumbling around looking for a breath mint and it was clear he wasn't going to offer her a seat.

Milena sat down all the same. The last time she was here, he'd suggested that if she really insisted on referring in her articles and lectures to the massacre at Srebrenica and other atrocities committed by the Serbian military, then she might at least refrain from using the word 'genocide'. Grubač had seriously proposed that she refer in neutral terms to 'incidents'. It had been a very unpleasant conversation.

Without a word he handed her a folder. It contained the briefing notes she had prepared for him ahead of the conference with the people from the Johnson Institute. She hadn't expected him to even glance at them.

'Last page but one,' he said.

She turned to it. It was the page accounting for all the honoraria that were going to be paid by the Johnson Institute, together with a list of expenses. Normally, such matters were of no interest to the head of the institute.

'Why,' asked Grubač, 'are you getting three times as much for your work than your Serbian colleagues?'

Milena put the folder back down on the desk. 'Every participant is paid the fee that's customary for their country of origin. As a German citizen, I'm automatically paid the German rate. But I can see why you're unhappy; that sort of thing can rankle. Look, I'm happy to share the financial benefit I'm gaining with my Serbian and Kosovan colleagues.'

'You want to forego the money? Out of the question. Of all of us, you need that money the most.'

'Then I don't understand...'

'The Johnson Institute really ought to be pulling their weight. Tell them it's not customary in Serbia to pay project specialists according to where they come from and that we're not willing to go along with these discriminatory practices.'

'Excuse me, Mr Grubač, but it's not that simple.' Milena leant forward. 'The Johnson Institute receives its funding from the German government, from the Federal Enterprise for International Cooperation. Since 1995 they've been bound by financial regulations that require experts be paid those rates. We can't just change them at a whim or dispense with them altogether.'

'That's not the only thing that's bugging me. What about the hotel? Why do the ladies and gentlemen from the Johnson Institute have to stay at the American luxury hotel on the other side of the Sava and not here, near us, in our beautiful Hotel Moscow?'

'Well, we got a better deal there for a start, plus we'll have access to a conference room with headsets and soundproof booths for the translators.'

'Why must you go and arrange everything over my head? The manager of the Moscow is a personal friend of mine and I'm sure we could come to some kind of arrangement. And honestly, do the translators really need soundproof booths?'

Why don't you look into that, then we can make the necessary changes.'

'Mr Grubač, you do realise the event begins in ten days? Contracts have been signed, and the tickets and the hotels are already booked...'

'Calm down. I'm not trying to put undue pressure on you. Look, the thing with the hotel – I'll take care of that; and you can investigate getting some extra money for our Serbian colleagues. But don't let yourself be taken in again! We must stick to our guns where the money's concerned. They want something from us, after all, and I for one am prepared to see the whole conference fall through if they dig their heels in. Let them go somewhere else to study legal reforms.'

'I beg your pardon?'

'I mean it.'

Milena sat up straight. 'Sabotaging the conference – is that what this is all about?'

'Of course not! But we're not going to be taken to the cleaners.'

'Then perhaps you'd kindly tell me why we didn't have this conversation two weeks ago, when there might have been some chance of making the changes you're asking for.'

'My dear Ms Lukin, you have no idea how many things pass across my desk every day. This conference is certainly not the only thing on my plate.'

'Then please explain to me where these requests for changes are suddenly coming from.'

'I've no idea what you're talking about.'

'Could it be you've had a call from the Ministry of Justice?'

'Your allegations are absurd.'

'So I'm right.'

'You know what you've got to do. You can go now.' Boris Grubač picked up his pen and pretended to study his files.

Milena didn't leave but remained sitting there looking at the photograph on the wall, which showed the director of the institute together with the pretender to the Yugoslav throne, Prince Alexander III and his wife Katharina Claire Batis, a Greek princess. The picture had been taken at a ceremony at which the royal residence was placed, free of charge, at the disposal of the grandson of the last king as a form of compensation, sixty years after the palace had been confiscated and nationalised and the then-king ousted and sent into exile in the United Kingdom. For Grubač, meeting the prince had been the high point of his life so far, and he had the photograph enlarged to such a size that it dwarfed the portrait of the Serbian president hanging next to it. For all that, though, Grubač was anything but a monarchist. In truth, he was nothing but a toady and a philistine. Milena felt the rage welling up inside her.

'If you let this fall through,' she said, straining to adopt a calm and measured tone, 'you'll destroy everything we've painstakingly built up: international contacts, connections and prestige. After a gaffe like that you can forget about getting your hands on any further funds for projects. Is that what you want?'

Boris Grubač tilted his head a fraction, puckered his lips and gave a worried nod. 'I've not looked at it like that. You're probably right.' He screwed the top back on his pen, folded his hands, looked her in the eye and said: 'I have a suggestion: let's not trouble ourselves about discrimination against our compatriots and leave the honoraria as they are. We'll also keep the hotel you've booked and throw a chunk of money into the greedy maw of the Americans. We'll go ahead with the whole thing as planned – together and pragmatically. But there's one small detail that must be changed.'

Milena leant back and watched as Grubač started leafing painstakingly through the file.

'It concerns two colleagues, project specialists Kurti and...'

'Redžepi.' Milena nodded. 'The specialists from Kosovo.'

'Right. Unfortunately we'll have to rescind their invitation and put them off until the next project that calls upon their expertise.'

'On what grounds?'

'Their presence simply isn't appropriate to either the timing or the subject of the conference.'

Milena stood up.

'You must understand.' Grubač was gesticulating wildly. 'If we go mixing a highly complicated legal reform, which we're forcing through against a lot of resistance, with the Kosovo question, then we'll make an already complex issue even more confusing and unnecessarily complicated.'

'Please excuse me.'

'I assure you, in the end it would only have a negative bearing on the outcome.'

'I still have a few things to take care of and time's running out.'

Boris Grubač's face had turned bright red. 'I'm serious, Ms Lukin!'

Milena was already at the door, when she turned around once more. 'I don't doubt it for a moment. But the participation of Professors Kurti and Redžepi isn't negotiable.'

'Then we need to discuss certain other matters in the not-too-distant future.' Boris Grubač was speaking so loudly Milena might already have been some way down the corridor. 'For example, your working practices in this institute.'

Milena walked back to his desk. Only the desktop separated her from the head of the institute. 'What about my working practices?'

'Well, for a start,' Grubač nervously stroked his bald head, 'you come and go as you please.'

'And?'

'And you allow your students to treat this building like some public institution. There are office and working hours, and they have to be observed by everyone, even by you and these – characters! There was another one of these types hanging round here just today.'

'What characters?'

'I had to throw him out myself. Make sure it doesn't happen again.'

'Him? Who are you talking about?'

'Some guy.'

Milena sank into the chair. 'What did he want?'

'No idea. He was lurking around your door.'

'What did he look like?'

'What did he look like? God, I don't know, the way all young people look like these days, I suppose: baggy trousers, wild hair – it doesn't matter now, does it?'

'Did he have a dog with him?'

'Don't change the subject. What I'm concerned about is your personal attitude to punctuality and work codes of practice and the laxness with which you interpret the rules of our institute.'

Milena had already left the room when she heard Boris Grubač call after her: 'Go home now. We'll talk again on Monday.'

There was no note, either stuck to the handle or slipped beneath the door. She put her bag down by her desk.

A guy, baggy trousers, wild hair.

She turned the key in her desk lock, picked up the telephone and dialled Siniša's number. No answer. After the beep on his answering machine, she said: 'Please call me back as soon as you can.'

She put the kettle on, and was mechanically shovelling coffee into her mug when a new thought flashed through her head. Frantically, she snatched up the phone once more.

No one answered. It rang and rang. The guy who had followed her was on his way to her home – the thought terrified her. Finally – Adam came on the line.

'Darling,' Milena exclaimed, 'what are you doing? Is everything okay with you over there?'

'Grandma Bückeburg has sent me five hundred Euros.'

Milena breathed a sigh of relief and asked: 'Come again? She's done what?'

'I can buy the PlayStation now.'

'It's not your birthday. Why's she done that?'

'It's for Paris, but Dad says that I should keep the money and that I don't need five hundred Euros spending money there.'

Really, Grandma Bückeburg might have spoken to her son before sending the money. The boy was being spoilt rotten by everyone. 'Have you called to thank her already?'

'Here we go – that's it: *Lara Croft Tomb Raider*!'

'If that's one of those violent computer games you can forget about it! – Have you practised your guitar?'

'But the game's brilliant.'

'And what about your French? You were going to prepare for your trip.'

'I wanted to, but grandma's too stupid to test me.'

'Don't talk that way about your grandma. And besides, you've got your French vocab cards.'

'She's grumpy and keeps complaining the whole time.'

'Can you put her on, please?'

It was quiet for a while, then there was a crackle. Vera was slightly short of breath: 'So much money – have you heard? What's her game?'

'It's not as bad as you think, Mum.'

'As if the boy didn't have enough fancy ideas in his head. Is this the way to turn a child into a responsible human being?'

'We'll take care of that.'

'The boy needs new winter shoes and a thick winter jacket. The basketball lessons have to be paid for, and the swimming lessons, and what about the painting class he wanted to attend? It's all well and good that the child's supposed to be encouraged to excel, but where's the money coming from, I ask you? And if he put a little aside, that wouldn't be a bad thing either. Instead, the grand old lady from Bückeburg can't think of anything better to do than teach her grandson how to become a spendthrift.'

'Let's talk about this calmly when I get home. What have you two got planned for this evening?'

'What?'

'Are you going to watch television?'

'The boy's stuck in front of his computer looking at catalogues, and I was planning to go for a walk round the block.'

'Mum...'

'Yes?'

'Please stay at home tonight.'

'Don't be ridiculous. It's a beautiful evening.'

'Sit on the balcony for a change.'

Silence on the other end of the line. Milena listened to the noises around her. Somewhere, she heard a door shut. Grubač was clearly leaving the building.

'What's going on?' Vera asked.

'For once, just do what I tell you and don't ask why. Lock the door and don't go outside. I'll explain later. I've got to go now. Ciao.' Milena replaced the receiver.

She buried her face in her hands and tried to erase the images: the black silhouette of her pursuer in the car behind her, the three-legged dog outside the church and in Dragan's cellar. She didn't know who this person was, the man in the cellar, and what he had to do with the two dead guardsmen in Topčider and the colonel's murder. She hadn't seen his face, but she suspected there was a connection.

She searched around for a handkerchief, blew her nose and ferreted around in her handbag. Finding a jelly banana, she squeezed it out of its wrapper into her mouth, where its sweetness spread, instantly calming her.

Perhaps there was a completely different, harmless explanation: Grubač had come across a student, who had lost his way at the start of the semester and had pitched up at the institute instead of at the university during office hours. She was getting hysterical and needed to stop driving herself and other people mad.

She opened the window. Air rushed in, full of the mellow fruitfulness of autumn. Outside, The Spring restaurant waiters were busy carrying full trays and plates between the tables, all of which were occupied. A boy was kicking a ball against the plinth of the Duke Vuk monument. The ball bounced back, the boy stopped it and kicked it again. Milena leant out of the window so she could see the pavement below. A few passers-by, residents with their shopping bags, nothing else. All peaceful.

She returned to her desk. She had to keep a clear head. She should do what she always did on a Friday: do some work on her thesis.

She opened the word-processing programme, clicked on the file marked 'Thesis', opened a new document, saved it under the name 'Chapter 5' and sat staring at the blank screen.

37

He gave the dog a kick, propelling it in the direction of the diners sitting on the restaurant terrace with woollen blankets over their knees, stuffing their faces. The dog obeyed and began creeping round the tables with a whimper. Surely someone would take pity and chuck the wretched animal a few morsels.

Pawle kept on walking, he was just a passer-by on the promenade. The girls outside the bar in their skimpy dresses were eyeing up guys, and the clean-shaven wide boys, drinks in hand, were busy chatting them up. They all knew sod all. They didn't realise their country was at war. The frontline was blurred and the enemy numbers were difficult to estimate. And the grey-brown building in front of him, the barracks from which the plaster was flaking off in large chunks, was enemy territory, an enemy he'd ignored for a long while. Next to the doorway, the polished brass plaque read: 'Institute for Criminology and Forensic Science'.

After the encounter in the cellar, he'd figured it out. He'd done his damnedest to evade Momčilo's people, hiding himself away in that damn cellar like a dog without realising that it was a trap set by his foe. This woman, Milena Lukin, was onto him. She was pursuing him. But it'd be a different story soon enough.

Stage one: Take up observation again. He was now carrying out the mission off his own bat, taking no orders or instructions from superiors. He had to gather intelligence and evaluate it; he had to assess the enemy and find out exactly who they were. Was the woman the boss and the silver-haired bloke with the silk cravat who sometimes tagged along her sidekick? And who else was involved? The babyface from the cemetery? And this rundown dump – was it the headquarters of a powerful organisation or just a hangout for a bunch of amateurs? His head was about to burst. So many questions, so many suspects, and he was alone, caught between the lines of a war being fought on two fronts. The old woman sitting on her cardboard box was staring at him. She'd had her eyes fixed on him for some time. He ought to change his position.

The ball that rolled in front of his feet was dirty, with red and blue patches. It appeared suddenly, out of the blue. He knew that ball. Pawle bent down and touched the cracked leather. Of course – still not properly inflated.

A boy approached him. Pawle looked straight through him, saw the village street, saw the children. Picking teams. Screaming. The little boys versus the big boys. Pawle was paralysed. He was sweating. What was wrong with him? It only took a single movement of his leg, one kick.

The boy hurriedly snatched up the ball and ran off as fast as he could.

Pawle took up position in the doorway. He had to keep his thoughts and senses under control, draw precise conclusions, react quickly and efficiently. That was the only way he'd win this war.

The vestibule reeked of urine. This was the place where the men who got pissed in the pub opposite came to relieve themselves. But for him it was the perfect spot. From here he had the whole square in view, could see the building, the entrance and the lit window; the only bright point on an otherwise dark façade.

Momčilo had underestimated the woman. They'd all underestimated her for that matter. He, Pawle, had to keep a cool head and try to anticipate her every move. He needed to be smart. It was up to him, and him alone, to decide when the observation phase was over and when stage two – action – had to begin.

38

Milena had typed words, even formed whole sentences, only to delete them again. She'd gorged on jelly bananas and stopped countless times to listen out for any noises inside the institute. The blank page disappeared from the screen once more, making way for the rocky coastline of Korčula.

She got up, went to the door, opened it a crack and listened. The fact that the lobby was absolutely quiet and the students weren't showing a film tonight spurred her into action.

She went back to the desk. Still standing, she moved the mouse and the rocky coastline vanished. She clicked on 'Save', closed the completely blank 'Chapter 5' and shut down the computer. She'd wasted almost an hour doing nothing of significance, but now she moved with speed and determination.

Hastily she put on her denim jacket, took her bag and switched off the desk lamp. She pulled the door shut behind her, locked it and hurried down the corridor. It was then that she heard the entrance door down in the foyer.

Milena stopped in her tracks and stood still. No doubt about it: footsteps on the stairs, muffled by the carpet. Panicking she turned around. Where to hide? The gents. Two steps.

Her heart was pounding as she stood in the darkness behind the door listening to the stranger come along the hallway. Evidently this guy knew exactly where he was going.

Through a tiny gap Milena peered out into the hallway. The person had passed the toilet door and was only visible from behind: A young man. Wearing a cap, and a jumper that peeked out from below his short jacket. He was holding an object in his hand. A hammer or a truncheon. Then he disappeared from sight.

She heard the stranger knock. He was standing outside her office door. She heard him depress the door handle. Then rattle the door. Then silence. Milena was sweating with agitation.

Footsteps again, this time walking back. Carefully Milena pushed the door to. She preferred not to see the man's face rather than be discovered in her hideout. At that moment the door slammed into her.

Milena crashed backwards and then braced herself with all her strength against the intruder. The struggle only lasted a few seconds; Milena screamed, something fell to the ground and suddenly the room was bathed in bright light. Milena saw thick eyebrows and two staring eyes directly in front of her.

'Dragan?' she asked in disbelief.

'Are you crazy?' He stepped back in a daze. 'What are you doing here?' he asked.

'Did you have to give me such a fright?' Milena felt her forehead. 'I was scared to death!'

'Sorry.' The object he picked up from the floor was a bicycle pump. 'Your colleague said Friday between six and eight would be a good time to find you here.'

'Interesting.' She looked into the mirror. 'And what time is it now?'

'I had a beer first, I'm sorry. Did you hurt yourself?'

'Giving me a call and arranging a meeting works quite well too, you know?'

'We're still working on that.' With a grin he pointed in the direction of the toilet. 'Can I just...?'

Milena unlocked her office again, switched the light back on and placed her bag by the desk. She was putting the kettle on when Dragan came in.

'Close the door,' she told him.

He did as he was asked.

'Coffee?' She took a second mug from the shelf, while Dragan stood looking at the photo of Adam across the pile of books and papers.

'I prefer tea,' he said.

'Sorry, I don't have any.'

'Have you got a cigarette?'

She spooned coffee powder into the mugs. 'I was at your mother's yesterday.'

'I heard. I was annoyed I'd missed you.' He leant back against the desk, making the pile of books wobble slightly. He swiftly straightened it. 'Actually, I wanted to ask you a question.'

'Sit down.' Milena poured hot water into the mugs. 'Has it got anything to do with the guy who almost knocked me unconscious downstairs in your cellar?'

He looked up at her, half-baffled, half-shocked.

'You know who I'm talking about?'

'That can only be the bloke from the cemetery.'

'Oh yeah? And who's he?'

'He's a total mess. I thought he needed help.'

'A homeless guy?'

'Could be.'

'So you took him to your cellar straight away?'

'I told him where he could find the key if he wanted to crash out there. I don't need the cellar right now.' Dragan scratched his head. 'I honestly didn't think he'd take me up on the offer.'

Milena put the mugs on the table. 'Do you know his name?'

'No idea.'

Milena shook her head. 'And it didn't cross your mind he might be dangerous?'

'You're worse than my mother.' He took a sip of coffee and pulled a face. 'The guy's just a poor sod. Maybe he got mixed up in something and needed to make himself scarce for a while. And when you showed up in the cellar he just freaked out. I can understand that. I got quite a fright too that time you came down there.' Dragan grinned. 'Did you see his dog?'

'Did I ever!' She walked to the window, gazed at the dark pane and thought for a moment. She didn't know if the man with the dog was the same one who had followed her in the car. But if he'd been hanging about at Nenad and Predrag's graves he must have known them. Maybe he belonged to the same unit. Maybe he was the murderer, the accomplice or a witness; maybe he was a deserter being hunted by the military police. There were so many possibilities.

She turned around to look at Dragan and propped herself against the windowsill. 'It was incredibly tidy in your cellar room.'

He looked at her in astonishment.

'Especially the blanket. Was it you who folded it so neatly?'

Dragan looked at her like he'd misheard. 'You're asking me whether I folded the blanket neatly?'

'Well, did you?'

'I can't remember. No.'

'Did you tell the man you were Nenad's brother?'

'No.'

'Why not?'

'Because I don't like harping on about it, that I'm the little sad brother of the great Nenad. And...'

'And what?'

'Because this guy isn't like that.'

Milena paced across the room. 'So what is he like?'

'He's not really a *social* guy, if you know what I mean.'

'Was he on drugs?'

'I don't think so. Am I being interrogated here? I just wanted to –'

'Don't you think the whole thing's a bit odd?' Milena leant across the table and looked at Dragan. 'This stranger shows up at the grave of Nenad and Predrag and you've no idea what he's called, how they're connected and what's wrong with him.'

'The bloke was in mourning! Maybe they were mates, what do I know? And honestly, the fact that they knew each other makes my saint of a brother a bit more likeable. – Can't you stop pacing up and down?'

Milena looked at him in surprise. She complied and sat down. 'Describe him to me: what did he look like?' She opened a packet of cigarettes. Dragan helped himself.

'There was nothing distinctive about him. Not particularly tall, more slight.' He thought for a moment. 'And his teeth, they were a bit gappy.'

'How old, do you reckon?'

'Late twenties. Early thirties, maybe.'

'Any distinguishing features?'

He waited for her to light his cigarette and exhaled. 'Hold it right there; I know what you are after. But shall I tell you something?'

She pushed the ashtray towards him.

'That whole story about Nenad and Predrag being murdered – it's all crap.'

Milena looked at Dragan attentively. 'How come?'

'My parents – they're clinging to this murder theory rather than getting their heads round the idea that their eldest wasn't as infallible as they'd always thought. Nenad and Predrag in the elite unit – maybe that wasn't the big success story it's always made out to be, and that nobody's allowed to contradict. In fact the two of them got themselves mixed up with a strange bunch when they joined this outfit with its blue uniforms – and I'm not saying that because I'm a pacifist. I mean to say, the colonel goes and blows his head off! Maybe there really was some sect trying to recruit them.'

Milena nodded. The report from Wiesbaden made no bones about it: the entry angle of the bullets clearly indicates that a third party fired the shots. And the forensic scientist had testified that the colonel's throat had been cut from behind. But she wasn't about to start an argument with Dragan now to try to change his mind. All she said was: 'Interesting, maybe you've got a point.'

'I'm not blaming you; mostly it's this lawyer who's getting on my tits. But still, my mum was pretty down again after you'd been.'

'I'm sorry to hear that.' She thought for a moment. 'I'm glad you've come here and that I know now what you think about the whole affair. Who knows, maybe we got a bit carried away.'

'But that's not really why I came here.' He put out his cigarette. 'I've got a girlfriend.'

Milena rubbed her eyes. 'I'm pleased to hear it,' she said. 'Congratulations.'

'Emilja can speak a little German. And we've been thinking about it. We want to go to Germany, to have a look around. There's a problem though: we don't know anybody there. So I thought you might give us a few tips, addresses and the like.'

Milena nodded mechanically. Maybe it wouldn't be such a bad idea if the boy was removed from the firing line. On the other hand...

Dragan raised his hand. 'I know what you're about to say: my parents – alone; me – far away, not speaking any German. I'm wise to all that already. I'll tell you right now, we just want to check it out, see what's going on there. After all, I need to see how to get ahead.'

Milena got up and opened the window. 'I'll think about how I can help you. But I can't promise anything.'

'Just in case.' He scribbled something on a piece of paper.

Milena took his telephone number and folded the paper in half. 'One more thing,' she said. 'I'll ask Siniša to get the lock on your cellar door changed. And you have to promise me that you won't hide the new key anywhere.'

He looked at her as if his thoughts were elsewhere.

'Did you hear what I just said, Dragan?'

'Pawle,' he said.

'What?'

'He's called Pawle.' Dragan stood up and put on his jacket. 'One time, he mentioned his name.'

'Pawle,' Milena repeated. A common enough name, but she remembered it being mentioned in a different context recently.

Dragan took one of her business cards out of the little box next to the telephone. 'Just in case I meet the guy again...'

'You keep away from him, d'you hear?'

'...I'll call you. Promise.' With his thick eyebrows and the defiant curve of his upper lip he really didn't bear much resemblance to his brother.

Milena handed him the bicycle pump and enquired: 'What would Nenad have said about you going to Germany?'

'He'd have objected, of course.' Dragan grinned. 'But I've always done the opposite of what my brother told me to do.' He took his pump. 'You know,' he said, 'there was one distinctive thing about the guy, this Pawle...'

'Yes?'

'He always kept his one hand inside his trouser pocket.'

39

The kerb on Milja Kovačević Street was so high that Milena had to bend her knees when she stepped down from the pavement onto the road. The cars were driving erratically, zigzagging round the potholes, while lorries simply drove right over them, making their loads bounce up and crash down on their flatbeds as they roared straight ahead. Milena pressed one ear shut and clamped her mobile to the other. All Tanja said was: 'Tonight at 9 pm. Stefanos is cooking. Can you make it?'

'I'll try.'

'It's your last chance. He's flying back tomorrow.'

'I can't promise you, though.' Milena looked left, then right, then left again.

'Where are you, by the way? It sounds like you're on a motorway.'

'I'll call you!' Milena pressed the red button and made a dash for it.

Once the furious honking had died down behind her, she switched off her mobile and slipped it into her handbag. She didn't need any assistance for what she was planning to do.

She wandered along the wall of dirty-yellow breeze blocks and rough sandstone, turned in through the big iron gate, walked under the arch with the cross and along the narrow tarmac drive. With each step the noise of the traffic outside grew fainter and more muffled. The cemetery keeper was there, sweeping up the leaves. A small child was calmly gathering up the golden leaves underneath an ancient elm tree and looking at each one in wonderment. Her mother kept casting worried looks up at the grey sky. Two elderly men she had often seen around here came towards her holding a watering can and nodded a friendly greeting. Milena stopped at the top of a little rise, from where she had a clear view over part of the grid of graves and paths. She hoped she'd see the dog somewhere, on its three legs, yet at the same time she feared seeing it.

She kept to the right, passing tombstones, inscriptions and countless little photos, then turned left, walked too far, picked the wrong row and eventually reached the graves of the two guardsmen. There was no one in sight. Milena clasped her hands together.

Around the wooden crosses, the Jokićs and Mršas had wrapped white linen sheets that reached down to the ground. On them lay various offerings of food: apples, pears and ornate boxes, probably containing *Lokum* and other delicacies that Nenad and Predrag had enjoyed. All around, between the low bushes, candles burned in little glass lamps. Almost imperceptibly, a light rain had started falling, wetting the ground and making the clods of earth glisten. Once a year of mourning had passed, the wooden crosses would be taken down and the graves sealed with stone slab and the bare earth where the fathers had knelt and cursed the day their sons had joined the elite unit would be covered over. It had not yet been six weeks since the colonel, cap in hand, had paid his last respects to the guardsmen before meeting his own death three weeks later. And it had only been a few days since Dragan had had his encounter at this very spot, a meeting that still greatly troubled Milena.

She opened her umbrella. She couldn't guess what the man would do next. Maybe the graveyard and the cellar were the very places he'd avoid in future.

She felt helpless. Her suspicions were mounting, but all she knew for certain was that he was left-handed. The more she researched and investigated the more people she got involved; it seemed sooner or later that every one of them got into the crosshairs of the criminals: the colonel; Samir, the kitchen boy; the Roma boy; Nataša Tošić; and now Dragan. If she was following any sort of strategy in her investigations it was probably the wrong one – as wrong as standing at the graveside with a red umbrella that stuck out like a sore thumb.

She made her way back slowly. She wished she could do what Dragan had suggested and just draw a line under it all.

The chapel behind the trees was built from the same red and yellow sandstone as the cemetery wall and resembled a miniature church. A mosaic, resplendent above the entrance, showed Lazarus with a golden halo, a grim face and a raised index finger. Milena mounted the steps and pushed open the wooden door.

Her eyes took a few seconds to adjust to the dim light that filtered in from the narrow windows beneath the cupola and which made the icons set in the black wooden wall glow mysteriously. And, as in every other Orthodox church the world over, here too were the ubiquitous old women, sitting in the wooden pews chatting, dozing and stretching their legs. Every so often one of them would get up, shuffle along the aisle to the front and clean the soot-smeared candlesticks and the glass screen protecting the Virgin Mary from the kisses of poor sinners.

Milena put down her umbrella, dropped a small-denomination banknote into the offertory box and picked up a handful of candles. As well as the old women there was a man kneeling in prayer at the far side of the church, and another one walking around and repeatedly glancing up at the cupola as if there were a magnificent ceiling fresco to be admired instead of the plain light blue paint that was actually there.

When he spotted Milena looking at him, he turned and disappeared behind a column.

Milena was not a particularly devout person; praying and crossing herself wasn't her thing at all. But after the death of her father and countless visits to the cemetery, she'd become used to lighting a candle now and then for her loved ones. In the process, she'd taken a shine to one particular icon, that of Petka Paraskeva. Three people were always uppermost in her thoughts: Adam, Vera and Tanja.

She set up and lit three candles but the man, who'd appeared again and was approaching her, started to irritate her. His padded jacket was zipped right up to the neck, his jeans were bleached out and his trainers were dirty. Despite his thinning hair he wasn't past his mid-thirties. In all likelihood, he was totally harmless.

She lit the next candle for her father. The little flame flickered, swaying to the right and left and struggling until it had grown to its full size. Then the slim flame burned high and stable. Milena blew her nose, before noticing from the corner of her eye that the strange man was now almost directly behind her and pointing something at her. She turned around with a start.

The man took a photograph, turned and walked on, with one hand nonchalantly in his pocket. Milena looked imploringly over to the old women. Two of them had fallen asleep, and the third was leaning on her walking stick staring into thin air. A draught made the candles gutter, the church door slammed shut and the man disappeared. Milena sighed. A tourist taking pictures of icons. She had to stop seeing ghosts everywhere.

She still had three candles left, so she lit one for Nenad Jokić, one for Predrag Mrša and the last for Danilo Djordan. She could do no more. She'd hoped and feared she would meet the stranger at the cemetery. But she couldn't engineer such a meeting. Feeling drained, she draped her bag over her shoulder and adjusted the strap. It was time to go home and help Adam practise his French.

She normally wouldn't have given the man who was praying a second glance and wouldn't usually have noticed a person making the sign of the cross. She only saw it in passing and was already halfway out of the chapel before she realised what was unusual about it: he'd crossed himself with his left hand. No one ever did that, not even left-handers. The tips of the thumb, index and middle fingers held together were the symbol of the Holy Trinity and the Orthodox rite demanded that these three fingers should first touch the forehead, then the lower chest, then the right shoulder and finally the left.

His right arm was hanging down limply. It was strange how his little finger and ring finger protruded while the other fingers weren't visible at all. They were simply missing – like they'd had been hacked off. As though he'd been caught doing something wrong, the man slowly hid his crippled hand in his trouser pocket.

Milena turned away quickly and walked on – ashamed by her nosiness and by the expression in the man's eyes: there was an emptiness in them, shame, hatred and a deep sadness.

All of a sudden, she realised what the hand reminded her of: the fist the Roma boy had extended towards her. She turned round again.

But the pew where the man had been kneeling was now empty. The church door slammed shut. Another draught of air made the flames flicker again. The man was gone.

40

He pressed himself against the wall and felt the cracked surface of the stones against his back. His hand, his bloody hand. It was sweaty, the scars hurt again and his heart was pumping like he'd sprinted across half the cemetery. And now the door was flung open and a shadow flitted out.

'...have seen him!' The voice faded away momentarily: 'Standing right in front of me. Call me back as soon as possible.'

The fact that she'd followed him into the church and he hadn't noticed a thing, that she'd suddenly been standing behind him and had looked at him like she knew everything about him – he hadn't expected that. He really had underestimated the woman. Only fools underestimated their enemy.

Carefully he peered around the corner. She was looking to her right and left and frantically pressing buttons on her mobile. She had seen his face and could now give a description of him. He'd never be able to come back here. The woman would have her people watching every corner. He tilted his head back and tried to breathe regularly.

The woman was tugging at her scarf in an agitated way while talking on the phone. In her nervous state, she wasn't going to notice a thing. She didn't even spot that he was standing right here, beside the entrance, behind a buttress. His hand gripped the knife handle in his trouser pocket and a strange calmness settled over him.

He pushed himself off from the wall and made for the bushes.

41

The raindrops were falling from the sky like sharp little needles. Milena could feel them prick her skin as she hurried along the narrow tarmac drive, looking left and right. She hadn't turned her back on the man for a minute, yet he'd vanished like he'd never existed. But she had seen him and his crippled right hand. A hand like that couldn't hold a knife. The slash across the throat had been made by the left.

She stopped and turned around slowly. In the gathering gloom of dusk some tombs loomed up like black giants while others cowered like hunchbacked dwarves. Milena set off again, faster and faster until she was running. Finally she reached the exit and emerged out onto Milja Kovačević Street, where the traffic and other people gave her a sense of security. Gasping for air she loosened her scarf from her neck and mopped her brow with it.

'You okay?' The flower merchant whose stall was right next to the cemetery entrance was just cranking the awning shut. Milena looked at her mobile. No one had called back, neither Siniša nor Tanja. She cursed under her breath.

'How about it?' With a smile the flower seller was holding out a bunch of yellow asters. 'Buy two, get one free!'

Milena put away her mobile. 'Did you see a man come out of the cemetery a moment ago?'

The seller put the flowers back in the bucket and lifted it off the pavement.

Milena followed him. 'Not quite your age, dark blue anorak, hair cut quite short.' She stepped aside. 'And sometimes he's got a dog with him, a bitch with three legs.'

'Do you mean him?' He nodded across to the other side of the street.

The flower seller indicated a bus stop, where the people with their shopping bags and briefcases were all looking in one direction down the street. Only one person was the odd man out. She could see his anorak and jeans, and noticed that he kept one hand in his trouser pocket, before the bus pulled up and blocked her view. Milena acted on the spur of the moment.

Seconds later the doors closed behind her and the bus started to move. Milena bumped into a man with a hat, apologised and tried to hang on to a pole. She hadn't thought about what she'd do if the guy suddenly confronted her. She had no plan. She looked about cautiously.

A huge guy with a woolly hat and headphones was singing along quietly and swaying to the beat of the music in his ears. Two women were discussing relationships. Somewhere a telephone was ringing and suddenly someone was huffing against the back of her neck. Terrified, she spun around.

'Are you getting off here or not?' A plump woman with a trembling little dog in her arms was looking at her.

Milena squeezed past a man reading a newspaper and realised it was her mobile that was ringing. She rummaged frantically in her bag. The ringtone was now insufferably loud and the display showed 'Siniša'. She answered the call.

'Are you alright?' He sounded concerned and upset, but it was good to hear his voice. 'Where are you?' he shouted.

'On the bus.' She whispered and covered her mouth with her hand as she spoke, while scanning the rows of seats.

'I've only just picked up your message,' Siniša said, 'have I understood you right? You've seen a man and something to suggest that he...Darling! I sincerely hope you're imagining things. And if not, I hope I don't have to tell you what you must do: give the guy a wide berth. Is that clear? Milena? Are you still there?'

At the front of the bus, in the second row of seats less than five metres away, the man was sitting in the window seat and looking in the direction of travel. She stepped swiftly back and hid behind the colossus with the headphones. At the other end of the line, Siniša gave a quiet groan. 'I understand,' he said. 'You're on to him. He's on the bus, too.'

'Listen,' Milena whispered. 'I'm on the Number 12. Heading out of town. Check the route and come after me as quickly as you can.'

'What are you thinking of doing?' he asked.

'As soon as I can I'll give you an exact location. I'll call you.'

'Don't go solo, do you hear?'

Milena ended the call and switched the phone to silent. She kept her eyes glued to the guy. His upper body swayed as the bus turned the corners, and his head wobbled like some large dummy that had been placed there and then forgotten. The man did not react to anything happening either side of him. Only after eight stops – she counted them – did he finally move. As if activated by remote control, he got up and walked to the door. He made no effort to look around the bus, but Milena still took care to conceal herself behind the other passengers. She let a few who were getting off go ahead of her. By the time she was out on the street and the bus was pulling away, the man had already started walking down the road in the direction of the traffic. Milena tried to get her bearings. The Danube Harbour was probably west of where she was, but she wasn't sure. The stop had no sign, nor could she see any street names.

'Excuse me,' she asked a woman with shopping bags who was about to turn into a path. 'What's the name of this street?'

'If you're looking for the new tile shop, it's two stops further on.'

The man kept walking briskly ahead. Milena switched to the other side of the street, so she could follow him less conspicuously, and in the dusk tried to remember landmarks that she could pass on to Siniša later: a low-rise office building painted red, a large house with several flats still under construction, and a window display with a sign and the ornate lettering 'Ladies Hairdressing Salon'. Suddenly the man had vanished from sight. He must have turned after the yellow house. She ran ahead and lost valuable time crossing the street. Carefully she peered around the corner.

The street was narrow, not particularly long and full of potholes. Along one side ran a tall hoarding, while on the other side there was a house that consisted of just a single storey and a flat roof. With glass bricks in its dreary façade, it resembled the back of a storage unit or a workshop. There was no door through which the man might have entered it, nor even a window. The entrance had to be where a delivery van sat parked at an angle. Milena clutched her bag tight and stopped to think. Of course, the sensible thing now would be to turn back, call Siniša and discuss how to proceed from here.

The gate was open and flanked by two pillars on which lanterns had been mounted. The driveway was paved with pretty red paving stones which extended all the way up to another building that also had a flat roof and was painted white and had cars parked outside. The crack in the window of the entrance door had been repaired in a makeshift fashion with sticky tape. The neon sign in the window emitted a warm yellow light: 'Driving School – all classes'.

She'd seen enough. She turned around and reached for the phone in her bag. In the same instant she saw the dog running towards her in the dark and out of the corner of her eye a shadow. Then everything went black.

*

He bent down to pick up her mobile which was lying on the floor next to her hand, pocketed it and slung her bag over his shoulder. He grasped the woman by the shoulders and lifted her upper body enough to allow him to slide his arms beneath her armpits like two levers. He found it hard straightening his legs and back to lift her. Step by step he started walking backwards, dragging her lifeless body with him. If only she'd come right up to the building! Every metre she'd approached would have been a great help.

With a final heave, he pulled her over the threshold and then a little further so he could close the door. Laying her down, he gasped for air and mopped his brow with his sleeve. In his trouser pocket her phone was vibrating, but he didn't pay it any attention. He searched her bag, found her purse, took out all the money, put it in his pocket and threw the bag onto a pile of junk in the corner. Then he shooed away the dog, shut the door from the outside and locked it.

The back of the main building lay in darkness. He knocked on the back door, rattled the handle and listened. Nothing, not a sound. It was a real shame that Momčilo had knocked off early, but at least Clubfoot should still be there.

He passed the dark office windows and turned the corner. The nettles growing under the narrow window with the iron bars almost reached up to his hips. He wasn't sure whether he'd spotted a light in the room where he'd once lived or whether it was just another light reflecting in the window-pane. He climbed on to a rusting roll of wire netting lying between old mattresses and other rubbish, but the window was too high and too far away, so he couldn't make out anything definite. He jumped down again, pushed his way through thorny bushes on the far side and emerged back where he'd started from, at the front of the house. Shielding his eyes with one hand, he peered into the classroom. The tables were all over the place and dirty dishes were piled up in the sink. The door leading to the hallway was ajar. And there was a light on. Pawle hammered on the window. 'Comrade? Open the door. It's me!'

The door closed very slowly.

Angrily Pawle banged on the window again. But nothing stirred. He clenched his fists in his trouser pockets and counted to ten. Then another five. Up to now the mission had been executed flawlessly. He'd manage the rest unaided, too.

He walked across the courtyard towards the side building, stood on tiptoes and fished the keys out of the gutter. He opened the large gate, and the familiar smells of petrol, oil and solvents wafted up at him. He switched on the light and squeezed between a Fiat and a Mercedes – both with masking tape stuck over their chrome work, ready to be resprayed – and walked around the car hoist to the big cupboard, which contained thousands of little compartments and drawers. The cables, as far as he could remember, were in the lower section, on the left next to the number plates. Yes, there they were. He put the longest he could find in his pocket, switched off the light and pulled the door shut behind him. On the way back to the shed he picked up the broom and with a few sweeps left and right brushed away the marks where he'd dragged Milena. Routine, pure and simple.

The woman still lay where he had put her down. He closed the door behind him, bolted it and leant back against it. The cold light of the energy-saving bulbs seeped in through the gaps. Strips of light ran symmetrically across the floor, bending when they hit her body and wandering on over it. He pressed the fingers of his left hand against his eyelids, but this only increased the burning sensation. He mustn't pass out now. Tomorrow morning, he'd tell Momčilo about how he'd followed the woman. How he'd caught her searching the compound. He'd been the only one to recognise the danger this woman posed. He had saved the lot of them.

She was stirring, groaning and slowly moving her head to one side. She almost always wore this denim jacket, but he was also familiar with her yellow anorak and her grass-green coat. And he knew about the petrol-blue Lada, her bathing suit, her weakness for cakes, her son and the grandmother. He knew more about this woman than he knew about most people. Why? He didn't want anything from her. He'd hated this mission from the beginning. He'd been trained for hit-and-run raids and quick results; this endless staking-out, hanging around, taking notes and pictures, that wasn't his kind of thing at all. He preferred the adrenaline rush to end-lessly ruminating on chewing gum.

The woman sat up. One side of her face was illuminated, the other in shadow. Her voice sounded different from what he'd expected, strangely surprised. The fear in her eyes calmed him down. One more night, just a few hours longer, and he'd be rid of her – forever, if everything went to plan. He hated her whining questions: Where-am-I?-Who-are-you?-What-do-you-want? His only response was to motion towards the pillar with his head and yell: 'Move it!' He took the cable from his trouser pocket.

How would Momčilo react when he handed him this tied and gagged mega-package? The matter was clear. First they'd lock him up, let him stew for a bit, debate behind closed doors and then finally punish him: insubordination, violence against a comrade, going missing, acting without orders – quite a list. He was going to be made an example of. But if they saw what he'd achieved they'd ultimately approve his action and rehabilitate him. After all, he had averted danger, saved the unit.

'Pawle?' Her voice was very quiet. 'Could I have a glass of water?'

How did she know his name? Why this strange expression in her eyes? He had to tie her up and gag her mouth with the scarf.

'Please,' she implored.

He didn't know why but he went over to the basin. In it there was a tin mug, and the tap was so tight that he could barely turn it. He had to use both hands.

'I know you visited Nenad Jokić and Predrag Mrša's graves,' she said and her voice sounded even softer and strangely far away. He had to hold his breath to make out what she was saying.

'I know you didn't kill the two. But maybe you were in the compound that night.'

The water flowed over the edge of the mug, over his fingers without him noticing. His hand trembled.

'Maybe you saw them. Maybe they suddenly appeared in front of you. You looked into the faces of the two guards and saw something familiar.'

He put down the mug. His hand, wet, cold as ice, could barely close the tap.

'You saw your friends from the past in their faces.'

'Shut up,' he whispered.

'The boys who played with your little brother, with Boris.'

'Shut up.'

'Pawle, I know you're from Bratunac. Your father was a carpenter. Your mother was a beautiful woman and your big sister Angelina was the spitting image of her.'

He pressed his eyes shut, and bent double.

'Pawle, can you hear me? What happened, Pawle?'

He was hunched on the floor, watching the naked feet in the shallow water and silvery fish swimming round them. He could see Boris and the boys with their short lederhosen. He watched the girls skipping, saw Angelina's flower-pattern dress, and how her ponytail bobbed up and down.

'Calm down, Pawle.'

He saw the furniture turned upside down and the lifeless dolls. The flower-pattern dress, the short lederhosen. Why was there no ground under his feet? An iron grip, he flew through the air, the carousel, the axe, bright colours, unbearable pain and yelling: So. You. Can. Never. Make. The Sign of the Cross. Again.

'It's over, Pawle. You're safe now.'

He panted and jammed the stump of his right hand into his left fist. He had to get to the forest. In the forest were the trees, the moon, the calm rustling.

'How did you end up here, Pawle? What do you do here?'

'The men,' he heard himself say, 'they found me.'

'What men?'

'The comrades.'

'Comrades?'

'They helped me. They gave me a place.'

'What place?'

'They showed me everything, they taught me everything.'

'They showed you how to kill.'

'To protect the General.'

'Did Nenad and Predrag have to die because of that?'

'The General has to be protected.'

'Is that why you killed the colonel?'

'I was following orders.'

'Because the colonel knew too much? Did he know about

the General? Did he know about the celebration inside the compound? About the subterranean tunnels? Did he have to die because he knew?'

'I was permitted to make up for my mistake, and I have made up for it.' Pawle angrily hurled the mug onto the junk pile. He grabbed the woman's arm, dragged her to the pillar and pushed her to the floor, panting. He took the cable from his trouser pocket.

Suddenly bright light flooded through the wooden slats of the door. Two headlights swung left, and then right before being extinguished. The engine was switched off. A car door slammed. Pawle left the woman lying on the floor, walked to the wall and peered between the gaps in the slates.

He saw Momčilo walking towards the main building and disappearing around the corner towards the back entrance. If he was returning to base at this hour, something must have happened. Clubfoot must have called him.

What did that damned dog want now? Pawle kicked it and pushed his sweaty hair back from his forehead. Everything was going to plan, wasn't it? Momčilo's arrival was timely. He'd hand the woman over to him, crawl on the floor in front of him like the bloody dog, lick his boots and beg for mercy and rehabilitation.

He peered through the gap again. Momčilo hurried across the driveway, followed by Clubfoot, who was talking to him nineteen to the dozen. They stopped outside the workshop. Clubfoot was searching the gutter for the key that Pawle still had in his trouser pocket. He'd forgotten to lock up again.

Momčilo pulled the door open, pushed Clubfoot inside, but remained outside himself, pressing himself flat against the wall. The light came on in the workshop. Pawle saw a gun barrel flash in the hand of that shit of a bookkeeper.

Somewhere the dog was panting, but he didn't care. He'd completely misjudged the situation. This wasn't about the woman, and the fact that he'd arrested her wouldn't cut any ice. In Momčilo's eyes Pawle was the enemy, and he wouldn't be able to get rid of him with just a kick. Momčilo meant to eliminate him.

*

Milena tried moving her arm. There was nothing broken, at least. The skin on her elbow was grazed, a minor wound, a mere scrape – nothing compared to what might have happened. This man was capable of anything. He would kill if he was ordered to. He'd slit Danilo Djordan's throat. What did he want with her? Was he going to murder her? Demand a ransom? Had he acted on his own or at the General's behest? She'd become entangled with a paramilitary unit and something major was afoot.

'Pawle?' A man's voice from outside – sharp and cutting. Pawle Widak didn't budge. He stood there motionless, staring out through cracks in the timber wall.

'I know you're here somewhere,' the voice screamed. 'Come out, you coward, show yourself!'

Milena embraced the pillar and slowly pulled herself upright. She peered through gaps between the slats.

Two men were standing in the beam of the security light in the driveway. The taller one was bald, with a beer belly hanging over his camouflage trousers; the shorter of the two had a leather jacket and a crew cut and was holding a cocked gun. He was slowly pivoting around, waiting to take a shot. 'Do you hear me, Pawle?' he yelled in a shrill voice. 'You don't stand a chance!'

She looked at Pawle from the side. His body was slender, almost slight. His face was pale, and his eyes lay in deep hollows. This man had witnessed so much evil, seen his family butchered and had then become a butcher himself. That night when he suddenly found himself confronted by Nenad Jokić and Predrag Mrša in uniform, he should have protected the General and shot the guardsmen. Instead, he'd recognised in their faces the boys from Bratunac, from home. The memory had paralysed him. He'd failed. The murder of the two guardsmen was probably carried out by his comrades. Was that why they were after him now?

'Give me my phone,' Milena said quietly.

Pawle clenched his fists.

'My phone,' she repeated. Her heart was racing, but her voice was utterly calm. 'I'll call the police. It's the only way, believe me.'

It was just a single movement, a slap in the face. Milena tumbled over, crashed into something and the wooden boxes collapsed on top of her.

'Shut your damned mouth!' he bellowed.

The dog, tail between its legs, cowered behind the old chest of drawers. Milena tasted blood.

'Good evening, Pawle.' The voice was suddenly directly behind the door and strangely gentle, almost tender. 'Be sensible now. Open the door.'

'Never!' screamed Pawle.

'It's over. Come on out with your hands up.'

Panting heavily, Pawle started tugging at the chest of drawers but could barely shift the unwieldy piece of furniture.

'For the last time: Open up! This instant! That's an order!'

The rattling at the door made the whole shed shake. The door fastening wouldn't hold out for much longer. Pawle pushed and shoved the heavy piece of furniture towards the door. His face was flushed with the effort. Milena didn't know which threat was the greater: Pawle or the men outside the door. Terrified, she groped around for a piece of wood.

The man outside now screamed: 'I'll set fire to the shed, do you hear?'

Pawle rammed the chest against the door and leant against it wheezing. Milena hid the short plank she'd found behind her back.

He wasn't paying her any attention. He stared at the floor, then looked at the back wall of the room where the chest of drawers had stood. Over a metre of floor below the wall had subsided enough for weeds to have encroached from the outside. The gap was large enough for the dog to be able to comfortably squeeze through it and escape.

'I'll light a fire under your arse! I'll smoke you out if I have to!' A kick against the door, then silence. Steps receding.

Silence fell around the shed. Pawle began digging at the floor with a shovel. As he was working, Milena crept up on him from behind. Now all she needed to do was take aim and hit him over the back of his head with the plank as hard as she could. She was standing there trembling when Pawle suddenly turned around. 'Call the police,' he ordered, tossing the mobile at her feet.

She was paralysed. 'I don't understand...'

'Get on with it!' He took off his jacket.

She dropped the plank and grabbed the phone. Twelve missed calls.

Pawle shovelled away the earth. He widened the gap below the wall. He was digging himself an escape route.

No sooner had she got a connection than Siniša was yelling at the other end of the line: 'Where the hell are you? Are you okay?'

Huffing and puffing Pawle lifted a stone out of the ground with the broken shovel as Milena whispered into the mouthpiece: 'Follow the bus route and after eight stops you'll come to a hairdresser, got it?'

'Yes. And then?'

'There you turn right, into the yard of a driving school. I am in the shed there. Call the police.'

'Filipow and his people are here with me.'

'The men here are armed.'

'We are close by. We'll be there soon.'

Milena rang off. Pawle lay on the floor and squeezed himself through the narrow opening, shoulders first. Milena would never be able to get through there. Once he was gone, she would be at the mercy of those men and their fury.

He emerged back into the shed with his face smeared with dirt and his cheek grazed. He'd miscalculated; the hole he'd made wasn't big enough to get his head through.

'Pawle!' She launched into an impassioned plea. 'You have to confess that you've committed murder. You've got to tell the police who these men are. You have to explain. You were completely under their thumb. You were a child; you have to tell them about your family, about the war and your escape and how you found yourself working for the General and his men. You must let them know where the General's hiding. Pawle, you must start talking! Do you understand me, Pawle?'

She heard the sound of splintering wood. An axe burst through the front wall. Milena screamed. Police sirens could be heard in the distance. The axe came down again. One of the men bellowed something she couldn't make out.

Car doors slammed shut, an engine sprang to life, tyres squealed.

As the sirens grew louder, Pawle desperately pushed through the gap below the wall, centimetre by centimetre. Now only his leg was still visible.

Milena grabbed it. Like shackles her hands closed around his ankle joint. With all the strength she could muster she held on to him. Finally – there was a blue revolving light. Commands were shouted, the babble from a walkie-talkie became audible, then Siniša's voice: 'Milena?'

'I'm here!' she screamed.

Pawle gave her a mighty kick. The last thing she saw of him was a dirty sneaker and the tread of its sole.

Epilogue

Immediately after being released, Milena Lukin issued a statement about everything she knew. She spent several hours with a police sketch artist who produced an identikit image of Pawle Widak. She also retrieved the map from the safe and showed Filipow the compound, the dotted lines and little crosses, and explained her theory that on the night of the eleventh to twelfth of July the two guardsmen had stumbled upon a secret system of tunnels, where the General and his men were celebrating the anniversary of the massacre at Srebrenica.

Filipow called in the military coroner Jovan Dežulović, who ruled that the little crosses and the writing on the tracing paper were insufficient evidence to reopen the investigation of the shootings at Topčider.

Pawle Widak remained at large.

The manager of the driving school, one Momčilo Bala, was released two days after his arrest. As was his assistant. The case against them focussed on possession of unlicensed firearms, car theft, tax evasion – small beer that probably wasn't even serious enough to have the business closed down.

Siniša pinned his hopes on a pamphlet that had been discovered in large quantities in a box at the driving school. It spoke of 'holiday/leisure camps', 'bonding' and an 'experience of nature'. Siniša was convinced that these camps were being used to train young men to fight and that the General's people were not only running the driving school as a front for money laundering but also as a way of getting new recruits for his paramilitary units. It was just a suspicion, which Siniša aired in a television interview which to date has not been broadcast.

On 21 October the Serbian newspaper *Politika* ran the following article:

> *In the early hours of yesterday morning, the body of a man was discovered on route 19–1 near the town of Ljubovija, just beyond the Bosnian border. The autopsy report states that the man died as a result of three shots to the back of the head. As no papers were discovered on the body, his identity could not be established. His crippled right hand was cited as a distinguishing feature. When it was found, the body was being guarded by a vicious three-legged dog, which had to be destroyed by local police marksmen before the corpse could be removed from the scene.*